PRAISE
NO ONE WILL MISS HER

"Both amusingly satirical and darkly bloody."

—*Washington Post*

"Deserves two big thumbs up. Readers will be gripped by this Byzantine and astonishing story in which one gasp-inducing twist follows on the heels of another. A unique page-turner that just begs to be turned into a movie."

—*Booklist* (starred review)

"A clever and surprising psychological thriller. . . . The superb character-driven plot delivers an astonishing, believable jolt."

—*Publishers Weekly* (starred review)

"A story that will completely throw you for a loop just when you think you know what's going on, *No One Will Miss Her* is an expertly written book with characters you'll find so interesting and a plot that is equally intriguing."

—Seattle Book Review

"Rosenfield fills the thriller with more twists than a talented gymnast, portrays her characters with razorlike precision, writes with brutal beauty, and invests what could have been an improbable plot with well-earned plausibility."

—*Free Lance-Star* (Fredericksburg)

"A blistering thriller. . . . Rosenfield so deftly engineers her novel's central twist, which falls ax-like toward the book's midsection, that her plotting rises to the level of architecture. . . . Lizzie Ouellette, eternally unappreciated, [is] ready for her close-up."

—*Portland Press Herald*

NO ONE WILL MISS HER

A NOVEL

KAT ROSENFIELD

WM

WILLIAM MORROW

An Imprint of HarperCollins*Publishers*

NO ONE WILL MISS HER. Copyright © 2021 by Kat Rosenfield. Excerpt from YOU MUST REMEMBER THIS © 2023 by Kat Rosenfield. All rights reserved. Printed in the United States of America. No part of this book may be used or reproduced in any manner whatsoever without written permission except in the case of brief quotations embodied in critical articles and reviews. For information, address HarperCollins Publishers, 195 Broadway, New York, NY 10007.

HarperCollins books may be purchased for educational, business, or sales promotional use. For information, please email the Special Markets Department at SPsales@harpercollins.com.

A hardcover edition of this book was published in 2021 by William Morrow, an imprint of HarperCollins Publishers.

FIRST WILLIAM MORROW PAPERBACK EDITION PUBLISHED 2022.

Library of Congress Cataloging-in-Publication Data has been applied for.

ISBN 978-0-06-305702-9

23 24 25 26 27 LBC 7 6 5 4 3

For Noah, who thought it sounded like a good idea

PROLOGUE

My name is Lizzie Ouellette, and if you're reading this, I'm already dead.

Yes, dead. Beyond the veil, passed-on and gone. A fresh-minted angel in the arms of Jesus, if you believe in that sort of thing. A fresh pile of chow for the worms, if you don't. I don't know what I believe.

I don't know why I'm surprised.

It's just that I don't want to die—or didn't, I guess, especially not like that. There one moment, gone the next. Erased. Obliterated. With a bang, not a whimper.

But like so many things I didn't want, it happened anyway.

The funny thing is, some people will say I had it coming. Maybe not in so many words, maybe not quite so out in the open. But give it time. Just wait. One of these days, maybe a month or two down the road, somebody will let it fly. Down at Strangler's, in that magic booze-emboldened hour before the neon Budweiser sign clicks off for the night and they turn on those death-glare fluorescents so that the barman can see what a mess everyone made, so he can swab down the sticky floor. One of the old-timers will toss back the dregs of his fifth or seventh or seventeenth beer, and stand up on unsteady legs, and hitch his sagging pants up to that under-the-gut sweet spot, and say, "It ain't like me to speak ill of the dead, but the hell with it—good riddance to her!"

And then he'll burp and shamble off into the restroom to splatter a poorly aimed piss everywhere but into the bowl. And with not so much as a meaningful look at the sink on his way out, either, even though his hands are crawling with a whole day's worth of dust and grit and grime. The old man with stains on his pants, dirt under his fingernails, a topographical map of busted capillaries racing over the strawberry bulb of his nose, maybe even a wife at home with a week-old yellowing bruise around her eye from the last time he hit her— well, he's the salt of the earth, of course. The hometown hero. The beating heart of Copper Falls.

And Lizzie Ouellette, the girl who started her life in a junkyard and ended it less than three decades later in a pine box? I'm the trash that this town should've taken out years ago.

That's how it is, in this place. That's how it's always been.

And so that's how they'll talk about me, once enough time has passed. Once they know I'm cold in the ground, or burned to ashes and scattered on the wind. No matter how terribly and tragically I died, old habits die harder. People can only pull their punches so long, especially when it comes to their favorite target, and even if the target isn't moving anymore.

But that part, that will come later.

Right now, folks will be a little bit kinder. A little bit softer. And a little bit careful, because death has come to Copper Falls, and with death comes outsiders. It wouldn't do to tell the truth, not when you don't know who might be listening. So they'll clasp their hands and shake their heads and say things like, "That poor girl was trouble since the day she was born," and there will be real pity in their voices. As if I had any say. As if I conjured trouble from inside the womb so that it was already there, waiting to catch me as I tumbled out, a sticky web that tangled up all around me and never let go.

As if the same people who are clucking their tongues right now and sighing over my troubled life couldn't have spared me from so much pain, if they'd spared just a little thought, a little grace, for their junk-yard girl.

But they can say what they like. I know the truth, and for once, I have no reason not to tell it. Not anymore. Not from where I stand, six feet under, finally at peace. I was no saint in life, but death has a way of making you honest. So here's my message from beyond the grave, the one I want you to remember. Because it will be important. Because I don't want to lie.

They all thought I had it coming.

They all thought I was better off dead.

And the truth, the one I realized in that last, horrible moment before the gun went off, is just this:

They were right.

PART I

CHAPTER I

THE LAKE

Just shy of ten o'clock on Tuesday morning, the smoke from the junk-yard fire on Old Ladd Road began to move east. The junkyard had been burning for hours by then. Unstoppable, marked by that putrid column, black and billowing, that could be seen for miles—but now the column was a front, pushed by the rising wind. The wispy points of its poisonous fingers crept down the road and went drifting through the trees, toward the lake, and toward the lakefront, which was when Sheriff Dennis Ryan sent his deputy, Myles Johnson, to start clearing out the houses there. Fully expecting to find them empty, of course. Labor Day was a month gone, and with it the tourist season, such as it was. The nights were longer now, and colder, tinged with the prom-ise of an early frost. That last weekend, pleasant little curls of wood smoke could be seen drifting above the houses, as the folks staying there lit their little fires against the evening's chill.

The lake was quiet. No droning motors, no shouting kids. Noth-ing but the rustling of the wind, the musical trickle of water beneath the wooden docks, a single loon crying in the distance. The sheriff's deputy knocked that morning at six houses, six empty houses with locked doors and vacant driveways, until the speech he'd prepared about the evacuation order died in his mind from lack of use. There were only two houses left when he pulled up to number thirteen, rolling his eyes reflexively at the name spray-painted on the mailbox. For a moment, he even considered skipping this one, thinking to himself that if Earl Ouellette's junkyard burning to the ground was a solid start, then his daughter choking to death on its ashes would be an excellent finish. Only for a moment, of course; he'd assure himself of that later, as he drowned the day in a bottle of Jameson, drinking hard to dull the memory of the horrible things he'd seen. A fraction of a moment. Just a blip on the mental radar, really, and certainly not enough to count, for God's sake. What happened to Lizzie had happened hours before he even knew he'd be coming down the shore drive, which meant it couldn't possibly be his fault, no matter how much a small, guilty voice in the back of his mind kept suggesting otherwise. By the time he knocked, she was already dead.

Besides, he did knock. He did. He took pride in his job, in the badge he wore. Skipping the Ouellette house was just a petty impulse, an old grudge reminding him that it was still there; he wouldn't actually give in to it. And besides, he realized, staring at the mailbox, there was Dwayne, Lizzie's husband, to consider. Lizzie might not be alone in the house—or she might not be here at all. The couple sometimes had renters at odd times. More than sometimes. If there was one person who was likely to flout the norm, to let folks stay at the place past season just to squeeze a few more bucks out of the year, it was Lizzie Ouellette. Likely as not it would be some city folks with a high-priced lawyer who inhaled a lungful of toxic fumes, and then they'd all be in the shit.

And so, he pulled into the empty driveway at 13 Lakeside Drive, stepping out onto a thick blanket of pine needles that released their scent under his feet. He knocked at the door with the words "fire," "danger," and "evacuation" fresh again in his mind—and then stepped back abruptly when the door swung inward at the first knock. Unlocked, unlatched.

Renting to outsiders, out of season, was just like Lizzie Ouellette.

Leaving her door standing open was not.

Johnson crossed the threshold with his hand at his hip, thumbing off the safety on his weapon. Later, he'd tell the guys down at Strangler's that he knew something was wrong from the moment he stepped inside—making it sound like some sixth-sense sort of thing, but in truth, any of them would have known. The air in the house was off, not knock-you-on-your-heels bad, but stale and scented with the low, sick notes of something beginning to rot. And that wasn't all. There was blood: a trail of it, thick circular splats on the knotty pine floor just inches from his feet. The droplets, deep red and still glistening, skirted the corner of the cast-iron wood-burning stove, dribbled over the kitchen countertop, and ended with a smear on the edge of the stainless steel sink.

He moved toward it, fascinated.

It was his first mistake.

He should have stopped. He should have considered that a trail of blood ending in the kitchen sink must have a beginning worth exploring before he explored anything else. That he'd seen more than enough to know something was wrong, and that he should call in and wait to be told how to proceed. That he should not, for the love of God, touch anything.

But Myles Johnson had always had a curious streak, the kind that made caution a distant second thought. For most of his life, this had been a good thing. Eighteen years ago, as the new kid in town, he'd instantly earned the respect of his peers by testing the ancient, knotted swinging rope that hung in the north woods on Copperbrook Lake, grasping hold and leaping into space without hesitation, while the rest of the boys held their breaths to see if it would snap. He was the one who would wriggle into the crawl space under the house to investigate a family of opossums that had taken up residence there, or walk right up to the ancient clerk at the post office and ask why he was missing an eye. Myles Johnson would take any dare, explore any dark place—and until that morning, life had never given him a reason not to. The young officer who stood in the lake house that morning was not just an adventurous, inquisitive man, but still an optimistic one, buoyed by a subconscious certainty that nothing bad would happen to him simply because nothing bad ever had.

And the slick drops of blood, that ominous smear on the side of the sink, were too tantalizing a mystery to retreat from. He moved forward, skirting the blood on the floor, eyes fixed on the mess in the sink—because it was a mess, oh yes, and the smear was the least of it. As he got closer, he could see: it wasn't just blood but meat, a splatter of small chunks and shards and gristle. There was something pink and wet and stringy peeking from the dark hole of the garbage disposal, and a smell like the back room of a butcher shop. And as Johnson peered at it, stretched a hand toward it, he felt the first small stirrings of a warning in his gut, and sensed the unfamiliar whisper of a new, strange voice saying, *Maybe you shouldn't.*

But he did.

It was his second mistake. The one he'd struggle to explain to everyone from the sheriff to the forensic team to his own wife, who wouldn't let him touch her for weeks no matter how avidly he scrubbed his hands—and the one he could barely comprehend himself, after the fact. How could he explain? That even in those final moments, as he moved to extricate the thing from the sink, he was just following the explorer's instinct that had always served him well. That he was only curious, and still so sure that nothing bad could come of that.

After all, nothing ever had.

The pulpy pink thing in the sink glistened. In the bedroom at the far end of the house, a cloud of flies lifted briefly, disturbed by an unseen force, and then settled once again to their business—on a blanket, damp and stained with red, draped over the thing on the floor that didn't move at all. In the air, the subtle scent of decay grew more pungent by half a degree. And just shy of eleven o'clock on that Monday morning, as the smoke from the burning junkyard began to creep between the houses at the westernmost cove of Copperbrook Lake, Deputy Myles Johnson reached two fingers into the garbage disposal and pulled out what was left of Lizzie Ouellette's nose.

CHAPTER 2

THE LAKE

The woods surrounding Copperbrook Lake had once been home to a logging outfit, abruptly shut down thirty years ago after the operation dissolved into bankruptcy. All that remained were the caved-in skeletons of old shacks, the odd saw blade forgotten, rusted, and swallowed up by blackberry bushes or thick clusters of jewelweed. The clearings where logs were felled and stacked were slowly being taken back by the forest, odd patchy places full of scrub brush and saplings, sat at the end of rutted dirt roads to nowhere.

Ian Bird was not from around here. He took two wrong turns down those roads, cursing when they dead-ended, before he found the turnoff to the shore drive. He pulled off the road at the mailbox that marked number thirteen, nosing in behind a van belonging to the forensic team. Like him, the techs had been summoned by the state police—as soon as possible, even though they privately griped that it would surely be too late to keep the local cops from trampling all over the place, marring the scene, sticking their ungloved hands into places they didn't belong.

Like the garbage disposal: Jesus Christ. Bird groaned out loud thinking about it. It was the worst kind of mistake, but you had to feel bad for the poor bastard who'd done it. Barehanded, no less.

That little gem, severed nose in the sink, had gone out over the radio while Bird was still on his way, which meant that some busybody with a scanner had probably spread it clear to the county line by now. Not that it really mattered. In a place like this, with a case like this, the details always leaked. Bird had never been to Copper Falls, but he'd spent time in enough towns like it, and he knew how it worked. City cops had to battle a hungry press to keep information close; out here, you were up against something much more primal. The people who lived in places like this seemed to be tapped into each other's business on a cellular level, sharing secrets through some kind of collective consciousness, firing it straight from synapse to synapse like drones all plugged into a single hive. And the juicier the news, the faster it traveled. This story would have blown down the shore drive and end to end through town before Bird made his first wrong turn.

Maybe that was all right, though. The more widespread the horrifying details about the murder of Lizzie Ouellette, the harder it would be for the husband to hide. Even friends and family would think twice about sheltering a guy who'd cut off his wife's nose . . . if he'd done it, of course. It was early yet, and all possibilities had to be explored—but this had all the hallmarks of a domestic dispute, something deeply, horribly personal. It was as much about the missing pieces of the puzzle: no signs of forced entry, no valuables taken. And of course, there was the matter of the woman's mutilated face. Bird had seen savagery like that just once before, only that time, there were two bodies: a murder suicide, husband and wife side by side. The man had taken an axe to her, saving the bullet for himself. It was a cleaner end than he deserved, and an infuriating mess for the investigative team. They had spent weeks interviewing friends, family, neighbors, trying to pin down the why of the thing. All anyone would say was that they had seemed happy, or happy enough.

Bird wondered if Lizzie Ouellette and Dwayne Cleaves seemed happy enough.

If they were lucky, they'd catch Cleaves in time to ask him.

Bird drained the dregs of his coffee, setting his cup back on the console, and stepped out. The wind had shifted, pushing the smoke from the burning junkyard north across the lake, but a faint acrid odor still hung in the air. He took his time making his way up the driveway, taking in the scene—the house nestled among the pines, coming into view as he rounded the final curve. Beyond it, the lake glittered, its waters stirred by the wind. Over the rustling of the trees, the faint *ka-thunk ka-thunk* of waves hitting the underside of a dock could be heard. Sound carried out here. On a quiet night, a scream might be heard all the way across the lake, if there was anyone around to listen. But every place in shouting distance had been vacant last night. No witnesses. Which made the killer either very lucky, or very local.

Bird knew which one he'd put his money on.

Myles Johnson was outside the door, looking faintly green. He stepped aside at the sight of Bird's ID and pointed down the hallway, where a half dozen people were crowded outside the bedroom door. Bird recognized the local cops from their uneasy looks—in over their heads, but still not pleased to see an outsider in their midst.

The remains of Lizzie Ouellette were stretched on the floor beside the bed. One of the techs shifted his body as Bird peered through the doorway, offering a brief glimpse of the corpse. The rise of a hip with a pair of red bikini bottoms stretched taut over the bone, a bare shoulder where her shirt had pulled to the side, hair matted with blood. A lot of blood—he could see flecks of it on her naked skin, and a spreading stain on the carpet beneath. Flies were buzzing, but no worms. Not yet. She hadn't been here long.

Bird scanned the area around the bed, noting the crumpled quilt on the floor. More blood. The quilt was stained, but not soaked.

"She was underneath it," said a voice, and Bird turned to see the young deputy who'd admitted him into the house standing behind him, his broad shoulders nearly brushing either wall of the narrow space. He was twisting a dishcloth in both hands, gripping it hard enough to turn his knuckles white.

The nose guy.

"You're the one who found the body, then?"

"Yeah. I mean, I didn't know when I moved the blanket; I thought she might be, you know, alive, or . . ."

"Alive," Bird said. "That would be after you found her nose in the sink? Is it still there?"

Johnson shook his head as one of the techs emerged from the bedroom, pointing ahead down the hall as she passed.

"He dropped it," she said. "We bagged it. It doesn't look like much."

Bird turned back to Johnson.

"All right, Officer. It's all right. Tell me what you saw."

Johnson grimaced. "I followed the blood. There was a trail from the kitchen, after I found . . . you know. And I saw the blanket, with more blood. I could tell someone was under it. I pulled it away. I saw her. That's it. I didn't try to—I mean, once I saw her, I knew she was gone."

Bird nodded. "So he covered her before he left."

"He? You mean, like—" Johnson shook his head furiously, clutching the dish towel. "No, man. Dwayne wouldn't—"

Bird's eyes narrowed at the sound of the husband's first name. "Yeah? Where is Dwayne, then? Did you try texting him? Did he answer?"

Bird felt a small flush of satisfaction as Johnson's face went red. The thing about the texts had been just a guess, but it had clearly been a good one. Johnson and the deceased's husband weren't just on a first-name basis; they were friends.

Sheriff Ryan had been leaning against the wall throughout this exchange; now he stepped forward, laying a hand on Johnson's shoulder.

"Hey, it's a small town. We all know Dwayne, some of us from way back. But nobody's trying to get in your way. We all want the same thing, here, and my men will give you whatever help you need. We already sent a car over to his and Lizzie's place in town. Nobody home. Lizzie's Toyota is around back, and they had one other vehicle, a pickup—it's not here, so best guess is that wherever Dwayne is, he's got it. We put out the description. If he's on the road, he'll get picked up sooner or later."

Bird nodded back. "So they lived in town, and then this place is what, a vacation home?"

"Earl—that's Lizzie's father—it's his place. Or was. I think Lizzie pretty much took it over, spruced it up and started renting it out. To folks from away, mostly." The sheriff paused, shifting his weight, frowning. "That didn't go over with some of the other homeowners."

"What does that mean?"

"We're a close-knit community here. Most folks with places on Copperbrook like to do things by word of mouth, you know. Family, family friends. People with a connection to the community. The Ouellette girl listed this place on some website, so anyone could rent it out. Like I said, it didn't go over. We had some trouble, some neighbors upset."

Bird raised his eyebrows, cocking his head in the direction of the bedroom, the blood, the body. "How upset?"

The sheriff caught his tone and stiffened. "Not like you're thinking. I'm saying, some of the folks she had up here, we don't know who they were or what they might have been into. You'll want to look into that."

There was a long silence as the men stared at each other. Bird broke eye contact first, looking down at his phone. When he spoke again, he kept his tone mild.

"I'll be looking into anything relevant, Sheriff. You mentioned the victim's father. He lives in town?"

"The junkyard. He has a trailer there, or did. I doubt it survived the fire. Christ, I can't even imagine . . ." The sheriff shook his head, and Myles Johnson stared down at his hands, twisting and twisting the dishrag. Bird thought the thing would rip in half soon.

"The fire," he said. "That's the father's place? That's a hell of a co-incidence."

"That's why I was here. The wind picked up, and I came around to tell folks to evacuate," said Johnson. "But the door—"

"Bird?" A forensic tech poked his head out of the bedroom, gestured with a gloved finger. Bird nodded, and made the same motion at Johnson.

"Let's have a look at her. Run me through it."

A moment later, he stood beside the corpse, reading aloud from the preliminary, scribbled notes someone had passed over for his perusal.

"Elizabeth Ouellette, twenty-eight years old . . ." He looked from the pad to the body, grimacing. The name was written in neat print, but the face was unrecognizable. The woman was lying on her side, her eyes half-lidded and dull beneath the blood-soaked hanks of gingery hair. They were the only part that still looked like what they had been; everything below was shredded, the kind of wound that some of the guys in the barracks referred to as "cherry pie." The missing nose was the least of it. Whoever had killed Lizzie Ouellette had put the barrel of something big under her chin—perhaps a shotgun, the one registered to and missing from the home she'd shared with Dwayne Cleaves—and pulled the trigger. The bullet had sheared her jaw away, obliterating her teeth and blowing the structure of the skull apart before exiting through the back of her head. A single pearlescent molar winked out from the mess, impossibly white and perfectly intact.

Bird grimaced, looking away, focusing on the rest of the room. There was a spatter on the wall, bone shards and brain, but he was still struck by the look of the place. Someone—the woman lying dead a few feet away, he guessed—had taken care with the decor. There was a threadbare but stylish oriental rug on the floor at the end of the bed, in a shade of faded blue that was echoed by the curtains that framed the picture window and the quilt, now stained with blood, that had covered the body. A pair of nice-looking lamps, brass or something like it, on matching bedside tables. A stack of old books artfully arranged on the dresser. Lake houses had a way of becoming a repository for mismatched furniture, old hunting trophies, novelty pillows with phrases like GONE FISHING emblazoned on them—Bird's own family had once rented a place up near the border that seemed to have a deer's head sprouting from every vertical surface. But this place was like something out of a magazine. He'd need to locate whatever website Ouellette had listed it on, but even now, he could imagine how enticing it must have looked to the city people browsing for a vacation getaway.

He turned back, bent toward the body. *Cherry pie,* he thought again. The dead woman's wallet, credit cards, and driver's license had been found in a purse on the dresser, but the face was a problem. And a question. He lifted his gaze to look around the room, from the techs to the sheriff to Johnson, who was now whispering quietly with two other, younger men who must also be local police.

"Who made the ID?" Bird asked, and in that moment, the energy in the room underwent a sudden, subtle shift. A stillness filled with uncomfortable fidgeting, the quick exchange of looks from man to man. The silence drew out a beat too long, and he stood, annoyed.

"Johnson? Sheriff? Who made the ID?" he repeated.

"It was, ah, sort of a joint effort," said a blond man who Bird didn't know. Johnson looked at the floor, biting his lip.

"A joint effort," Bird said, and there was another beat, another set of looks, before Johnson stepped forward and extended a finger, pointing down at the body.

"It's there," he said. Bird followed the pointing finger, and saw. He'd missed it at a glance, amid all the blood and the dark, fat bodies of the buzzing flies. The dead woman's shirt was bunched up toward her neck, and on the inner curve of a pale breast was a dark blob, the size of a housefly, but solid. And static. The flies rose in a hovering cloud; the spot stayed still. He squinted.

"Is that a mole?"

"Yes, sir," Johnson said. "Identifying mark. That's Lizzie Ouellette, no question."

Bird blinked and frowned, not enjoying the sense of having missed something, enjoying the changed energy in the room even less.

"You're sure about that," he said, and noticed that Johnson wasn't the only one nodding. He looked at the rest of the men. "All of you? You all know that well what Elizabeth Ouellette's breast looks like?"

Johnson coughed and turned red. "Everyone knows, sir."

"How?"

The question hung in the air, and Bird realized: the men were trying not to snicker. To snicker was an instinct, somehow, even now. He could see it, see them nearly quivering with the effort to hold it back.

Nobody wants to say it, he thought.

But incredibly, someone did. The blond cop, his mouth twisting just a little—not smiling, exactly; nobody could accuse him of smiling—met Bird's eyes and replied.

"How do you think, man."

It wasn't a question.

Bird sighed and went to work.

CHAPTER 3

THE CITY

It was just shy of ten o'clock, sunlight streaming through the wall of south-facing windows, when the couple in the multimillion-dollar town house on Pearl Street finally began to stir. She woke first, and all at once, which was unusual. All her life, Adrienne Richards had been a reluctant riser, fighting her way out of sleep in a long series of kicks and groans and false starts. Now, the woman lying cocooned in the king-sized bed came awake with a single blink. Eyes closed. Eyes open. Like Juliet, awakening in her tomb—only with Egyptian cotton sheets, minimum twelve hundred thread count, in lieu of a marble slab.

I do remember well where I should be,
And there I am.
Where is my Romeo?

She could have rolled over to see him, but she didn't need to; she could feel him beside her, could hear the slow, even breaths that meant he wouldn't wake for an hour yet, unless she shook him. Just one of the many things she knew by instinct, after nearly ten years of marriage. She knew the sound and shades of his breath better than her own.

She'd have to shake him, of course. Eventually. They couldn't sleep all day. There were things to be done.

I do remember well where I should be.

She did.

She remembered everything.

There had been so much blood.

But for several long minutes, she lay awake and unmoving, contenting herself to let her gaze roam around the bedroom. It wasn't hard to stay still; the cat, a big gray boy with green eyes and silky fur, had settled into the crook of her body overnight and was warm and purring against her, and the pillow where her cheek rested was soft and clean. The room was painted a lovely dark blue—Adrienne had gone through a color therapy phase, and this one was supposed to promote wellness, better sleep, and better sex—and curtained in the bargain, so that even now, in this last hour before morning gave way to midday, the shadows draped heavy as velvet in the corners and crevices, pooling underneath the furniture. The dress she'd worn last night was lying like a ponte pancake in the place where she'd unzipped and stepped out of it—a stupid mistake; it would probably need to be dry-cleaned—but otherwise, the room was perfect. Simple. Magazine-ready. The personal touches were confined to a nearby shelf: a brass figurine of a ballet dancer, a pair of sapphire earrings left in a saucer, and a photograph, framed, of the new-minted Mr. and Mrs. Richards on their wedding day. A memory from happier times. Adrienne was blond and slim and smiling in a white silk dress; Ethan was tall and broad-shouldered, already sporting a closely shorn haircut that masked a receding hairline. He had been thirty-four on their wedding day, twelve years older than she; it was her first marriage, his second.

Not that you'd know this from looking at the picture, she thought.

They both looked radiantly happy, thrilled at the novelty of it all. Newlyweds at the start of their lifelong adventure, together, forever.

She envied them. The young couple in the picture had no idea what they were in for. A horror beyond imagining, only she didn't have to imagine it. It had happened, and in the few hours she'd slept, had seared itself on her memory in terrible, vivid detail. Last night . . . she had been in shock, she supposed, and so had he, on that long drive home. The two of them sitting in stunned silence as it all disappeared into the rearview: The town. The lake. The house, and everything in it.

The bodies.

The blood.

There had been so much blood.

But it was easy to feel, as the mile markers flashed by in the dark and the events of the night receded behind them, that it had all been a sort of bad dream. Even the mundane homecoming had that sense of being not entirely real. She had nosed the Mercedes into the alley behind the house, and all she could think was that they were almost home. She'd gripped the keys all the way to the door, white-knuckling them with her mouth pressed into a thin line, her husband standing grim beside her. They must have spoken at some point, if only to agree that further discussion was best left until morning, but all she remembered was silence. The two of them moving carefully down the darkened hall, finding their way to the bedroom, not even bothering to reach for a light switch. She had kicked her shoes away, unzipped the dress, stepped out of it and into bed. The last thing she remembered was gazing into the dark and thinking that she'd never fall asleep, that she couldn't possibly.

But she had.

She couldn't lie still anymore.

The cat gave her a reproachful look as she shifted her weight, leaping softly to the floor when she slid out from beneath the duvet. Beside her, her husband stirred. She paused.

"Are you awake?" she whispered. Softly. Testing.

His eyelids fluttered but remained shut.

She left him sleeping and left the room, arms crossed protectively over her bare breasts, following the cat out and down the hallway toward the kitchen. She flinched from the sunlight coming through the wall of windows. The place had a lovely view of the neighborhood, but God, it was bright. All that glass, miles of windows, the stone facades of the houses across the street blazing back at her in the sunshine. It was dazzling. Above the narrow streets, the sky stretched blue and cloudless.

The cat twined around her bare legs, meowing. Hungry. She would need to cancel the cat sitter.

"Okay, buddy," she said softly. "Let's find you some breakfast."

She was sipping coffee at the countertop, wrapped in a sweater and tapping at a laptop, when her husband appeared at the end of the hall. She'd heard him get out of bed twenty minutes before, but the door had stayed shut; instead, there was a brief silence followed by the sound of running water. At first, she was stunned. Out of bed and into the shower, as if this were just an ordinary morning. As if there weren't urgent conversations to be had. Then the surprise gave way to relief. There were worse things a man could do under the circumstances than adhere to his routine. It meant he was handling things.

He paused in the same place she had, gazing at the view through the wall of windows. He was wearing an old college sweatshirt, and he'd shaved. There were bits of toilet paper clinging to his face; one came free as she watched, coming to rest on the sweatshirt's frayed neckline. She cleared her throat. Time to get down to business.

"Hi."

He turned slowly at the sound of her voice. His eyes were red—from lack of sleep, she thought. She hoped. Surely he hadn't been crying. She peered at him, but his facial expression was unreadable.

"Come on. There's coffee."

She pointed a polished finger at the cabinet beside the sink. He opened it as if in a daze, pulled out a mug, sat down beside her.

"I fucked up. I cut myself," he said. His voice was gravelly. "It's going to bleed all day long."

"It's fine," she said. "You're going to stay in today anyway. Out of sight. I don't know how long we have. I made a few appointments and I'm leaving within the hour, to see how fast we can get some things together. All right?"

He set the mug down. "What's going on?"

"They found her."

All the color drained from his face.

"What about him?"

She shook her head, leaning forward to read aloud.

"We are seeking the public's assistance in locating Ouellette's husband, Dwayne Cleaves," she said. "Anyone with information, blah, blah, blah. There's a phone number to call. That's it."

"Shit. How? How could they even—"

"The fire at the junkyard," she said, evenly. "The wind came up this morning. They must have gone around to evacuate. But it'll be fine—"

He wasn't listening. He shook his head, beating an open palm against the countertop. "Shit. Shit, shit, shit. Dammit, why did you have to . . ."

He looked up, saw the look on her face, and decided not to finish the sentence.

"It'll be fine. Do you understand? It'll be fine. It is fine. They've got the right idea. Dwayne Cleaves killed his wife, and now he's on the run."

There was a long silence.

"They're going to find him," he said finally.

She nodded. "Eventually. Probably. But who knows when. You saw what I did. It could be a long time."

"So what do we do?"

"We? Nothing. You stay here. Out of sight. I'm going to get the money, and then we'll make a plan. A real plan. We've been lucky, but I want to be smart, even if that means taking a few days. It's fine. We don't need to run, not when nobody is chasing us."

He hated her right now. She could feel it coming off of him in waves, could see the tension thrumming in his jaw as he ground his teeth together. He'd always hated when she took this tone, which made it all too clear that she thought she was the smart one between them. *Well, tough shit,* she thought. She was smart. She always had been, and she had always known it, whether people like her husband cared to acknowledge it or not. And if she had to piss him off to remind him what was at stake and who was in charge . . . well, she preferred his wounded anger to some of the alternatives. That red-eyed, haunted look he'd had when he first came out of the bedroom, gazing out the windows like he didn't know who or where he was—no, she didn't like that at all. If he couldn't keep it together, they were both screwed.

"What if the cops show up?" he said finally.

"And why would that happen?"

He shrugged, looking down. "I don't know. The Mercedes? People are going to remember seeing it, if they saw it. Out-of-state license plate, out of season, big fucking luxury car that sticks out like a sore thumb. Especially after that bullshit at the market last year. You and the fucking yogurt? They're going to remember, and they're going to come asking questions, and—"

"Then I'll tell them what they need to know," she cut him off, glaring. "I will tell them. Look at me. Look at me." He did. For several long seconds, he stared at her as she gazed back. She laid her hand on top of his and spoke with fierce conviction. "We are so close to finishing this. You just have to let me handle it."

Finally, he nodded. He believed her; she could see it in his face. But the lost look—that was still there, too. She sighed.

"Say it. We can't afford to play this game, not now. Say whatever you're not saying."

He gazed into his coffee cup. He'd barely tasted it, and now it was cold.

"It's just . . ." He trailed off and squared his shoulders. "They're going to figure it out. What we did."

She shook her head furiously.

"They won't."

He sighed, twisting the band on his finger. A familiar nervous habit. Seeing him do it made her heart ache—but she had to be firm.

"Listen to me," she said. "Lizzie and Dwayne are dead. It's over. There's nothing we can do. But we are alive. We have a future. And we have each other. Right? You have to trust me."

His shoulders sagged, and hers did, too, with relief. He was giving in to her, the way he always did, the way she always knew he would. But his eyes stayed haunted, and when he spoke again, she nearly screamed aloud.

"I can't stop thinking about—" he said, and she leaned forward, gripping his shoulders, unable to bear it.

"Don't."

But he couldn't help it. Couldn't hold it back. The words escaped in a whisper, and the air in the condo hung heavy with dread.

"The way she looked at me."

CHAPTER 4

LIZZIE

For the record, I never fucked that guy.

You know the one I mean. The one who just couldn't help himself, standing over the bloodied, battered corpse of a murdered woman, having a good solid gloat with the hometown fellas about how they'd all seen her tits before. Pure class, those Copper Falls boys. Truly. Especially that line. Such a perfect combination of crass and coy that it became a little bit famous. Someone who was there told someone who wasn't—*You won't believe what Rines said to that trooper*—and before long, people were repeating it like a catchphrase clear across the county. You remember it, don't you?

How do you think, man.

Jesus fucking Christ.

You probably thought I was kidding. Or exaggerating, deluded, just being dramatic. It's all right; I've heard it before. *She's making it up. She's just looking for attention. Everyone knows that Ouellette girl is a sack of lying trash.* These are, of course, good churchgoing people we're talking about. Salt-of-the-earth, New England working folks. It's hard to believe in such casual cruelty unless you've seen it with your own eyes.

But now you have. Now you know. Visit beautiful Copper Falls! Where the air is clean, the beer is cheap, and the local cops will slut-shame a girl at the scene of her own goddamn murder.

His name is Adam Rines. The blond with the crooked little almost-smile, Mister How Do You Think. And despite what he wants every-one to believe, I never slept with him. I never slept with any of them, except Dwayne, and that was different and later on. Much later. It had been a good five years by then, since that early summer day, the moldy shingles of the hunting shack moist between my shoulder blades, the jeering of six ugly boys ringing in my ears.

How do you think, my ass.

I'll tell you how. Or you could even guess. All it takes is a little imagination. Like this: Imagine that you're thirteen years old. Ninety-five pounds and not yet a woman, but not a little girl anymore, either. Imagine your body, all gangly arms and knob-kneed legs that never look right no matter how you arrange them together, and your hair, a ginger-colored mess that's always lank and dirty, the ends all uneven where you had to cut it yourself with a pair of dull scissors. Imagine your ignorance: a mother long dead, and a dad who just doesn't know, doesn't realize that a thirteen-year-old girl is old enough to need a bra, and a box of maxi pads, and a conversation about what they all mean. He doesn't see you growing up.

But everyone else does. They see what's happening to your body. They see it even before you do.

Imagine.

They caught up to me while I was riding my bike home on the last day of school, five dusty miles, my backpack so heavy that I had to get off and walk every time I hit a hill. There were a half dozen of them. Some of them were older, and all of them were bigger. I left the bike in the road, front wheel spinning. I ran into the forest ahead of them and tried to disappear between the trees, but they caught me. Of course they caught me. I counted myself lucky afterward that pulling my shirt over my head was all they did.

I'd had that mole forever. You couldn't miss it, raised up like it was and so dark against my skin. I knew it was ugly—even then, I was careful not to let the other girls see it during those quick-change moments in the locker room after gym class—but there was nothing I could do to hide it that day, backed up against that falling-down shack a hundred yards into the woods with my arms raised out in a T and a boy leaning hard against each of my shoulders. I couldn't even see past the hem of my T-shirt, stretched tight over my face, damp with sweat and spit. I wasn't wearing anything underneath, and one of them jabbed a finger against the dark blemish below my breast, hard enough to make a bruise, making a disgusted noise while he did it.

They all saw it. And the ones that didn't see it, like Adam Rines, all heard about it. It was its own local legend, my mole, growing in the retelling like the giant prehistoric carp that was supposed to live down in the deepest part of Copperbrook Lake. I still remember that first time with Dwayne, when I stepped out of my dress and stood there uncovered like he wanted, letting him look at me, he gazed at that dark spot and said, "I thought it would be bigger." I said, "That's what she said," which I thought was a pretty solid comeback, but Dwayne didn't laugh.

Dwayne never laughed at my jokes. Some people thought I was funny, but not Dwayne Cleaves. My husband was like a lot of men. Always making noise about how he loved comedy, but no sense of humor to speak of. All but the dumbest jokes would go over his head, and the ones he liked best were always at someone else's expense. He loved, I mean *loved,* those prank-call radio shows, where the hosts would get someone all riled up with a fake story, dragging it out while they got more and more upset, and only come clean after the poor bastard totally fucking lost it. God, I felt sorry for those folks. Not that I have any business giving out marriage advice under the circumstances, but if this sounds like your man? Don't marry him. Because he's an idiot, and probably mean to boot.

Of course I wasn't smart enough to take my own advice. Not that I had options, either. The boys weren't exactly banging down the door of Pop's trailer to take me on dates or give me a diamond ring. Dwayne would never have admitted we were even together if not for what happened that summer after graduation, and you could feel the shame coming off him in waves—that crawling, squirming humiliation that's so potent, everyone else gets embarrassed for you. It was thick in the air the day we got married. People looked at their feet and grimaced when he said "I do," like he'd just shit his pants in public. That's the thing about being an Ouellette in Copper Falls: just being next to you is embarrassing. Like those sad maids in India. Untouchable.

Of course, untouchable is not the same thing as unfuckable, which is why this whole messed-up story ends the way it does.

The police won't hear any of this, either. The men who come around, collecting evidence and asking questions, will get only half the truth—or outright lies, from people like Adam Rines—and I didn't leave behind a diary to set the record straight. Maybe I should have. Maybe people would actually listen to me now, the way they never did when I was alive. Maybe they'd even understand.

I wouldn't start at the beginning. I don't even remember the beginning. Some people say they have memories from way back, clear ones, distinct little glimpses of their lives at age two or three or five. It's all just a blur to me. Partly, it's that nothing ever changed: the trailer, the junkyard, the woods beyond. Pop asleep in that shitty recliner in front of the old TV with the rabbit ears on it. The sour smell of last night's spilled beer. Day after week after year, the same. The only way to tell if a memory is from before or after is that sometimes my mom is there, hovering in the background. I can't remember her face anymore, but there's the shape of her. Reddish hair that had started to fade to brown. And her voice, harsh and dusky like the cigarettes she was always smoking—although I don't remember ever seeing her do that, either. Maybe she never smoked in front of me. Or maybe I've just forgotten. I do remember that my father punched a hole in the wall of the trailer the night that Mom skidded out on the county road between Copper Falls and Greenville, going so fast that she flipped over the guardrail and took a long plunge down into the brush. She died on impact. She'd been driving too fast. Stoned, too. Pop never told me that part, but the kids at school all knew, and they were at just the right age to make it hurt. It was an exciting day there at Falls Central when someone in Miss Lightbody's fifth-grade class realized that my given name, "Elizabeth," rhymes with "crystal meth."

I remember the two state policemen standing on the drop-down step outside, one behind the other, holding their hats against their chests. They probably teach them that at the academy, to never give someone bad news with your hat on. I wonder if Sheriff Ryan will take his off when he tells Pop I'm gone.

Maybe I don't want to tell this part after all.

And I don't want you to think my life was all bad. It wasn't. My father did love me, which is more than some people can say. He gave me what he could, and the mistakes he made were out of ignorance, not meanness. Even when he was drunk, and he was drunk plenty, he never raised a hand or said a cruel word. Plenty of people hurt me in my life—hell, I married a man who did almost nothing else—but Pop wasn't one of them. That house on the lake, the one where I died? He bought it cheap from Teddy Reardon the year after my mother's accident. He bought it for me, to fix up and rent out for the college education he thought I might want someday. He actually thought that was possible. That I'd amount to something, never mind what everyone said about us.

And when it all went sideways and I ended up with Dwayne, Pop handed me the key to the place and called it a wedding present, and you'd never have known he was disappointed except for the way he couldn't quite meet my eyes.

CHAPTER 5

THE LAKE

Bird's first thought, as he scrolled through the history on Lizzie Ouellette's Facebook page, was that she didn't like having her picture taken. Some girls were downright obsessed with their own faces—his last girlfriend had been one of these, her social media feeds an endless scroll of self-portraits, overlaid with those weird glowy filters that made her look like some kind of cartoon doll. Whatever you called that kind of girl, Lizzie was exactly the opposite. Her profile photo had last been updated three years ago, a grainy picture taken from a distance as she faced into the sun. One hand was lifted to shield her eyes, a can of Coors Light clutched in the other, and her face was a featureless squint—it was impossible to tell what she looked like beyond the basics: pale, thin, red-haired. Bird kept swiping. The next several photos didn't have Lizzie in them at all; one was a picture of a sunset over the lake, another a blurry shot of something brown and furry—a rabbit? a cat?—nestled in a patch of grass. At some point, she'd tried to take a close-up photo with the camera on her computer, her features so blown out that all you could see were her eyes, her nostrils, and the thin line of her mouth. But finally, he found her. Ten years back, right up close, glancing over her shoulder and into the camera with wide eyes and parted lips, like she'd been caught off guard. She was wearing a strapless yellow dress and a wreath of flowers on her head, her hair twisted up beneath it in a series of elaborate coils, and her cheeks were full and pink. Ten years ago . . . Bird did the math. She would have been eighteen here. Just a kid, off to her senior prom.

He gazed at the picture for several seconds longer before it clicked: the flowers, the makeup, the outfit. The prom, he'd thought, but it wasn't.

It was her wedding day.

The last time Lizzie Ouellette had willingly let herself be photographed—or the last time that someone else cared enough to point a camera in her direction, and the more Bird scrolled back and forth through her feed, the more sure he was that it was the latter. Facebook profiles only told you so much about a person, but there was something incredibly lonely about this one. Some people didn't post much online because they valued their privacy. But for Lizzie, it seemed more like she simply hadn't bothered, because no one would care.

They cared now, of course. In the past few hours, Lizzie Ouellette's timeline had come alive with comments. They read like macabre yearbook entries: *I can't believe it. RIP Lizzie. Lizzie we were never close but I know your having fun in heaven, stay sweet girl.* Bird dutifully wrote down their names, but he was already certain none of them would be any help. These people didn't know the girl, didn't spend time with her. With one exception, a Jennifer Wellstood, they had never liked a single one of her photos or even wished her a happy birthday. Certainly, they would have no idea what she'd been up to in the last few days of her life, which was Bird's job to piece together and proving near impossible. That moment at the house, just a few hours before—the barely suppressed snickering over that mole on the woman's breast—had been the tip of a town-wide phenomenon. Somehow, everyone in Copper Falls knew about Lizzie Ouellette, but nobody kept company with her.

Even her own father wasn't sure where she'd been that past weekend, what she'd been up to, why she would have ended up at the lake instead of the place she and Dwayne owned in town. Earl Ouellette had been Bird's first interview, conducted in a corner of the police station, where the EMTs had left him just after dawn on account of the fire. Earl's stubbled face and gnarled hands were smudged with grease and soot; as he talked, he kept scrubbing absentmindedly at one blackened knuckle with his thumb. Bird wondered if he might be in shock. By any reasonable measure, he should be. It was a hell of a thing for a man to bear, his livelihood and his family both gone in a single morning. Lizzie had been his only child. Earl Ouellette was now alone in the world. And yet . . .

"I don't know what help I can be. We didn't keep in contact much," Earl said. He gazed straight ahead, his eyes bloodshot and glassy from the smoke, or grief, or both.

"Even with her living so close?" Bird asked.

Earl had shrugged. "Everything's close here. The whole town ain't but a mile end to end. Lizzie kept herself to herself. She always did, even when we was under the same roof."

"At the junkyard?" Bird had passed by on his way here, just to see the charred remains of the single-wide that had been his victim's childhood home. "That must have been hard. Close quarters. Even just for two."

"She had her own room. I tried . . ." Earl paused so long that Bird thought that might be it, the whole sentence. I tried. But the older man coughed, retrieved a handkerchief from his pocket, spat a thick gob of brown mucus into it. "I tried to give her space," he said.

Earl's thumb passed back and forth over the soot stain. Working it.

"Have they figured out how the fire started?" Bird peered at him. Earl shrugged. "Haven't heard. Could be anything."

"You had insurance, I'm guessing." He tried to keep his tone casual, but the man's shoulders stiffened all the same.

"Ayuh."

Bird didn't press; the fire was a strange coincidence, but it wasn't his to investigate. And anyway, Earl Ouellette had been dead asleep behind the wheel of his truck in the parking lot at Strangler's for most of the previous night, as was apparently his weekly habit. Half a dozen people had seen him—or heard him snoring—which meant that Earl was officially off the hook for arson and murder alike. For several seconds, the men sat in silence. Bird was considering his next question when Earl Ouellette suddenly turned and stared directly at him. The old man's eyes were an unsettling shade of blue, like an old pair of jeans bleached nearly colorless by years of wear.

"They asked where she went to the dentist," Earl said.

"The dentist," Bird repeated, then shook his head as the realization clicked. *Shit.* "Oh. To make an ID. They didn't tell you . . . ?"

Earl's gaze stayed steady, puzzled but no less piercing.

Goddammit, Bird thought.

"The police identified your daughter at the scene by a distinguishing mark on her, ah, upper rib cage." Bird watched as the blue eyes narrowed, the wiry brows knit together. "I'm sorry, Mr. Ouellete, there's no good way to say it. Your daughter was shot. Her face was badly damaged."

Some men would have broken down at this moment. Bird was grateful that Earl Ouellette did not. Instead, the older man fished a cigarette from a crumpled pack and lit it, ignoring the posted NO SMOKING signs and a gray-haired receptionist who turned and glared at the first whiff of tobacco.

"It would be a help to have medical records," Bird said. "Any records. Dentist, or—do you know which doctor your daughter went to?"

"Can't say that I do. She saw Doc Chadbourne for that business ten years ago." He paused. "You'll have heard about that."

Bird had. He nodded, and Earl did, too.

"Chadbourne passed away, though. Maybe four years back. Nobody to replace him, so most folks go to the clinic down in Hunstville, if they go anywhere."

Bird scribbled a note to himself as Earl dragged deep on the cigarette. He was gazing into the distance now, working his jaw. He cleared his throat.

"A distinguishing mark, you said."

Bird nodded. "A mole. I assume . . ." Earl cut him off with a curt nod.

"Had it since she was a kid. They said she could get it took off with a laser, but I never had the money."

"I understand. Sir, I know this is a difficult time, but as a family member—what I mean to say is, if we showed you a photograph of the mark, would you recognize it?"

Earl nodded again, his one-word reply coming out on a cloud of smoke.

"Ayuh."

Ten minutes later, Bird turned off the cruiser's engine and glanced in the rearview mirror, running a hand through his hair. It was shaggier than he liked it—miles from the no-fuss buzz cuts he used to give himself back in his early days on the force—but the longer it got, the more you could see the early grays coming in at his temples, and so he'd put the clippers away and started letting it grow. It made him look a little older, a little graver. Not a bad thing for a cop, and especially not on a day like this. Although if he really wanted a trim, he supposed he was in the right place.

The building in front of him was a trailer, with a canvas awning mounted over the door and a custom paint job. Bright purple, the same shade as the hand-lettered sign that stood close to the road. In keeping with small-town tradition, the salon's name was an atrocious pun: this one was called Hairs 2 U. The paint was fresh and well-maintained. The parking lot, cracked and pocked with jagged potholes, was not, which squared with what Bird had heard and observed about Copper

Falls overall: people were doing their best, and the summer people were a help, but not even the yearly influx of tourists could reverse the town's protracted death from neglect. The roads crumbling, storefronts shuttered and cloaked with dust, the Victorian farmhouses standing vacant at the edges of unplowed fields, their walls beginning to buckle under the repeated weight of the winter snows. The carcasses of roadkilled deer were left to decay by the side of the county highway, because there was no budget anymore for the guy whose minimum-wage job it had once been to drive out in his pickup and scrape them up with a shovel.

Every year, the population of Copper Falls shrank just a little bit more as people gave up, lost hope, fled south in search of easier lives—or didn't, and died where they sat. Bird had taken a glance at the numbers. Even before Lizzie Ouellette turned up with her face blown off in the house beside Copperbrook Lake, life expectancy in this rural county was well below average, for the usual reasons. Accidents. Suicides. Opioids.

He got out of the car and mounted the steps below the awning, the door squealing on its hinges as he pushed it open. The junkyard was still burning, the air still faintly acrid, even here at the edge of town. The scents inside the trailer—shampoo, peroxide, something vaguely, chemically grapefruity—were pleasant by comparison.

There was only one person inside, a brunette with a heavy jaw and a phone in her hand. She glanced up at him, then back at the screen.

"Jennifer Wellstood?" Bird asked, already knowing the answer. The brunette nodded.

"Sheriff said you'd be by. How long will this take? I have a client coming."

"When?"

She shrugged. "An hour?"

"That's fine. I just have some questions. My name is—"

"Yeah, I know." She sighed at the phone, then set it aside. "I don't know how much help I'll be. I barely knew Lizzie."

"Funny, everyone says you were her closest friend in town," Bird said. The woman looked at her feet. "If that's true, it's sad," she said. Then she shook her head. "Fuck. It's probably true."

The thing you needed to understand, Jennifer said, was that Lizzie didn't make it easy. Yes, folks were shitty to her. Her dad, too. Earl Ouellette had come to town as a young man to work at the logging outfit, married a local girl, and taken over her father's junkyard all within a span of ten years or so—which made him inherently untrustworthy, as far as a certain set of local diehards were concerned. It didn't matter that this had been four decades ago, give or take; no matter how long you stayed, or how many roots you put down, they didn't run deep enough to impress the families who'd been here for five generations. And as for your kids—

"You ever hear that saying? 'Just because a cat gives birth inside an oven, that doesn't mean the kittens come out biscuits'?" Jennifer said, smiling wryly.

Bird nodded. "Yeah, I've heard it."

"Then you know how it went. It didn't matter that Lizzie was born here. She was still an outsider, as far as folks were concerned who cared about that stuff."

And she made an easy scapegoat, Jennifer said. Not just because of her dad, or that trash heap where they lived, or the fact that Earl Ouellette sometimes hunted squirrels for stew meat—something that might have been normal wherever it was that he came from, but folks around here frowned upon it, and he didn't even have the decency to act ashamed. It was Lizzie herself. Earl was complacent in the face of the town's disapproval, but Lizzie, she gave it back to them. And it just kept on and on that way, until the loathing was all anyone remembered, until people hated her—much, much more than they'd ever hated her daddy. It ran dark and deep like a river between her and everyone else. Unbridgeable.

"But you were friends," Bird said.

Jennifer shrugged. "We weren't, really. But we didn't have bad blood. If I saw her out, I'd say hi, she'd say hi. I didn't always get along with Lizzie, but I guess . . . I kind of felt sorry for her. Dwayne was always showing up to stuff without her, barbecues or whatever, like we were still in high school and the guys would bust his balls if he brought her out. I mean, they *were* married. It was messed up. So I'd invite her sometimes."

Bird thought of the picture of Lizzie squinting into the sun with a can of beer. Had that been Jennifer's doing? A pity invite to hang out in somebody's yard?

"When did you last see her?" he asked.

"Hard to say. I ran into her at Hannaford—it was a while back. Beginning of summer, maybe? We didn't talk very long. She was keeping busy, with work and then the house. The lake place. You saw it?" Bird nodded; she did, too, smiling a little. "She made it nice. She was good at that stuff. I was happy for her."

"I hear not everyone was."

Jennifer shook her head. "People are ridiculous. I mean, honestly, it's pure jealousy. Nobody *wants* to rent at a discount to their wife's second cousin Charlie. They'd all like to do what Lizzie did, tell Cousin Charlie to screw off and put it on Airbnb, get some city people with deep pockets to rent it out. That one couple, I can't remember the name, but they were loaded. They took Lizzie's place for a full month last year, and then again this summer. The woman pulled up here in her big black SUV once, asking if I could tone her."

"Did you?"

"Nah, I would have had to special order it," she said. "She had unique hair."

"Unique?"

"Color treated. You know what balayage is?"

"Bally-what?"

She rolled her eyes. "Never mind. Anyway, I guess it started out rose gold or something, but the water up here was messing with it—

between the lake and the sun she was getting real brassy. Honestly, it looked like shit. I told her the best I could do was take her back to her natural color."

"How'd that go over?"

Jennifer snorted. Bird laughed in spite of himself.

"Anyway, that was the last I saw her. Too bad. I could've probably charged her triple."

Bird cast a glance around the space. Like Lizzie, Jennifer had an eye for decorating—products lined up neatly along the wall, a potted plant offering a pop of green beside them. It wasn't bad for what it was, but it was still a hair salon in a trailer.

"What about Lizzie? You ever do her hair?"

"Once, actually. For her wedding."

"I saw a photo. She looked very pretty."

Jennifer chuckled. "Lizzie? Pretty? Must have been a good picture. The hair turned out nice, though. I was still in vo-tech then; I was just a kid. But yeah, it was just that one time. She doesn't come here"— she paused, checking herself—"I mean, *didn't* come here. Lizzie wasn't much for haircuts. Or chitchat."

"She didn't confide in you, then," Bird said.

"Not me. Not anyone, I don't think. Dwayne, maybe."

"Tell me about Dwayne."

Jennifer shrugged. "I don't know where he is, if that's what you're asking. I guess you think he did it, huh?"

Bird didn't blink. "How about him and Lizzie? You knew them both, sounds like. How'd they end up together?"

She snorted. "They were eighteen, Officer. I bet you can guess."

"So she was pregnant," Bird said. He'd known this, of course. It was one of the first things he'd learned about Lizzie Ouellette once he started asking questions, the first thing that most people seemed to think he needed to know about her.

"She was," Jennifer said. "She lost the baby, I guess. But she got the guy."

"It sounds like you think she got away with something."

Jennifer sighed. "Look, I was two years behind Lizzie and them in school. I didn't run with those kids. But I don't think I was more than four years old the first time someone told me the Ouellettes were trash and I should stay away. They said Lizzie had herpes and if you got too close, you'd catch it. We didn't even know what herpes was, but you know how kids are."

"Sounds like this was more than kids being kids," Bird said.

"It definitely kicked up a notch around the wedding. People were angry about what she did to Dwayne."

"What she . . . did?" Bird tried to keep his face neutral, but Jennifer caught his tone and smirked.

"Oh, you know. Ruined his life." She rolled her eyes. "Like she got knocked up all by herself, right?"

"Is that how Dwayne felt?"

She shifted her weight, suddenly uncomfortable. "I don't know. Everyone was surprised that they stayed together, after. He didn't talk about it very much. I think he felt trapped once they were married, baby or no baby."

"Were either of them ever involved with someone else? Affairs?"

"I wouldn't know about that," Jennifer said quickly. But her eyes slid to the side as she did.

Bird would come back to that, if he needed to. For now, he finished his questions and thanked Jennifer Wellstood for her time.

He was halfway turned around, shifting the cruiser into gear to pull out of the parking lot, when the door of the purple trailer banged open. He dropped the car into park, instead, then rolled down the passenger-side window as Jennifer approached. She had her arms crossed tightly beneath her breasts, hugging herself, and she looked back and forth, up and down the empty road, before bending at the waist to peer through the window.

"Miss Wellstood," Bird said.

"Look," she said. "I don't want to cause trouble."

"Trouble for who?" Bird said, and again, she looked chagrined. Good. Sometimes, people just needed a gentle nudge in the direction of decency—or at least, not being overly worried about damaging the reputation of the guy who'd dismantled his wife's head with a shotgun.

Jennifer leaned in farther. "A while back, I went by Lizzie and Dwayne's place to drop some stuff. It would've been right after the holidays, I had my husband's whole family for Christmas and she let me borrow her big roaster pan. She answered the door with two black eyes."

Bird raised his eyebrows and held her gaze, waiting, sure there was more. Jennifer bit her lip. "She was trying to keep me from getting a good look. And I didn't ask. I didn't want to ask." Then she shifted her weight, and for the second time, her eyes slid sideways. Guilty. "I guess I should have asked."

Bird leaned toward the window.

"You think Dwayne was hitting her?" he said, but Jennifer stiffened and stood, stepping back and looking out at the road. A car was approaching from the west. It slowed as it passed, the driver's face a pale moon behind the glass. Watching. Jennifer waved. A hand flashed in return. When the car was out of sight, she stood back, recrossing her arms.

"You didn't hear this from me."

CHAPTER 6

LIZZIE

My husband was a lot of things. A high school dreamboat. A lowlife bully. An athlete who could've gone pro, if only. A junkie. A jerk. And yes, he was a killer. Eventually—and eventually, we'll get to that part. I mean to tell you everything. But it's not enough, just to tell the truth; I'm telling you a story, and I want it to come out right. You have to know how it all began to understand the ending.

My husband could be a real bastard.

But he wasn't a wife beater.

Even during the worst times, when he was really raging, drunk or stoned or both. I could see in those moments that he would've liked to hit me. But he didn't, and I think it's because he knew if he did, I'd hit back. And I'd make it hurt. I knew where his soft targets were.

He'd never have risked it. For all his legendary abilities on the ball field, the rocket arm that might have made him a star, my husband wasn't a man who enjoyed a challenge. The Prince Charming of my

fucked-up fairy tale preferred his fights unfair, his opponent hope-
lessly outmatched, and his outcomes guaranteed. In high school, he
was the big guy who'd stick out a boot in a crowded hallway just to
watch some puny eighth grader go sprawling. He was the kind of
man who took a weird, grotesque joy in following a spider around
the house, letting it scuttle almost all the way to freedom before he
brought down a shoe or a rolled-up magazine and turned it into a
smear on the floor. Or the goddamn bug zapper—he loved it. He'd
watch it like a movie, sitting there, beer in hand, while mosquitoes
and blackflies floated out of the twilit woods, drawn by the hypnotic
blue glow of the Flowtron in our backyard. If you closed your eyes you
could hear them hitting it: *Bzzt! Fzzt!*

Dwayne would let out this idiot's chortle every time one of them
incinerated itself, this *duh-huh-hurr* sound from deep in his throat,
and eventually he'd drain his beer and pitch the can away into the
yard and say, "These bugs are so fucking dumb."

That was my man: half-drunk on a Tuesday, reveling in his supe-
riority to something that doesn't even have a central nervous system.
Picking on someone his own size would have taken a kind of integrity
he just didn't have.

But the men in Copper Falls were like that. Not all of them, maybe
even not most of them, but enough. Enough to make it a trend.
Enough so that if you were one of them, you could look around and
assume that the way you were was the right way to be. Your own father was probably the same; he would be the one who first taught you
that there was a sense of power to be had in stamping on spiders, zap-
ping flies, snuffing out a life so much smaller than yours that it hardly
meant anything at all. You'd learn early, while you were still a boy.

Then you'd spend the rest of your life finding little things to crush.

It happened the summer that I was eleven, still young enough to feel
that the place we lived had a kind of magic to it. Our trailer sat at
the end of the lot nearest the road, the heaps rising up behind it like

an ancient, ruined city. It felt like the edge of another world, and I liked to pretend that it was, and we were its keepers, my father and I—sentries at the borderland, charged with guarding ancient secrets from trespassers and plunderers. Snaking corridors of hard-packed dirt wound back between the piles of scrap metal, splintered furniture, broken and discarded toys. There was a line of busted-up cars marking the property line to the west, stacked like oblong building blocks, so old that they had been there not just since before I was born but since before Pop took the place over. Pop hated them; he worried out loud that they would topple one day, and warned me away from ever climbing them, but there was nothing to be done. The machine that had been used to lift and stack them had been long since sold off to pay some debt, and so the cars stayed, slowly rusting. I would weave my way back to the place where that line ended, where the heaps stopped and the woods began, a narrow path of yellowed grass winding into the trees just beyond the bumper of a crushed Camaro. This was the oldest part of the property, from some long-ago time before it became a repository for unwanted things. A hundred yards into the trees was my favorite spot: a clearing where the rusted-out husks of three ancient trucks sat facing each other, sunk into the earth up to the wheel wells. Nobody knew who they'd belonged to or how they'd come to be left there, nose to nose like they were paused in the middle of a conversation, but I loved the shape of them: the curvy hoods, the heavy chrome fenders, the big, black, bug-eyed holes where the headlights used to be. They were part of the landscape now. Animals had nested in the seats over the years; vines had threaded themselves through the chassis. One of them had an oak tree growing straight through it, rising out of the driver's seat and through the roof, blooming into a lush green canopy overhead.

It seemed beautiful to me. And even the ugly parts, that line of stacked cars or the piles of busted junk, seemed like something exciting, dangerous, a little mysterious. I hadn't figured out yet that I was supposed to be ashamed—of the trailer or the heaps behind it, of our cheap furniture, of the way Pop would pluck toys or books out of the boxes of crap people left at the junkyard, clean them up, and present them to me at Christmas or birthdays all wrapped up with a bow on top. I didn't know they were trash.

I didn't know *we* were trash.

I have Pop to thank for that. For that, if nothing else. I was able to imagine for a long time that we were the blessed guardians of a strange and magical place, and I realize now that it was because of him, that he took it upon himself to keep the world's meanness at bay so that it wouldn't interrupt my dreams. Even when things were tough, when the winter had lasted a month longer than usual, and the car broke down, and he had to spend our grocery money for a new transmission, he never let on that we were desperate. I still remember how he would walk into the woods at dawn and come back with three fat squirrels strung over his shoulder, the way he'd grin when he said, "I know a lucky gal who's getting my nana's special limb-chicken stew tonight." He was so convincing with his "special" and "lucky" that I clapped my hands with joy. One day, I would realize that we weren't lucky but broke, and that our choices were squirrel meat or no meat at all. But in those early days, neatly clipping the feet off my dinner with a pair of bloodstained tin snips, undressing them out of their skins the way Pop had taught me and his daddy taught him, it all felt like an adventure. He shielded me from the truth about who we were for as long as he could.

But he couldn't do it forever.

I was alone a lot that summer, just me and the heaps and the junkyard cats. We'd always had a few skulking around, raggedy feral things that I rarely saw except out of the corner of my eye, a lightning-quick flash of gray slinking low from between the heaps and into the woods. But there had been a litter of kittens that winter; I could hear them mewing from somewhere near the trailer, and one day I saw a lean tabby cat disappear down a passageway into the trash with a freshly killed mouse dangling from her jaws. By June, the tabby had left for parts unknown, but the kittens were still there, grown into three curious, leggy adolescents who would sit on the heaps and watch me every time I walked through the yard. Pop gave me a long look the day I told him I wanted cat food from the grocery store.

"Them cats can hunt for themselves," he said. "That's why we don't chase 'em away, 'cause they keep the yard clear of vermin."

"But I want them to like me," I said, and I must have looked truly pathetic, because I saw him suck in his cheeks to keep from laughing—and the next time he went to the market, he came back with a bag of cheap kibble and a warning: no cats in the trailer. If I wanted a pet, he said, he'd get me a dog.

I didn't want a dog. Not that I didn't like them, understand. I always liked animals, liked them better than people for the most part. But dogs, they were just so much. The slobber, the noise, the desperate desire to please. The loyalty of a dog is overrated; you get it for nothing. You could kick a dog every day and it would still come back, begging, wanting to be loved. Cats, though—they're different. You have to work for it. Even the new kittens at the junkyard, the ones who hadn't learned yet to be wary of people, wouldn't take food from my hand right away. It took days before they didn't run from me, more than a week for me to earn their trust. Even when they would take scraps from my fingers, only one of them ever let his guard down enough to crawl into my lap and purr. He was the smallest of the bunch, with a white face and gray markings that covered his head and ears like a cap, and a funny pair of front legs that bent inward like a pair of human elbows—what some people call a "twisty cat." The first time he crawled out of the heaps, I laughed out loud at the sight of him, hopping forward and sitting up on his hind legs like a kangaroo, appraising the situation. He didn't seem to know that he was broken, or if he did, he didn't care. I loved him fiercely and immediately. I named him Rags.

My father didn't understand, nor share my warm feelings for broken things. The first time he saw Rags come creeping out of the heaps, his face darkened.

"Oh, hell, girl. He can't hunt with those cockeyed forelegs," he said. "He won't survive the winter. The kind thing to do would be to put him down, before he starves."

"He won't starve if I feed him," I said, balling my hands into fists and glaring. I was ready to fight, but Pop just gave me that dark look again, frustrated and sad, and walked away. That summer more than most, he didn't have time to battle it out with a stubborn kid over the sad, brutal facts of life. He'd worked it out with Teddy Reardon to buy the house at the lake—it was on the verge of collapse then, a hundred years old and barely used for the last twenty-five—and would leave me to watch over the junkyard most afternoons while he worked to fix it up. I took the job seriously for about three days, which is how long it took me to realize that everyone in town knew what Pop was up to, and nobody was going to come around looking for scrap metal or car parts when he wasn't here.

I didn't mind. I was used to spending long hours alone, playing elaborate make-believe games based on things I'd read in books. I'd cast myself as a pirate, or a princess, and imagine that the heaps were high walls surrounding a strange and mysterious land that I was trying to either escape or plunder, depending on the day. I was good at pretending, and I preferred doing it alone; other kids would always mess up these games, breaking character or breaking the rules, and shattering the fantasy along with it. By myself, I could occupy a single story for hours or even days, picking up where I left off as soon as Pop's car had disappeared down the road.

The weather that morning was ominous. The day had dawned gray and grim, the sky already heavy with low-hanging clouds. Pop had glanced at them, grumbling; he was still patching the roof of the lake house, and unhappy at the prospect of the work being interrupted by what seemed like an inevitable storm. To me, though, the massing clouds were just part of that day's story: a witch had taken up residence in the woods, I decided, and had cast a curse that was slowly spreading like a dark sickness over the sky. I would have to make my way to her lair, and battle her black magic with my own. I filled a glass jar with the makings of a counterspell: clover blossoms, a length of ribbon, one of my baby teeth from a box where I kept odds and ends. (The tooth fairy had stopped showing up at our trailer as my father's drinking grew worse, though I wouldn't make the connection for years yet; in the meantime the unclaimed teeth made themselves useful at times like this.) When Rags crept out of the heaps, I gathered him in my arms and added him to the game: all the other cats in the yard were the witch's servants, I decided, but this one had changed his allegiance after she cursed him with twisty legs.

I didn't hear them arrive; I don't know how long they'd been there, watching me. I was moving slowly and carefully through the heaps, making my way back toward the magical spot where the three rusted trucks sat nose to nose: if ever there were a spot to perform magic, that would be it. Absorbed in the game, lugging Rags along while he contentedly napped against my shoulder, it took me by surprise to realize that I wasn't alone. A group of three kids, two boys and a girl, stood staring from beside the long stack of cars, blocking the yellowed grass path into the forest. I knew all three, of course, from school and from town. Two of them, a girl and a boy with dirty blond hair, were Brianne and Billy Carter, twelve and thirteen years old, the children of our nearest neighbors on the other side of the woods that abutted the back of the yard. Once upon a time we'd played together, back when my mother was still alive to facilitate such things, but that friendliness had disappeared when she did; now they only ever showed up to throw rocks at the cars, and my father had spoken to them more than once about not crossing onto our property. Clearly, they hadn't listened.

The other boy, DJ, was younger—he'd sat a row behind me in Miss Lightbody's fifth-grade class the previous year—but he was big for his age, so that he and Billy stood almost shoulder to shoulder.

From the smirks on their faces, I guessed they must have been watching me for a while.

"Oh my God, it's disgusting," Brianne said loudly, and her brother grinned.

"I told you," Billy said. "She kisses it and everything."

"Oh my God," Brianne said again, and let out something between a giggle and a shriek.

It took me a beat to understand that they were talking about the cat, who was still obliviously snoozing in my arms with his funny forelegs tucked up under his chin. It took me longer to understand the full meaning of that "I told you," to realize that this wasn't the first time Billy Carter had crept onto our property and watched me while I played in the yard with Rags. He had been here before, maybe more than once, maybe hanging back in the woods so I wouldn't see him— or maybe I'd just been so lost in my stupid games that I never noticed I wasn't alone. Now he was back, and he'd brought an audience.

Billy and his sister sneered and laughed as I gathered Rags more tightly to my chest, but it was DJ who stepped forward.

"You shouldn't be touching that cat," he said. "My dad says cats like that have a disease. He's gonna give it to the other cats and soon they'll all be messed up like him. He shouldn't even be alive."

I bit down on my lower lip, unable to form my thoughts into words. My mouth was dry and my mind felt fuzzy, like I'd just jolted awake from a vivid dream, and my skin was prickling all over with the unpleasant shock of being intruded on. I wanted them all to go away. I hated Brianne and Billy, who had come through the woods and onto our property even though they knew they weren't allowed, even though they'd been warned. Pop had told them that the next time they trespassed he was going to call their folks, or maybe even the cops, and yet here they were, so sure that they could just tromp and stomp all over our yard and get away with it. But it was DJ who made me more nervous, the way he kept taking little steps forward, the way he looked at Rags with a mix of disgust and fascination. The way his red, wet mouth formed the words, *He shouldn't even be alive.*

I should have run. I could have run. I knew the yard better than anyone, and I was fast; I could have made it back through the heaps to the trailer and shut myself in, and Rags, too, safe behind the locked front door. We could have waited there until the intruders got bored and went away. Even though Pop said no cats in the house, he would have understood that I had to, that breaking the rules was the only way to keep the terrible thing that happened from happening.

But I was too slow. Too stupid. Too innocent to understand that we lived in a world where some people liked to stomp on little things— and where they'd tell you afterward that what they had done was a sort of kindness. I remembered all at once what Pop had said, the meaning of which I had stubbornly refused to really hear.

You ought to put him down before he starves.

DJ, the little boy with the red mouth, was fast, too. And unlike me, he had come with a plan: I would find out later that he'd tagged along with the Carter kids just for this reason, to do this thing he'd been taught was necessary. He grabbed Rags out of my arms before I knew what was happening. One moment my arms were wrapped around the cat; the next they were empty, and Rags was dangling by his armpits from DJ's hands, which held him fast as he squirmed. I tried to rush forward.

"No!" I screamed.

"It's gotta be fast. Keep her back," DJ said, his mouth set in a grim line that made him look older all of a sudden, like a grown-up man with a job to do. The low, gray clouds overhead had started to mass and darken, and from inside my head, from the part of my mind that could keep me preoccupied for hours with make-believe stories, a small voice whispered, *It's too late; the curse is spreading.* Brianne and Billy obeyed instantly, running to me, grabbing my arms, pushing me backward as DJ carried the squirming cat away, and I was screaming because I finally understood, too late, what was about to happen. What he was going to do. He shifted his grip on Rags, flipping him in the air, holding him by his hind legs. A single drop of rain sliced against my cheek as I struggled against hands that held me fast. DJ stopped in front of the stack of crushed cars, so tall and solid and unforgiving. I saw him shift his weight like a ball player, pivoting his knee, bending his elbows, his body coiling with pent-up energy as Rags swung helplessly by his hind legs—and then from inside my head, another voice spoke up, one that sounded like my own, but older and tired and ice-cold.

Don't look.

I squeezed my eyes shut.

There was a yowl, abruptly cut off by a terrible, echoing clang.

The hands that held my arms let go.

The rain began to fall hard, harder, dampening my T-shirt against my skin.

"Hey," said DJ's voice beside me. "Hey, look . . . it didn't suffer."

I didn't answer.

The rain kept falling.

I sat in the mud, shivering, eyes closed, until I was sure I was alone.

Pop arrived home not long after, and found me sitting on the folding stairs in the rain. I was soaked to the bone and holding Rags's limp body in my arms, my T-shirt covered with blood and matted fur.

"Lizzie?" he said. "Jesus, what in the hell . . ."

I looked up, and said, "It's okay, I didn't bring him inside, because you said—you said—" and then I was sobbing, and my father was scooping me up in his arms, me and poor, dead Rags together, and carrying me inside, where I eventually stopped crying and told him what had happened. I remember the look on his face as he listened and then stood up, grabbed his keys, and set out down the road in the direction of the Carters' house: it was the same look I'd seen on DJ's face an hour before, the determined expression of a man with an unpleasant but necessary job to do. He told me he would be back in ten minutes, but it was much longer, closer to an hour, and whatever he said, Billy and Brianne never set foot on our property again that summer—and come September, they were gone entirely, the whole family moved down-state never to be heard from again.

DJ was another matter, a more delicate one. His daddy was the preacher at the hilltop church in the village, and his family name was among the oldest in town, even engraved on the founders' monument that stood on the green. My own father, who'd grown up far from Copper Falls and shared blood with nobody in town but me, had to tread carefully—this was what he told me as we dug a grave for poor, sweet Rags in the clearing behind the yard, and I laid a bouquet of clover blossoms and dame's rocket on the freshly turned earth. He made me tell the story again, and then a third time, listening care-fully as I repeated the sequence of events. The appearance of the kids at the edge of the yard. The way Rags was in my arms, and then wasn't. The way DJ flipped him, head to tail. The terrible resonant clang as bone covered by fur collided with the fender of a crushed Camaro. The feeling of the rain soaking my shirt, my hair, as I sat in the mud with my eyes closed—and then the sight that greeted me when I opened them. He asked me, gently but with great seriousness: Was I sure about what DJ had done? That it was, indeed, him? Even with my eyes closed? And just as seriously, I nodded. Yes, I was sure.

The next morning, Pop shaved his stubble, combed his hair, put on a clean shirt, and drove into town. He was gone a long time; the sun was midday high when he finally came back. He wasn't alone. As I stood watching from the folding stairs, a second car, newer and nicer and cleaner than Pop's old pickup, pulled in behind. The preacher was at the wheel. There was a smaller figure in the passenger seat.

"I'll be inside," Pop said, then cast a look back over his shoulder at DJ, who stepped out of his father's car and stood with his hands stuffed deep in his pockets. "This boy got something to say to you. Isn't that right?"

"Yes, sir," DJ said.

I watched as he approached, my arms folded carefully across my chest. I thought I'd be sick at the sight of him, at the memory of what he'd done, but I wasn't; instead, I felt curious. The boy walking toward me seemed like a different person from the one who'd taken Rags from my arms. That grown-up look was gone from his face. He looked young, unsure, unhappy. He stopped a few feet away, shifting from one foot to the other.

"My dad says I owe you an apology," he said finally. He kept his eyes down. "He says that even if it's right on principles to put a cat like that out of its misery, I shouldn't have done it. Because, um, because"—he cast a quick look back at the figure behind the wheel of the car—"because it wasn't my place, Dad says. So he drove me over here to tell you."

"To tell her what, boy?" said my father's voice, and DJ and I both startled; he was standing just inside the trailer door, a shadow beyond the screen, and I felt a flush of gratitude that he had stayed to see this through.

"I'm sorry," DJ said.

I didn't know I was going to speak until the words were already out.

"Are you?" I said, and for the first time, the boy lifted his eyes and met my gaze.

"Yeah," he said, and then, so quietly that only I could hear him: "I wish I hadn't done it. I wished it right away."

Of course, there was no undoing it. Sorry or not, Rags was dead, and so was the part of me that believed in fairy tales, in magic spells, in saving broken things from a world that wanted to hurt them. I stopped playing in the heaps after that. I never fed the junkyard cats again. I didn't tell myself pretty stories about our place in the world. When I stepped out the door, I knew who and what I was: a girl who lived at the center of a mountain of trash.

And now it's all gone, and so am I. I bet you can see the smoke from that burning yard for miles. If you squint, maybe you can see my soul floating skyward along with it, lifted on a column of putrid, billowing black. I wonder where my father is, if he'll finally leave. He should. Business torched, daughter dead; there's nothing to keep him in Copper Falls.

But wait: this story isn't over. I almost left out the best part.

Because after the forced apology and sudden expression of regret, DJ nodded and turned away, and walked with hunched shoulders back to where the preacher's car sat with the engine still running. The man in the driver's seat rolled down the window, and a cloud of cigarette smoke curled out through the opening and into the hazy air.

The preacher said, "All done now, Dwayne Jeffrey?"

The boy said, "Yes, sir."

Because that boy, the one who killed my cat—reader, I married him.

CHAPTER 7

THE CITY

"Adrienne Richards?"

She'd been waiting so long and listening so intently for the name to be called, she was out of her seat on the first syllable. The leather sofa where she'd been perched squeaked rudely as she rose.

"Yes."

The woman who'd called Adrienne's name was young and impeccably dressed, from the trademark red soles of her Louboutin heels to her trendy, oversized glasses. She smiled in a practiced way, tight lips and no teeth, pure professionalism; if her client's more casual sneakers-and-leggings look was out of place, she gave no indication.

"Through here, please, Ms. Richards."

"Thank you."

The Louboutins clicked away and she followed, steeling herself to walk smoothly, to act normal. To pretend this was a day like any other. Just a woman having a meeting—business as usual, nothing to see here.

It wasn't easy. She'd already had one scare that morning, just a few blocks from the salon where she'd booked a walk-in appointment with the first available stylist for highlights and a haircut. She'd intentionally chosen a spot fully across town from the condo—equally far from both Ethan's office and any of Adrienne's usual haunts—in part to avoid the possibility of running into anyone who might know them. Thus far it had worked perfectly. Nobody had given her a second look, and the young man who'd styled her hair had given her exactly what she asked for: a long, wavy bob with rose-gold highlights, a perfect match to the picture Adrienne had saved on Pinterest under the tag "hairspiration."

When a finger tapped lightly on her shoulder as she stood on the sidewalk, fumbling for her keys, she nearly shrieked aloud. She whirled around and found herself face-to-face with an apologetic-looking blonde wearing the same head-to-toe Lululemon-inspired style that also dominated Adrienne's wardrobe, like a uniform that allowed members of the city's female leisure class to know one another in the wild. A closer look revealed that they were in fact wearing the same leggings, in slightly different cuts.

"I almost didn't recognize you!" the blonde chirped, and there was a moment of pure, gripping panic: *Fuck. Who are you?* The woman's face was familiar, but only in the sense that Adrienne's world was full of women who looked like this, generically beautiful, with thick, patrician brows, their faces as artfully sculpted by cosmetics and injectables as their bodies were by boutique fitness classes. Then the blonde spoke again, and the panic released.

"It took me a minute to remember your name—Adrienne, isn't it?"

She smiled back, instantly adopting the same apologetic tone.

"Yes! Of course, hi! I'm so sorry—this is embarrassing, but I've completely forgotten—"

"It's Anna," the blonde said, laughing. "SoulCycle, the early Saturday class. I know, right? I'm so terrible when I run into someone from the studio in real life, it's like, a different context? I almost walked right past you, but then I spotted your bag . . ." She broke off to gesture at Adrienne's gym tote, which was indeed hard to miss: not just the print, loud and colorful, but the logo emblazoned across one side, a conspicuous announcement that the bag had likely cost at least two thousand dollars. Anna's gaze landed briefly, enviously, on the label, then bounced back to eye level. "Anyway, I thought I'd say hi. Your hair looks great! Did you do something?"

"Sort of," she said. She desperately wanted this conversation to end, but Anna was clearly one to keep small-talking; being uncharacteristically curt would be unwise. She smiled in a way that she hoped seemed self-deprecating, a little intimate, and leaned in. "To be totally honest, I've had this color before. It was last year's big fall trend, but I just can't let it go." She paused, allowed herself to giggle. "Is it awful that I think it really works on me?"

"Ohmigod, no, totally," Anna said, with so much earnestness that it was hard not to burst out laughing. "You'll probably make it re-trend! You should post it on social. So have you been to spin lately? I don't think I saw you there this weekend, or . . . wait, did you have a vacation planned?"

The panic was back. For someone who claimed a faulty memory, Anna was way too knowledgeable about the details of the Richards family's travel schedule. *Dammit, Adrienne,* she thought. She'd always talked too much.

"I guess I've been off my routine," she said. Another self-deprecating smile, tone friendly enough. Still, she worried it was the kind of cryptic nonanswer that might pique Anna's interest.

But Anna wasn't interested. She'd stopped listening, maybe even without hearing the start of the answer to her own question, and was instead staring down at her phone and tapping furiously at it.

"Anna?"

"Oh, dammit," Anna said. "Adrienne, I'm sorry, I have to put out a fire, but maybe I'll see you . . . you know . . ."

"Sure," she said, and Anna looked relieved—at being able to return her attention to the so-called fire, or maybe just at not having to explicitly commit to attending a SoulCycle class with Adrienne, who she hardly knew and had probably only ever pretended to like.

Either way, that had been the end of it. She'd air-kissed at Anna, who had twinkled her fingers back in a twee little wave, and it was all over with no apparent suspicions aroused. Her next stop was back downtown, and she'd passed the drive in a sort of ecstatic fugue state, terrified but also strangely exhilarated by the surprise run-in. She had been totally unprepared for it, had been waiting the entire time for the inevitable moment when Anna realized that something was very, very wrong. Halfway to her destination, she'd been gripped by another wave of panic and had to pull over to examine her reflection in the rearview mirror, suddenly haunted by the horrifying possibility that she'd missed a spot, and that she'd been chatting away to Anna-from-SoulCycle with a fine spray of someone else's blood prominently displayed on her face.

But of course there was nothing there. And Anna hadn't noticed a thing. Whatever mark last night's horrors had left, however powerful the sense that she'd woken up this morning as an entirely different person and everyone would know, it was now clear that she could still be, or at least seem, normal. The realization made her giddy.

I could get away with this.

Everything she had done since last night was predicated on this being true, but until now, she hadn't truly believed it. Even though some people would be quick to point out that this wasn't the first time Adrienne Richards had gotten away with murder, in the most literal sense of the word—but that had been different. Adrienne had been young, and dumb, and reckless, and the man's death had been an accident. A very different thing, all told, from putting a shotgun under someone's chin and looking at her face as you pulled the trigger.

There had been so much blood.

She shuddered and shook her head furiously, trying to obliterate the memory, or at least blur it out.

And yet, the other thought was still there in her head, impossible to ignore.

I could get away with this.

There was just one thing: it was definitely "I," and not "we." She was seeing things clearly now, and that included the unignorable fact that her husband was going to be a problem. Everything had happened so fast, there had been no time to consider the obvious pitfalls of choosing him as a partner in crime—and it wasn't as though she had a choice, not when he had chosen her first. This whole mess was his fault, and here she was, cleaning it up. Not for the first time. Good little wifey, stepping in. There had been a time when she wanted to play that role, and then, eventually, "want" stopped having anything to do with it. Every marriage has its well-worn grooves. This was theirs. It was how things worked between them. The blood spatter had been still warm and wet on her cheeks as she turned to him and told him that it would all be fine, she would take care of everything. And she'd meant it.

But this, she thought, was the last fucking time.

The woman in the Louboutins showed her down the hall and through another doorway, the clicking of her heels suddenly hushed; the marble floor underfoot had been replaced by gleaming wood covered with a richly woven oriental rug in subtle shades of red and ochre. A small gold plate beside the door read, simply, RICHARD POLITANO, and then, beneath that, PRIVATE CLIENTS. They passed through an inner waiting room—empty but for the rug and a few other pieces of tasteful, plush furniture—and then a second doorway, where her escort cleared her throat and said, "Adrienne Richards," like she was a servant in a Jane Austen novel announcing the arrival of a noble-woman in the drawing room. There was a huge mahogany desk in the room, and a small man sitting behind it, who rose at the sound of Adrienne's name.

"Mrs. Richards," he said, smiling in the same practiced way as the woman in the Louboutins. He extended a hand, an exact half inch of shirt cuff showing past the sleeve of his perfectly tailored suit. "So nice to see you. It's been ages."

"It's Adrienne, please," she replied, matching his smile. "And it has been ages. I was trying to remember when I was last here."

There was a soft click from behind her, and she turned to find that the heavy door through which she'd entered was now shut. The woman in the Louboutins had left, and left them their privacy. She suddenly understood the purpose of that superfluous lobby, an empty room in a building where square footage came at a serious premium: it was a symbol, a hundred-thousand-dollar buffer between you, the *private client,* and the ordinary business practiced elsewhere in the firm. In here, you were special. In here, you were safe.

"Adrienne, then," said Richard Politano. "And you'll call me Rick, of course. As for your last visit, weren't the two of you here together? You and Ethan? Just the once, I think. It would have been quite some time ago, during that . . . well, unpleasantness."

She nodded. "That's right."

"Well, we meet today under better circumstances, then. Have a seat," he said, sweeping his hand to one side to indicate a pair of arm-chairs, cozily arranged at angles to a polished coffee table. "Can I offer you a coffee? Or a glass of wine? I'm sorry to have kept you waiting. I had to shuffle a few things to fit you in, but of course I'm always happy to make time for you, and Ethan. How is Ethan?"

"Ethan is fine . . ." She trailed off, pressing her lips together, shifting in her seat—and noted with pleasure the way Rick shifted forward incrementally in his, leaning hungrily into the space where something was clearly being left unsaid. She decided there was no need to beat around the bush: "But as you can see, Ethan is not here."

It was a statement designed to elicit a response, and she wasn't disappointed: in the split second it took for Rick Politano to temper his reaction, she saw a series of emotions flit across his face. Amusement, surprise, intrigue, excitement. *Good,* she thought. She offered him a smile, tentative and sly.

"Rick. I'm going to speak candidly. I can do that, can't I? You've always struck me as a man who takes confidences seriously."

"Of course," he said, and this time, he made no effort to hide his interest. His tone didn't change, but his smile did; the upper lip crept up by a millimeter, and in an instant, Rick Politano's expression shifted from friendly and businesslike to positively vulpine.

"I'm asking because I need an advisor. Someone I can trust," she said.

"I'm not sure I understand," Rick replied, cocking his head in a way that suggested he understood her perfectly.

She leaned forward, keeping her eyes locked on his, and said, "I don't want to be one of those women who gets blindsided by life. One of those women who lets the husband handle everything, assuming she's safe and taken care of, and then the shit hits the fan, and it turns out she has nothing."

"I see," Rick said. "Is there something I should know? To borrow your expression, Adrienne, has the shit hit the fan?"

"No," she said. Then: "I don't know. Not yet. Maybe it won't. But if something happens, if something is coming, I want to be prepared. I want to know where I stand. And ever since the . . . unpleasantness, I feel I'm lacking that information. Ethan doesn't tell me much. I feel . . . I feel as though I'm not in control. And it feels terrible."

Rick Politano had thick black eyebrows under a swoop of thick white hair, and as she finished speaking, he knit them together in disapproval.

"I'm surprised to hear that," he said. "A man who keeps his wife in the dark is walling himself off from a valuable ally, especially—if you don't mind my saying—if she's as ambitious and intelligent as you are. I always thought Ethan understood that, but . . . well, who's to say. Perhaps he didn't want to trouble you."

"Perhaps," she said. "But here I am, troubled."

"Well, we can't have that," Rick said, smiling. "So let me assure you, every possible scenario has been considered and planned for. It's thorough but not complicated. I'm happy to walk you through it."

"Yes," she said. "Please do."

CHAPTER 8

LIZZIE

There's still so much I haven't told you. About the life I had with Dwayne, and the life we made together. The baby, so small and so still, in the glimpse I had before they took him away. Dwayne's accident, and the addiction that followed. The way things soured and festered over the years, the way our happiness rotted from the inside, until it all ended with a bang, literally.

But there will be plenty of time for all that.

It's time I told you about Adrienne Richards.

Adrienne Richards was not the kind of person who frequented Copper Falls, and Copper Falls was not the kind of place that would've appealed to her. The town itself was un-lovely, all those falling-down houses and boarded-up storefronts, dust gathering in the plateglass display windows that lined our little main street. Some of the towns farther south had cute little rows of shops for the summer people and enough seasonal business to sustain them; we only had one, the dairy bar, run by a lemon-faced woman named Maggie whose right forearm was forever bigger than her left from years of working the ice-cream scoop. Besides Strangler's—and lord help the out-of-towner who tried to set foot in that shithole—there was nothing to attract tourists except the lake itself, which was beautiful but remote. Fifteen miles outside the un-lovely town, down a series of winding gravel roads that were tiresome to drive at the best of times, treacherous at night, and well out of reach of the nearest cell tower, which freaked a lot of city people out. The ones who did come usually wanted the place for a weekend, a week at most, and the only question they ever seemed to ask was whether it had Wi-Fi. (It didn't.) It's why I thought Adrienne's message was a prank at first, some local jackass trying to have a little fun. It was like a parody, the way she pretzeled herself to make clear without saying it outright that she and Ethan were a Big Dang Deal. She wanted to book a full month ("money is no object"), she wanted to confirm that the lake and the house were as isolated as they looked on Google Earth, and she wanted to confirm that our "staff" (I laughed at that one) were discreet, because she and her husband took their privacy very seriously.

Later, I realized why she chose Copper Falls, and my house, when everyone with that kind of money was vacationing in fancy places, the Hamptons or the Cape: she needed to be where they weren't. She wanted the anonymity of Copper Falls, where nobody was sophisticated or interested enough to know her backstory. She wanted to escape her reputation, if only for the summer.

We had that in common. I think that's why, eventually, she chose me, too.

For most people in Copper Falls, Adrienne and Ethan were irritating but uninteresting, just another rich couple who weren't from around here and weren't to be trusted, but whose money they'd grudgingly accept as long as they insisted on hanging around. The details of their lives, and the extent of their wealth, were irrelevant; when poverty has always been right next door, in your neighbor's house if not your own, the difference between a millionaire and billionaire is just an abstraction. It's like trying to calculate the travel distance to Mars, as compared with Jupiter. What's another hundred light-years, when what really matters is that it's totally out of reach and you're never fucking getting there? Even when I realized that the Richardses weren't just your average upper-middle-class couple, I couldn't wrap my head around what it meant to have that kind of money.

But the way the world felt about them—that, I understood. When I did an internet search for Adrienne's name, right after I received her prepayment in full for the month, it was suddenly clear why "discretion" was so important to her. She and her husband were famous for all the wrong reasons.

Ethan Richards was a criminal. The soft kind, one of those fancy, white-collar bad guys who floats away on a golden parachute and lands gently in a pile of cash while the company he looted burns to the ground. The scandal was old news by then, but stories like this always ring the same bells. Shady dealings, hidden losses, men with corner offices tiptoeing along the finest of lines between *unethical* and *illegal* in order to line their already-overstuffed pockets, and stepping all over the little guy on their way to wealth. When the shit finally hit the fan, hundreds of people lost their jobs, and even more lost their life savings. The scope of the whole thing was hard to grasp, but the impact was plain enough. Somewhere, someone's grandma is going to spend her retirement eating Fancy Feast in an unheated apartment because of what Ethan Richards and his friends did—and of all the men involved, Ethan got away without a slap on the wrist.

That night, I stayed up for hours reading all the stories about his arrest and subsequent release, and all the outraged op-eds that came later, about why the laws needed changing so that people like Ethan Richards would pay for their crimes down the road. He was never charged, but it almost didn't matter. As far as the press and the public were concerned, he was guilty on all counts, with Adrienne as his codefendant. It was funny how that worked out. People were angry at him, but, lord, they really hated her. You could see why: she made the perfect villain, a gorgeous picture of shallow privilege with her little vanity projects, her Instagram sponsorships, her totally unearned life in the lap of luxury. And then there was the callousness; she seemed either ignorant or indifferent when it came to the havoc her husband had wrought, and some of the articles even slyly suggested that she might have had a hand in it herself, a flawlessly highlighted, fashion-forward Lady Macbeth urging on her man from behind the scenes. Later, after I got to know her better, I would decide that they were probably wrong about that. Adrienne just wasn't ambitious or imaginative enough to mastermind a billion-dollar accounting scandal. But the more I read that night, the more I couldn't help admiring Adrienne Richards. The corporate drama, the news stories, the possibility that her husband might be indicted for fraud and go to prison, leaving her with nothing—a lot of women would have lost their minds, but not Adrienne. More than anything, it all seemed to bore her.

I couldn't tell her any of that, of course. I wouldn't have. I'd already decided to treat them like any other guests, save for an offer to stop by once a week to do a little light cleaning and change out the linens, and that's only because they were staying so long. The day they arrived, I handed over the spare set of keys, gave them the five-minute spiel on our local attractions and the ins and outs of the house, and left them to themselves.

It was pure coincidence that I happened to be in the market a few hours later when Adrienne came in. She was something to see in that moment, swanning through the aisles in her espadrilles, leaving a perfumed trail and half a dozen annoyed locals in her wake. At first she just flitted from section to section, making disappointed noises over the selection of cheeses, grimacing at the vegetables ("Where's the *kale*," she murmured), putting nothing in her basket while people looked on and rolled their eyes. I had half a mind to sneak out before she could spot me. A couple old-timers were starting to shoot dirty looks in my direction, too, because there was only one person in town who would rent to a visitor so obviously not-from-around-here. One of them muttered something to the other under his breath; I caught the words "that Ouellette girl" and decided I'd rather not hear the rest.

But then Adrienne walked up to the register and started asking Eliza Higgins where the organic Icelandic yogurt was, and Eliza just kept saying, "What?" in this obnoxious fake-clueless tone, like she'd never heard of either yogurt or Iceland and maybe didn't speak English at all, and then Adrienne would repeat herself sounding more annoyed each time, and I found myself getting angry. Angry at both of them. I wanted to slap Adrienne, not just because she seemed not to realize she was being mocked, but because she should've known better than to give Eliza the opportunity, to think she could ask for any fancy thing she wanted in a place like Copper Falls. In fact, this turned out to be one of her great talents: to make it seem like *you* were the weirdo, the world's most adorable idiot, for not knowing about free-range alpaca milk, or freeze-dried yogurt-dipped bumblebee eggs, or bespoke vagina steaming, or whatever other expensive shit Gwyneth Paltrow had recommended in her stupid newsletter that week. But that was Adrienne, and then she'd somehow act surprised, all wide *Who, me?* eyes and bafflement, when everyone in town fucking hated her.

But then again, they fucking hated me, too—which put us on the same team. Would I have done what I did, if not for that? Would things have been different?

Because what I did was march up to the register myself and say, "Jesus fucking Christ, Eliza. She wants yogurt from Iceland. It's not that fucking complicated. Just tell her you don't have it, because you don't, because everyone in town only just stopped freaking out about that time three years ago when you started stocking Oikos and they had to learn to pronounce a new fucking word. And then point her to where the Oikos is, since it's the next best thing, so she can finish her shopping and get back to the lake. Also, she and her husband are gonna be here all month"—I turned to address the small crowd that had gathered behind me to gawk—"That's right, guys, the entire fucking month, and part of August, too, so you can go ahead and get your underpants in a big fucking twist right now"—and then turned back to Eliza to finish, "so maybe you'll find it in your heart to order a case of the Iceland stuff. If there's any left after they leave, I'll buy the rest from you myself. It's good, right?"

Eliza just gaped at me, but Adrienne jumped in like we'd been doing this routine together for years. "Oh, it's delicious," she said. "It'll change your life."

Twenty minutes later, Adrienne Richards paid for her groceries and we walked together into the parking lot, leaving Eliza Higgins scowling at her register. The sun glinted off Adrienne's hair—it was a silky blond back then, before she dyed it that trendy rose-gold color that the sunshine and lake water would eventually turn orange—and she glanced cautiously over her shoulder before letting out a husky, conspiratorial cackle.

"Oh my goodness," she said. "That was an adventure. I'm not sure I can ever go back there."

Her laughter was contagious, and I couldn't help myself; I giggled. "It might be a little bit awkward," I admitted. "If it's a problem, you can let me know what you're low on at the end of the week, and I'll bring it by when I come to do the housekeeping."

Adrienne raised an eyebrow, looking sidelong at me. "I'm not sure you can ever go back there, either," she said.

"Oh, they're used to me. I've known Eliza all my life," I said.

"She won't be angry?"

I laughed. "I didn't say that. But if you never had someone's good opinion to begin with, there's no need to worry about losing it."

I'll be honest: I didn't feel as cavalier as I sounded. We'd been out of the store for less than a minute, but the news of what I'd done would have spread town-wide by now, just another entry into the annals of Lizzie Ouellette, Trash Bag Bitch. I would probably hear about it from both Dwayne and my father before the day was done, and neither one of them would find it entertaining the way that Adrienne seemed to.

But in that moment, I found I didn't care. I wanted her to like me, to be the kind of person she would like. She was so *golden*. The way she wasn't even rattled by Eliza's rudeness, the way she walked through the parking lot with her chin lifted and her hips swaying, like she was floating down a runway. Walking beside her, matching my gait to hers, I allowed myself to hope that whatever magic she had inside her might rub off on me, just a little. And maybe I was imagining it, but something about the tone of her voice and the tilt of her head as she spoke made me think that a line had been crossed—that she did like me, that maybe we'd even be friends.

I think that was when I first realized: Adrienne Richards was lonely. I had read, in some gossip rag, that their friends all shunned them after what happened. Those magazines can be full of bullshit, but in this case, it was obviously the truth. They had no kids, no family, nobody to stick by them on the basis of shared blood alone. I imagined what that would be like, for someone like her. For the phone to stop ringing, the invitations to stop coming. To have people start whispering when you walked into a room. I studied her social media accounts: they used to look like a nonstop party, but now the photos never had other people in them. Mostly, they were only Adrienne, her face or her nails or her hair; occasionally, there would be a picture of a book or a coffee cup sitting on the same glass-topped table in her apartment. She and Ethan must have spent a lot of nights in there, just the two of them, staring at each other. I think their vacation was more about interrupting the boredom of their mutual exile than anything else. Not that they did anything differently during their month at the lake, but at least there was more space and different scenery to do it *in*. Sometimes, it seemed like they'd escaped to the lake just to escape from each other. When I visited the house, something I was doing every other day by the end of July, they were almost never together. She'd be on the deck, usually with a self-help book in her lap, always with a glass of wine that she'd refresh to a more photogenic level before asking me to take her picture. He'd be inside, napping, or out on the water in one of the Costco kayaks I'd left for guests to tool around in. Not paddling, just drifting. He'd take the boat a few hundred yards out and just sit there, staring into space, the paddle resting on his lap. I'd wave. He either didn't see me, or just didn't wave back. And then sometimes he wouldn't be there at all. The first time it happened, I saw the big black Mercedes missing and asked where he'd gone.

"He went back to the city," Adrienne said.

I frowned, not understanding. "Bummer. He couldn't stay?"

"No, he could. He just didn't." She yawned. The sun was getting low and golden, and out on the lake, a loon shrieked. Adrienne didn't react. She might have been drunk, or more than drunk. Had she already started using by then? I like to think I would've known, but she was good at hiding things.

"I'm sorry," I said.

Another yawn. "Whatever. Hey, Lizzie, take my picture?"

She leaned against the railing, the lake behind her, the wine in her hand, while I used her phone to snap a photo—and then another, and another, since Adrienne was fussy about her angles. I didn't mind. She was beautiful, and later, in the privacy of my bathroom, I would practice tilting my head and pursing my lips the way she did, and imagine being that beautiful, too. That poised, that "blessed," the word she always used to describe herself and the life she lived. And when I thought about Ethan, it was only to wonder why a man who was married to a woman like that wouldn't take every chance, every available opportunity, to be with her.

It seemed so strange.

It doesn't anymore.

CHAPTER 9

THE LAKE

The house in town where Lizzie and Dwayne had lived was a feature-less little saltbox: gray vinyl siding on the outside, old green carpet and wood-paneled walls within. Bird, who was six foot three, ducked involuntarily as he passed through the front door. In the west, the sun was dipping lower, drenching the early evening in golden light as a faint chill crept into the air, but inside the house it seemed that night had already fallen. The ceilings were low, the rooms dark.

Bird wasn't alone: Myles Johnson had met him out front, still look-ing as spooked as . . . well, as a man who'd started his day by pulling a severed nose out of a garbage disposal. Bird grimaced at the sight of Johnson's hands, already red and chapped from repeated washings. They were going to bleed before the day was done.

"You been here before?" Bird asked.

Johnson peered around, scanning the room from left to right. Bird followed his gaze. The doorway opened into a den that contained a torn fake leather sofa, a plaid recliner, and a pair of mismatched end tables. It was hard to believe that the same woman who'd so painstakingly decorated the lake house had also lived here.

Johnson replied, "A few times. Deer season, usually. I'd pick Dwayne up and we'd go hunting. I never stayed long, though."

"Anything look out of place?"

Johnson shook his head. "Not to me. But I can't be sure."

Bird moved toward the kitchen and Johnson followed, hunching as he passed through the doorway. The house was neat but claustrophobic. The rooms were airless and cramped, the furniture bulky and a little too big for the space. It wasn't a crime scene, at least not as far as anyone knew—one of the techs had swept through briefly and found no traces of blood, nothing in disarray. The shotgun registered to Dwayne was the only thing apparently missing. Dwayne and Lizzie's clothes still hung in the closets. The refrigerator was stocked. Someone's dirty plate sat in the sink, with something yellow—egg yolk, maybe—dried to a hard crust on the rim. None of it looked like anything to Bird. Sometimes, with a case like this one, the victim's home would have a haunted feeling, every scuff on the woodwork or stain on the carpet suddenly imbued with meaning, harbingers of eventual tragedy. Sadder still was when there were signs that she'd seen it coming: a suitcase packed and stashed in a closet, a wad of bills socked away in a drawer, the address of a shelter or a divorce attorney's business card tucked between the pages of a book. In the life of a battered woman, there would never be a day more dangerous than the day she tried to leave. In one heartbreaking case, the suitcase had been by the door, the woman it belonged to lying facedown a few feet away. She'd dropped it when he shot her.

Lizzie Ouellette didn't have a suitcase, or a secret cash stash, or a diary detailing her escape plan from years of abuse. Nor had Dwayne left behind a written confession, or a suicide note, or a telltale internet search for travel to Canada or Mexico. But Bird thought the house would be valuable all the same, if only for what it could tell him about the people who'd lived there, revealing things about Dwayne and Lizzie that the people of Copper Falls might prefer not to say. Jennifer Well-stood had been more forthcoming than most, but even she seemed to be part of an unspoken agreement among the locals to only reveal so much. This house, though, with the mismatched shitty furniture, the dingy carpet, the shelves that contained no books or mementos, the walls on which not a single photograph was hung—it all told a story. The two might have bedded down here together each night, but the shared space contained no sense of a shared life, no "us." The fake leather couch had a long dent down the middle where Dwayne must have regularly sprawled out alone. A few empty beer cans sat on the table at the end where he would have put his head, the one with the better view of the television. Lizzie could have taken the chair, of course, but the chair looked comparatively unused, with a pair of battered work boots with one broken lace lying on the floor right in front of it. Even with what little Bird knew of her, he couldn't picture Lizzie sitting there.

He left the kitchen and moved toward the back of the house, Johnson following at his heels. A doorway on the right opened into the bedroom: messy, with a sour aroma emanating from the piles of dirty laundry on the floor. Bird paused and glanced back at the deputy.

"How about this?" he asked. "Anything different?"

"I don't know, man. I was only ever in and out; they weren't invit-ing me into the bedroom," Johnson said, giving Bird a bewildered look. "But it looks . . . normal? For Dwayne, anyway. He's kind of a slob. You should see his car."

"How about Lizzie? Would this have bothered her?" Bird asked.

Johnson shifted uncomfortably. "I see what you're doing," he said.

"What's that?" said Bird.

"You want to know what it was like between them, were they fight-ing or whatever. I mean, I get it. But I just don't know, you know? People like their privacy around here. My own folks used to go into the basement if they were gonna have it out, because it was the one place where they could scream at each other without the neighbors hearing. If Dwayne and Lizzie were having problems, I never saw it. Hell, I hardly saw her at all. She kept her distance from Dwayne's friends and that was fine with us."

"Why's that?"

Johnson blinked, looking surprised, and Bird repeated the question. "Why's that, I said? Your buddy was married to her for ten years. You never wanted to get to know her? Or you just didn't like her?"

"I mean . . ." Johnson said, and trailed off. "I guess I never thought about the why. There wasn't any one reason. Things with Lizzie, it was just, you know. It was how it was."

Bird turned away. He'd heard that one a few times today: *It was how it was.* Why did the town still find Earl Ouellette faintly suspicious even when he'd lived here for decades, owned a business, married a local woman, fathered a child who'd grown up alongside their own? *It was how it was.* What made Lizzie such a unique combination of punching bag and pariah, a girl who everyone casually loathed from a distance without ever stopping to ask why? *It was how it was.* Copper Falls was a place where your role was assigned early and permanently; once people had decided who you were, they'd simply never allow you to be anyone else. Your label was what it was, for better or for worse.

For Lizzie, it had been worse. Bird had no doubt about that, even as he ran up against the community's tendency toward close-mouthedness combined with the broader taboo against speaking ill of the dead. People talked around it, allowing the ugliness to squat unsaid in between the lines.

Poor Earl. Lizzie was always a challenge. He tried to keep her in line. Maybe if he'd been around more, but . . . well, she took after her mother. God rest her soul. Both of their souls. Billie was always in trouble, too. Always wild, with something to prove. She was little older than Lizzie when Earl came to town. If the Cleaves boy had just been a bit more careful, if you know what I mean, maybe none of this would have happened . . .

Bird grimaced, letting his gaze drift around the messy bedroom. *The Cleaves boy.* That was the other thing: Dwayne Cleaves was thirty years old and the prime suspect in the murder of his wife, but people couldn't quite stop talking about him like he was some kind of hometown hero whose life had been unfairly derailed. *So much promise, such a shame. He was going to play major-league baseball. Or maybe it was minor-league. A scholarship? Well, whatever. Point is, he had a shine on him. He could've made something of himself. He gave it all up. And for what? Some folks say she was never even pregnant.*

The silence stretched on a beat too long, and Myles Johnson cleared his throat.

"I think they had a room upstairs, like an office," he said. "You check that out yet?"

"Not yet. Lead the way."

The men bumped against each other as they reached the back of the house and then turned to climb the narrow stairs beneath the sloping ceiling. It was warmer on the second floor, and brighter. Bird stepped onto the landing and nodded as he looked around: there was a sense of intention in this room that echoed the carefully decorated lake house. This upstairs space would have been where Lizzie spent her time, then, while Dwayne sprawled out with his beer and television on the story below. A low, narrow sofa was set against one wall, a potted plant in a stand beside it. There was a shelf at the other end filled with books, yellowed paperbacks mostly, and opposite the sofa was a small desk. The cheap laptop which had been sitting on top of it was missing, dutifully removed by the cops who'd visited the house that morning. The machine wasn't password-protected and had already been examined and declared uninteresting, or at least unhelpful. Lizzie used it to manage the booking calendar at the lake house—the names of everyone who'd rented the place that summer was supposed to land in Bird's inbox any minute—and to visit a handful of websites. The usual stuff, nothing scandalous: Facebook, Netflix, Pinterest. She'd been most active on the latter, curating little collections of "pins," bookmarks, and images; Bird had never heard of the site, but whoever had reviewed the laptop (a woman, he guessed) called the collections "inspiration boards." Lizzie kept them in half a dozen categories under various headings: interior design, makeup, landscape, style, crafts, and one eclectic board called "dreams." Bird had scrolled that last one expecting to see some sort of frou-frou fairy-tale tableau: Cinderella ballgowns, diamond earrings, billion-dollar mansions, the French Riviera. But Lizzie Ouellette's collection of "dreams" was banal, if not outright boring. A softly lit cabin in a snowy forest. A martini in a sweating crystal glass on a dark wood bar. Someone's feet in a pair of sturdy leather boots. A set of fingernails painted cherry red. A woman standing with her back to the camera, silhouetted against a peachy sunset. Bird, recalling the images, felt a twinge of pity mixed with annoyance. You'd think someone who lived in such a small place, lived such a small life, would dare to dream a little bigger.

He turned back to Johnson.

"You said you didn't spend much time in the house. I assume you didn't come up here?"

Johnson looked around, shrugging. "Nope. First time I've seen it. It's . . . nice."

"Reminds me of the lake house," Bird said, and the other man nodded.

"Yeah. Like, put together." He shrugged again. "You asked why she didn't hang out with us, right? But she had stuff like this; she had her own thing going on."

"The way I heard it, she would've had to find something else to do. Isn't that right? I heard that people gave Dwayne a hard time about marrying her. I heard that folks would invite him out, but not her."

Johnson squirmed. "I don't know. Sure, people liked to joke around. Bust his balls. It didn't mean anything. But in high school, Dwayne could get any girl he wanted, and Lizzie was kind of . . . you know. The junkyard. And her weird dad. And she was kind of high on herself, considering . . ." Only Bird made the mistake of leaning forward, a little too keen, and Johnson clamped his lips shut and started furiously rubbing his hands together again. He took a breath.

"I don't want to talk bad about Lizzie," he said. "I feel awful about what happened to her. I feel awful about everything. And I know anything I say, you're going to read into it, and I don't want that, either. I still don't think Dwayne would hurt her. All I'm trying to say is, being with her wasn't good for him. It kinda seemed like, once he got involved with her, everything started going wrong."

Bird tried another tack. "Like his career? I heard he was going to play major-league ball."

Johnson snorted a little. "Uh. No. College. D-1, maybe. But it was something, yeah, and then he couldn't. He had to get that job at the logging company because of the baby, and then there wasn't a baby. And then he had his accident. You've heard about that."

Bird nodded. The accident was a major plot point in the story of Dwayne Cleaves, Tragic Hero—a mishap involving a fully loaded logging truck and a faulty tie-down. Dwayne had suffered a crushing injury that left him minus three toes on his right foot, and lucky he hadn't lost the whole thing. A lesser-known but more interesting plot point, one that Bird had put together on his own, was that Dwayne had received a decent payout from the logging company for his troubles—close to six figures per toe—and used it for a down payment on a local business. Plowing in the winter, landscaping in the summer, equipment included. The original owner, a man named Doug Bwart, had since fled to a retirement community in Florida, but when Bird reached him on the phone, the man still remembered the transaction like it was yesterday. Most interesting of all, what he remembered most wasn't Dwayne.

It was Lizzie.

"Damn near gave it away, didn't I?" the man had grumbled. "Dwayne was a good feller, but that wife of his—damnable girl. She nickel-and-dimed me. She come in, waving around all kinds of paperwork, jawing on about emissions this and compliance that. I would've knocked another twenty-five thousand off just to shut her up."

That was before Bird informed Doug Bwart that Lizzie Ouellette was dead, at which point the man stuttered, backpedaling, assuring Bird that he'd never have spoken so harshly if he'd known. But like the house, with its upstairs-downstairs split personality—and like Myles Johnson, who had all but said outright that Dwayne would be better off without Lizzie around—Bwart's story was illuminating. And complicating.

Bird's thoughts were interrupted by the sound of Johnson clearing his throat.

"Sun's getting low," he said. "Have you seen what you needed to see?"

"Yes. And I appreciate you coming by," Bird added. "It's a help, having someone who knows the town."

The two men returned wordlessly down the stairs and exited through the front door, both inhaling deeply as they stepped into the deepening evening. The chill in the air was refreshing, the scent of smoke from the burning junkyard finally chased away. The yard itself was unsalvageable, Earl Ouellette's livelihood burned down to nothing but a pile of sodden ashes—and in another couple days, he'd have his only daughter's ashes to scatter on top. Loss on top of loss. A ghastly thought. Bird shook his head, dug in his pocket for his keys. Beside him, Johnson hovered. He was twisting his hands again.

"Sir?" the deputy asked. "Do you really think Dwayne did it?"

Bird stared into the distance.

"I think I'd like to ask him that question," he said finally. "Good night."

The saltbox house receded in the rearview as he drove away, but inside Bird's head, he continued to pace its rooms: the dark den, the messy bedroom, the short staircase, the airy office. Maybe the house, where the two had lived together yet so very separately, was a sign not of cooperation or compromise but of trouble brewing, bubbling, eventually boiling over. And yet: when Lizzie Ouellette had wound up pregnant, Dwayne Cleaves had stepped up and married her. Then tragedy, Dwayne's injury, had turned into opportunity, and Lizzie had stepped in to negotiate . . . and he'd let her. He'd *trusted* her. Granted, that had been years ago. A lot could happen; a lot could change. But the truth, the one that Bird couldn't ignore, was this: in two of the most challenging moments of their lives, moments that could easily have split them apart, Lizzie and Dwayne had come together.

CHAPTER 10

THE CITY

Adrienne's gym bag was heavy on her shoulder as she crossed the lobby of the downtown bank, stepping through the front entrance just as the clock struck five. The sidewalk was swarming with people and she draped an arm over the tote, holding it close to her hip, keenly aware of the catastrophic consequences should someone try to snatch it. She had left Rick's office hours before, but his warning words were still ringing in her ears.

"There's no need to rush this process. And a cashier's check of that size? My dear, it's simply not done. It's not just unorthodox, it's dangerous. I could never recommend a client take that kind of risk."

"But," she'd protested, which was when Rick leaned in and placed a hand on her knee. The touch was more fatherly than lecherous, but still startled her into silence.

"Adrienne, this money is yours," he'd said. "I want to be absolutely clear on that. You are in control, and I can distribute these funds any way you like." He grinned at her, that vulpine smile. Cunning and hungry. "But it's very important to me that you and your assets are well taken care of, and I believe I have a solution that can satisfy both your immediate and long-term concerns, without doing anything rash. This way, your interests are protected on all fronts . . . including from the greedy hands of the IRS."

She'd capitulated then. She couldn't very well explain that her immediate concerns were far more immediate and far less nebulous than she'd led him to believe, that the IRS was the least of her worries. That two people were dead and she was living on borrowed time.

She grimaced as she walked, hurrying to keep pace with the fast-moving crowd, office drones rushing to catch their trains home. Nobody looked at her, but she still felt horribly conspicuous, exposed. She had walked out with a check after all, albeit for just a fraction of what was in the accounts she'd hoped to liquidate entirely. But a fraction was a lot of money. More than she'd ever held at once. Rick was right: Ethan had planned for every imaginable scenario, including but not limited to his incarceration or death, to ensure that his wife was well taken care of. Whatever happened to him, Adrienne could be assured of living on in the manner to which she was accustomed, as the saying went. Or at least close enough.

"I don't want to pry," Rick had said, while the grin stayed in place, suggesting there was nothing he wanted to do more. "But perhaps we ought to review and discuss the potential division of assets? You'd be entitled to far more than this if, just for instance, you were anticipating a divorce—"

"Oh no, no. It's nothing like that," she'd said, quickly and with a laugh, as though the idea of divorce was shockingly ridiculous.

Oh no, Rick, she imagined herself saying. *It's something so much worse. Tell me, Rick: have you ever seen what happens when a shell full of Mag-Shok turkey shot connects with a human jaw? Her face literally exploded, Rick.*

And were her immediate concerns satisfied, as her trusted advisor had so elegantly put it? Thanks to Ethan's thorough planning, the answer might actually be yes. Adrienne had known about some of it—like the safe-deposit box, freshly emptied, its contents now safely packed into the bag on her shoulder. It had been a struggle not to gasp when she opened it, but she'd taken everything. Who knew when she'd have another chance? Better to collect it all, even if it meant walking around with hundreds of thousands of dollars stuffed into the zip pocket inside her gym tote.

The cashier's check, plus the diamonds. Now, those had been a surprise. Lord knew when Ethan had decided to acquire them, or how much they might be worth, but they were marvelously easy to transport.

She would have to wait to count it all. To calculate, estimate, decide whether what she already had was enough—which meant she'd have to decide exactly how much she needed, a question that only brought a dozen more in its wake. Enough for what? Enough for who?

Enough for two? she thought, and gripped the bag tighter still. To know what was "enough" required knowing what came next, and she didn't. She'd been half-convinced that it would all fall apart before she could make it even this far.

Instead, it was all going better than she'd dared to hope, even with the setbacks. Her greatest fear was that Richard Politano would stand in the way of her getting what she needed; instead, he'd been all too eager to help. Of course he didn't believe her about the divorce. He'd probably started stewing on that little possibility well before she arrived, calculating that Adrienne's side would be the more lucrative if she and Ethan split up. But there was something else, too: a palpable sense, running throughout their conversation, that Rick had never really liked Ethan. That he not only enjoyed helping Adrienne, but also got a little kick out of doing it by moving money around behind her husband's back. All the available funds were now in her name, spread through a series of brand-new accounts that Rick had promised she'd be able to access within forty-eight hours.

She wondered if she could wait that long. Or if she should. What if the additional money made the difference between getting away and getting caught? How much did a person need to make herself disappear? To become someone else and get the hell out of town, maybe even out of the country, a long drive south and across the border into Mexico—except that neither she nor her husband spoke Spanish. These were the things she needed to think about, should have already been thinking about. But even as she tried to focus, to plan ahead, her mind kept insistently circling back, revisiting everything she'd said and done so far that day. The commuting crowd on the sidewalk swept her along, and she drifted with it, holding the bag close but allowing her thoughts to wander. She picked through her memories, mulling over her missteps, realizing she was more worried about what she didn't remember. How many mistakes had she made without knowing they were mistakes? It occurred to her, suddenly, how many security cameras would have picked her up as she journeyed from place to place today. Sitting in the waiting room at Rick's office, crossing through the lobby at the bank. She had been smart enough to avoid toll roads on the drive back last night, to obey all traffic laws on the endless red-light-green-light slog down the nearly empty Post Road. But the city, with its noise and its bustle, had lulled her. As though she'd already begun to disappear, just another face in the crowd.

Now her face was on a half dozen cameras all over town, something she should have thought of earlier. If the police came knocking, if they decided to snoop, would they be able to track her movements? Would they think to look more closely? Her stomach lurched at the prospect, and she swallowed hard. She wondered how long it would take for them to match Ethan's prints, which were all over the house at the lake, with the ones they'd taken two years back. It was a stupid, showboating arrest that went nowhere, but that little bit of damage was done: he was in the system now, his fingerprints permanently on file. And despite her confidence that morning, all that bold bravado—*We are so close to finishing this, you just have to let me handle it*—she knew that "we" would not be doing anything. Ethan wouldn't be talking to anyone; if the cops showed up before they could run, it would be Adrienne who met them at the door, offered them coffee, answered their questions. Her husband would have to make himself scarce; even if he kept his mouth shut, one look at his guilty face was all it would take for them to realize the truth. And when they asked where she'd been since Sunday night, she would need to sell the lie.

I don't know nothin' about no murder, Officer. I'm just the beautiful wife of a wealthy financier, having a normal weekday.

Normal: a trip to the salon, a run to the bank, a meeting with the financial planner, and . . . dammit. Because she'd already screwed it all up, hadn't she? Rick said it himself: her visit was "an unexpected surprise." Adrienne hadn't seen him in years, and he'd shuffled his schedule, maybe even canceled other clients, to accommodate the appointment. Not normal. Not normal at all.

She'd have to be more careful. She should stick to her routine. Do the kind of thing women did when they had nothing to hide, and they had all day, every day, to do whatever they wanted. She should buy a green juice for fifteen dollars. Get a manicure, a pedicure, or both. She should go to the stupid SoulCycle class after all, spend an hour riding to nowhere as fast as she could, post a picture of her glistening décolleté and hashtag it *#SweatIsGold*.

"Excuse me," she said, suddenly, hoisting the bag into a more secure spot on her shoulder and darting through the pedestrian crowd. She had an idea: there was no SoulCycle in sight, but there was a coffee shop on the next corner. She made a beeline for it, slipping through the door and falling into line behind a gaggle of college-aged girls who were ordering pumpkin spice lattes. She asked for the same. Skim milk, one pump, no whip. The barista picked up a cup in one hand, a Sharpie in the other.

"Name?"

"Adrienne," she said, stressing the last syllable like always, because people never seemed to get the spelling right. "With two *N*s and an *E*."

Five minutes later, she picked up the steaming latte and found a seat at the countertop, resting her feet on the gym bag as she settled into position. Her phone in one hand, the cup with her name on it in the other. Something had gotten lost in translation—the cup read ADRINENN—but that was all right. The photo was what mattered: she opened the front-facing camera and scrutinized the screen as she brought the cup to her lips, turned so that the shop's logo could be seen, and widened her eyes above the rim. She tilted her head, and the rose-colored waves fell lightly alongside her face. She selected a filter that brought out the richness of her hair, and captioned the picture: SUGAR, SPICE, EVERYTHING NICE. #FALLHAIRDONTCARE #PUMPKINSPICESEASON #CAFFEINEJUNKIE #AFTERNOONPICKMEUP

Even without whipped cream, the latte was cloyingly sweet. She managed to drink half of it before it went lukewarm, forcing herself to sit, wait, watch through the plateglass window as people passed by. A few of them glanced her way, their eyes skating past hers, but nobody approached her. For a moment, she was cocooned once more in that luxurious sense of having already disappeared, of being nobody at all.

On the counter, her phone buzzed briefly. She picked it up, punched in the code. The picture she'd posted had a smattering of likes, and one new comment.

It said: *Privileged bitch.*

She laughed in spite of herself, a high, hysterical giggle. A few heads turned, but that was all right. Adrienne was used to being looked at.

It was, after all, just a normal day.

CHAPTER II

LIZZIE

She really was a privileged bitch, you know. Adrienne Richards, née Swan, the heiress to a modest fortune made by a great-grandfather who owned a furniture company. The family had its roots somewhere south, near the Blue Ridge Mountains, and even before she married rich, Adrienne was definitely one of *those* girls. Private-school-educated, Southern debutante, sorority darling, a card-carrying member of the NRA. The kind of woman who still talked about going to college for her "M.R.S." degree. I learned all this the same way everyone else did. It wasn't hard to find; you've probably heard the stories, too. There was the splashy magazine spread on her million-dollar wedding. Or the time she insisted on building a basement spa, complete with plunge pool, in their hundred-year-old town house on the Green—when Adrienne told a local reporter that the neighbors who complained about the noise were just "jealous haters." There were the rich-lady start-ups, from organic perfume to a line of vegan leather handbags to astrology-based interior design, all blithely abandoned when Adrienne's attention span ran out and she discovered, to her horror, that running a company required actual work. There were the legendary tantrums. The obnoxious Instagram account. And then, eventually, there was the sleazy husband who made a billion dollars ruining people's lives, people for whom Adrienne Richards couldn't seem to muster a shred of sympathy, not even to save her own skin when the press came calling and their friends demanded answers.

And because of all that, you probably thought you knew every awful thing there was to know about Adrienne Richards. Maybe you even appreciated her in a twisted sort of way, for being such a perfectly drawn villain, the kind of woman people just love to hate. You wouldn't be alone. But you didn't know the truth.

Adrienne wasn't just a privileged bitch. She was bad, cruel, rotten, in the way people are when they've never had to care about anything or anyone else. The stuff in the news was just the tip of the iceberg; it was the stories she kept hidden that really told you who she was. Like the time she adopted a shelter dog as part of some social media campaign, then sent it back to the pound three days later because it peed on the carpet, and when the rescue asked why she wouldn't keep him, she lied and told them the dog had bitten her and should probably be put down. There was her mother, diagnosed with early-onset Alzheimer's and left to rot in a shitty nursing home down south. Adrienne hadn't visited even once, she explained with a shrug, because "Why would I bother? She'll just forget I was there." And there was the underage drunken driving accident that her daddy's fancy lawyer got bargained down to a misdemeanor and then purged from her record, even though the guy in the other car never walked again. He died of pneumonia five years later, right around the time that Adrienne was picking out the table settings for her wedding to Ethan.

This was the stuff about Adrienne that nobody knew—except me, because she told me. Would you believe that I was flattered at first? It made me feel so special, the way she sought me out. At first she would just ask me to stay for a drink when I came to tidy up the house, but soon I was driving over every other day just to sit with her and talk. She really was lonely, abandoned by her friends, no family but Ethan left to speak of. And I thought we had a connection, something like sisterhood, only better: two women, both set apart and misunderstood, bonding across the barriers of class and culture because we shared something deeper, something real. She told me her secrets, and like an idiot, I told her mine. The pregnancy. The accident. The pills, and everything that came after. I told her how we struggled, and she told me I wasn't alone. She'd wanted babies, too, she said. But Ethan had gotten a vasectomy during his first marriage, and either couldn't or wouldn't have it reversed. It was the kind of heartbreak all the money in the world couldn't solve, and we shared it. She knew what it was like to be ten years married, bound to a man who dragged you down with him every time he stumbled. We'd even gotten married on the same day, August 8, 2008. Of course, her husband remembered theirs.

I thought we were in it together. But I was fooling myself. She didn't confide in me because we were friends.

She did it because we weren't, and never could be.

She'd gaze at me over the top of her wineglass, her soft blue eyes all sleepy in the light of the late summer sun, and say, "I just love our talks, Lizzie. I feel like I can tell you anything," and it took me such a long time before I started to hear the part she wasn't saying. I can tell you anything—*because who are you to judge me?* I can tell you anything—*because I don't have to care what you think. Because you're country trash, junkyard girl, and no matter how low and shitty and grasping I am, I'll still be better than you.* Confessing her sins to me was comfortable, liberating, precisely because I was nothing. She might as well have whispered her secrets into the ear of one of the junkyard cats that still skulked the heaps at night, looking for vermin. Go on, unburden yourself. After all, what's that mangy cat gonna do? Who's it gonna tell? Who would believe it, even if it did?

When they came back the following year, I started to understand what I was to her, even if Adrienne didn't. If you asked her, she'd probably tell you that we *were* friends, or better yet, that she was some kind of mentor to me. A big sister, worldly and generous, guiding a local yokel in the direction of self-actualization. She'd never admit that she kept me around because she liked having someone to feel superior to. That it made her feel magnanimous to feel like she was doing me a favor.

So I played along. I promised to be honest, and this is the truth: I gave Adrienne Richards exactly what she wanted. I told her I was so glad she felt that way, because I knew I could tell her anything, too. I'd gaze at her with big, moony eyes, the dirtbag ingenue, just dying for my beautiful patron to bestow her wisdom and blessings on me. I pretended to be thrilled when she handed me a shopping bag full of twice-worn couture, thousands of dollars' worth of beautiful things that were utterly useless to me. As if I had anywhere to wear clothes like that.

"I was going to donate these," she cooed. "They don't fit me, since I went on paleo. But then I was getting ready to come up, and I thought, *Lizzie could wear them!* They might be a little snug on you. But you're so handy, you know how to sew, don't you? Maybe you can let them out."

I took them. I thanked her. I didn't bother pointing out that we were exactly the same size, that the red bikini and soft striped slub shirt she always wore at the lake had belonged to me first. That I gave them to her that very first week, when I came to deliver their groceries and change out the beds, because the pine trees were shedding like crazy and she was worried about getting tar on all the fancy-shmancy shit she'd packed. I didn't remind her how she sashayed out, wearing my bathing suit, and crowed, "Oooh, it fits! We could almost be sisters, I mean, except, you know," and I said, "Except you're the one who grew up in a fairy-tale palace and I'm, like, the hunchback twin raised by wolves," and she giggled. "Well, you said it, not me."

I kept my mouth shut, and went home, and hung the beautiful, expensive clothes deep in the closet I shared with Dwayne. They still smelled like her, a musky mix of shampoo and perfume that would waft out and travel through the house. The scent was so strong, so foreign, that I would sometimes catch a whiff of it as soon as I opened our front door.

Sometimes, when Dwayne was passed out downstairs or out God knows where, looking to score, I would put on a diaphanous strappy gown that was one of Adrienne's hand-me-downs and lie on the upstairs futon in our cramped little house, pretending I'd just gotten home from some sort of big, fancy party. A charity ball, an awards show, a dinner where you had six different silver forks, one for each course. The kind of events the Richardses used to attend, before they became pariahs. If I scrolled a couple years back in Adrienne's social accounts, I could see pictures of her wearing it, smiling in a ballroom, her arm linked with Ethan's. The dress was made of something silky, in a shade of green that reminded me of forest moss. Maybe it even *was* silk; I wouldn't have known the difference. It swirled around my ankles when I walked, and slid deliciously up my thighs every time I swung my legs up to lie back on the sofa. Like an invitation, except that nobody was ever there to accept. I sometimes thought about creeping downstairs, waking Dwayne, letting him slide the dress up to my waist as I lowered my hips to meet his, but I never did. It had been ages since he touched me by then, but that wasn't what stopped me. It was something worse: the awful feeling that he'd look at me and laugh. I wouldn't even have blamed him. When I passed a mirror, the fantasy would fall away and I would see myself for what I was: a grown woman with premature lines on her face and bruises on her shins, playing dress-up.

Maybe that's when I started to hate her. I didn't even know yet that she would give me so many reasons to. That second summer, she came armed with a list of special requests that never stopped growing. Could I come to change out the sheets every other day, instead of once a week? Could I drive an hour downstate to buy some string lights for the deck? Could she have some packages delivered to our house in town? I didn't mind bringing them over, did I? Of course I always did what she asked. Like I was goddamn delighted to be at her beck and call. I spent so much time smiling and nodding through clenched teeth that my jaw started to ache.

I should have been glad when she started asking for Dwayne instead. Suddenly, all the jobs that needed doing required his skills instead of mine. A dead branch was dangling over the roof and needed to be cut down. There were noises coming from the bedroom walls; she thought a bird or a bat might have gotten trapped inside. The drain in the bathtub was clogged again, something that only seemed to happen when Adrienne was staying in the house. She shed like a long-haired cat, all over everything; you always knew where she'd been. I wished she would wear a shower cap, and stop forcing someone to come by every three days to pull a big, nasty clump of her hair out of the plumbing.

This is the saddest part: there was some pathetic piece of me that still wanted to be that someone. Would you believe that instead of being relieved to be off the hook and happy to let my husband be the one at her beck and call, I was jealous? Not because she was getting Dwayne's attention, but because he was getting hers. It made me feel crazy. The more I loathed Adrienne, the more I wanted to keep her all to myself. To remind her that I was the special one, the one who accepted her when nobody else did. After all, it was me, not Dwayne, who understood her, who she confided in, who knew her secrets. I was the one who did her shopping, anticipated her needs, who remembered to put her favorite chardonnay on ice so it would be perfectly chilled when she arrived. I was the one she handed her phone to when she wanted a picture taken, who didn't even need to ask for her pass code because I knew it by heart, just like I knew exactly where to stand and how to tilt the camera to capture all her best angles.

And worst of all, I was the one who remembered that she once told me she'd love to see the lake after the season had ended, who had the bright idea to invite them back. "Peak fall is my favorite time of year up here," I said. "It's beautiful. You'd love it. Why don't you come up then, stay another week? I'll hold off on closing up the house. I'll even give you a discount."

She laughed at that. But then she said yes, they'd love to come back, and I felt a flush of triumph. Because the house was mine and that meant it was me, only me, who had the power to give Adrienne Richards what she wanted.

So you see, I have only myself to blame. That's what kills me—and yes, that's what killed me. I thought I was so fucking smart. But when I penciled Adrienne in for another week, it was my own dates I was marking.

Elizabeth Emma Ouellette, November 4, 1990–October 8, 2018.

And every terrible thing that happened that night, happened because of me.

CHAPTER 12

THE LAKE

Deborah Cleaves had a honey-blond bob and the studied manners of a preacher's wife who'd been by her husband's side through twenty-nine years of sermons, social calls, and church dinners—manners that persisted even though the preacher had passed away two years back. She offered Bird his pick of coffee or whiskey, and served the former on a tray accompanied by an antique sugar bowl and a little matching pitcher of cream.

"I'm sorry I don't have decaf," she said. "I keep the regular on hand for guests, but I don't drink it myself."

"Regular is fine," Bird said. "I'll be up awhile yet."

"Will you be staying here in town?"

"For the moment."

She nodded. "Of course. I'm sorry to be meeting you so late. I drove out this morning to visit my sister and wasn't checking my messages. If I'd known . . ." Her voice began to tremble, and she trailed off, shaking her head, and dabbed at her eyes with a tissue. "And you don't have any idea where he is? Dwayne?"

"We were hoping you might," Bird said, and Deborah Cleaves shook her head harder. She twisted the tissue between her hands.

"No, no, no. I couldn't imagine, I can't imagine. That w . . ." she started to say, and snapped her mouth shut, coughing to cover the faux pas, but Bird caught it. *That woman,* or maybe, *that wife of his.* Either way, he was guessing that Deborah's tearful concern was reserved largely for her son, with very little love lost for her now-deceased daughter-in-law. He also guessed that she would be very careful not to slip up like that again.

"Excuse me," Deborah said, recovering. "It's just, I haven't seen much of my son lately. He's always so busy—he owns his own business, you know—and then there was quite a lot to do at the lake this summer, as I understand it. Of course I wished he would stop by more often, but once they're grown, you know, it's hard—it's hard . . ." She broke off again, pressing her lips together, gathering herself. "But something must have happened. Dwayne wouldn't just disappear. Can't you do DNA? Or fingerprints, or something? Whoever did . . . that . . . to Elizabeth Ouellette, that person could have kidnapped him, or—"

The idea of Dwayne being kidnapped was absurd, but Bird nodded and broke in gently. "Did Dwayne have enemies? Someone who would want to hurt him?"

The tissue had started to disintegrate. "I don't know, I don't know."

"Could he have been in trouble? Money? Or drugs?"

Deborah Cleaves stiffened, her hands clenched into fists.

"My son doesn't do drugs." She glared at him. Her voice grew shrill. "Have you asked Earl Ouellette if his daughter did drugs?"

"We spoke to Earl," Bird said mildly. He allowed the silence to stretch for another few beats, while Deborah fidgeted. There was no obvious reason to think that the murder was drug-related, but the vehemence of her reaction gave him pause. If nothing else, addiction could put a lot of stress on a marriage. If Lizzie had been using, and if her husband had been unhappy about it . . .

"Detective? I'm sorry, I want to help. I just don't know what I can do. I don't know where my son is," Deborah said, breaking the silence.

"You can help by telling us right away if he calls you," said Bird.

"Of course, but—"

Bird smiled. "We want him found just as much as you do."

His conversation with Deborah Cleaves concluded, Bird drove back through town and turned right on the county road, crossing over the Copper Falls town line and into a no-man's-land of loosely developed plots. There was an auto-body shop that seemed to double as a repository for broken-down farm equipment; the grocery store with its windows brightly lit, the evening's last few shoppers pushing carts across the lot to their waiting cars; a gas station with a flagpole mounted on the roof, the Stars and Stripes hanging limply in the windless night, faintly lit by the streetlights below. Then, nothing. The lights faded behind him as the dark closed in and thick stands of pine trees rose up on either side of the road. A few minutes later, the bar called Strangler's loomed ahead, the last stop before the county road widened from two lanes to four and the posted speed limit jumped from forty to fifty-five miles per hour. Bird spotted it at a distance, set back a hundred feet from the road. The building was lit by floodlights and advertised by a dingy fluorescent sign that looked like it was floating, unanchored in the dark: one word, BAR, in red letters against a white background.

Bird sighed. It had been a frustrating day. Dwayne's friends and family swore up and down that they didn't know where he was. An APB on Dwayne's truck had gotten no hits so far, which was disappointing but not a surprise. There simply weren't enough men to monitor the hundreds of miles of country road that surrounded Copper Falls, not when Dwayne could be traveling in any direction, and was staying off the highways if he had a shred of sense. No LoJack in the truck, either. For all they knew, he wasn't even driving it. He could have just as easily ditched the vehicle somewhere in the woods off any of a hundred random dirt roads, where it could sit undiscovered until the following spring. But it wasn't just that they had no real idea where Dwayne might have gone; they also couldn't figure out where he'd been. The couple's movements in the days preceding the murder were infuriatingly vague. People remembered seeing both Lizzie and Dwayne around town within the past week, and every week previous, but all they could say was that everything seemed normal. Lizzie was back and forth to the lake, managing a rotating calendar of renters. Dwayne and his landscaping equipment had been in the woods all summer, clearing brush and downed trees on one of his buddy's ATV trails. If the couple had been fighting, nobody saw, or was willing to say so.

Then, the phone records: Lizzie's cell phone, a basic flip model, had been found at the lake house in the same handbag that held her wallet and ID. Dwayne's phone, the same as his wife's, had last pinged the only nearby tower around ten o'clock on Sunday night, then nothing. Discarded or dead, most likely. Because the area's cell coverage was so unreliable, most people in Copper Falls still had landlines. Dwayne and Lizzie had two, one at their house and a second at the lake; those records showed a call from the latter to the former just before three o'clock on Sunday afternoon. The call had lasted two minutes, but it was impossible to know who had made it, who had answered, or what was discussed. Basic maintenance, maybe. The summer was over, and people tended to close up their properties for the winter by the end of September, defrosting the fridge, draining the pipes, filling the toilets with antifreeze so that there would be no damage when the temperature dropped. But even though the last renter on Lizzie Ouellette's books had left after Labor Day, the house was still set up for guests, and there was a small note on Lizzie's calendar for that Sunday, the day she was killed. It said, *AR 7?*—just like that, with the question mark. One of the old-timers on the local police force thought it was a reference to the vintage firearm, especially since both Lizzie and Dwayne had been registered gun owners and competent if not avid hunters; Lizzie had sometimes made extra cash during the season by dressing small game for people who didn't want to do the messy work themselves. But the AR-7 wasn't a hunting rifle, and there was no evidence that either member of the couple had been interested in collecting guns.

And then, Bird thought, there was the weird curveball: a guest with a criminal record. The answer to Deborah Cleaves's question was that yes, they'd dusted for prints. The house was full of them, sets on top of sets, about what you'd expect for a property that had so many people coming and going. Lizzie and Dwayne and a rotating series of guests, plus probably a few fresh smudges from local law enforcement who either didn't know or didn't care about preserving the scene. They hadn't had time to run them through the criminal database, but thanks to the recently disclosed rental records, Bird now knew that at least one would be an immediate match.

Ethan Richards.

That Ethan Richards.

It stood to reason that Richards and his wife were the couple Jennifer Wellstood had talked about, the rich city folks who came from the internet and rented out Lizzie Ouellette's house for an entire month at a time. He was on the roster two years in a row, arrival date in mid-July, with a bunch of surcharges for additional cleaning and weekly deliveries; it looked like Lizzie had squeezed some extra cash out of the deal by doing their grocery shopping. Of course, nobody thought Ethan Richards had something to do with the murder. His crimes were the kind you pull off with a calculator, not a shotgun. Still, just seeing the man's name made Bird's stomach turn and his hands automatically clench into fists. He'd seen it right up close, the chaos and despair that Richards's corporate greed had wrought. His own parents lost their life savings when their financial advisor turned out to be one of many who'd invested in Richards's bullshit funds. An absolute goddamn catastrophe. The guy had invested a good deal of his own money, too, and couldn't even remember afterward where he'd gotten the tip. So many lives ruined. What Bird remembered best was his mother's voice when she called to tell him what had happened.

"I don't understand! Gary's a good man! He said it was 'risk-free arbitrage'!" she kept saying, over and over, until the words dissolved into a wail.

What he remembered second-best was the hunch of his father's shoulders at the table that Christmas. It was all over by then. The DA had declined to indict, and Ethan Richards and the rest had walked free. A lawyer might be able to help them recover some of what was lost, Joseph Bird told his son, but they couldn't afford one, and when Bird said he'd pay for an attorney, his father waved the offer away.

"Nah, son. It's all right," he said, smiling. "The way I see it, there's time. Worst-case scenario, I'll just work until I die."

Bird gritted his teeth at the memory. Dad had been close to a well-deserved retirement when his assets all but disappeared. When he made that crack at Christmas, he'd probably assumed he had another ten good years in him, maybe more.

Eleven months later, he dropped dead of a heart attack, and Amelia Bird had to sell the house just to pay for her husband's funeral.

It was a weird coincidence for that white-collar scam artist to be somehow connected to a case that Bird was working, but a coincidence was probably all it was. It was too bad; he wouldn't have minded a little trip to the city, a surprise knock on the door of Ethan Richards's billion-dollar mansion, a flash of the badge followed by a few needling, borderline antagonistic questions about his relationship with Lizzie and Dwayne. Nobody liked getting a visit from the police, no matter how wealthy they were, and he would have enjoyed the opportunity to make Richards's life just a little bit unpleasant.

Instead, Bird's next stop would be the hospital in the next county over, where he'd have the distasteful responsibility of watching the medical examiner perform Lizzie Ouellette's autopsy. He'd crack her sternum, pull the organs out of her body, weigh them, and finally state the blatantly obvious.

Manner of death: homicide.

Cause: single gunshot to the head.

Time: Sunday evening, which meant that at least twelve hours had passed before Myles Johnson discovered her body. Now the critical forty-eight-hour period following the crime was halfway gone, maybe even more than, with very little to show for it.

There were a dozen cars parked outside Strangler's, trucks and beat-up sedans, mostly American, and all with in-state plates. He pulled into a spot away from the rest and strode across the parking lot. The door squealed as he opened it, and the abrupt silence as he entered gave Bird a sudden flashback to eighth grade, the first day of school, and the paranoid sense of having walked into a room where everyone had just been talking about him. For a second, every pair of eyes in the bar seemed to be aimed his way. Then the moment passed, the stares stopped, and the buzz of conversation filled the room again. Bird found a seat at the far end of the bar and ordered a Budweiser from the man behind it, a craggy fellow with big, bushy brows who wrenched the cap off the beer like he was wringing its neck.

"You're that cop," said the bartender.

"That's right."

"You here to talk, or to eat?"

"Both. I'll take whatever's quickest," Bird said.

"Burger?"

"Sounds good."

"It comes with fries."

"Great."

Bird drank his beer and casually observed the rest of the bar's occupants. There was one younger couple in a corner, heads bent together, their eyes periodically flicking in his direction. Otherwise the patrons were all men, in work shirts or T-shirts, hands clasped around bottles of Bud or Molson with several empties collected on the table in front of them. No cops, although Bird recognized one man with a dark, sooty smudge above his brow as a member of the volunteer fire department who'd offered to drive Earl Ouellette to the morgue to identify his daughter's body. He wondered where Earl was now. Staying with friends, hopefully.

The bartender retreated into the kitchen and returned with a plate and a bottle of ketchup, sliding both in front of Bird with a curt nod.

"Were you working last night?" Bird said.

"Last night and every night," the bartender said. "And like I told the sheriff's man earlier, I didn't see nothing unusual, unless you count Earl sleeping off a few beers out in the parking lot around closing time."

"From what I hear, that wouldn't count as unusual," Bird said, and the bartender chuckled a little.

"The man likes his routine. Earl's all right. But nobody in here had anything to do with that business with his daughter."

"How about his son-in-law? I hear he's one of your regulars."

The bartender gestured at his clientele. "These folks are the regulars. If we're open, they're here. Dwayne, we'd get him in once a week, maybe, but he did his drinking at home. You see that feller there?"

Bird looked toward the corner and found that the couple sitting there were both staring at him. He lifted his chin, a nod of acknowledgment, and watched as they bent their heads back together, whispering.

"You might talk to him about Dwayne," the bartender said. A hardness crept into his voice. "You might do me a favor and arrest him while you're at it."

"For what?" Bird asked.

The woman at the table pushed back, stood up, picked up her purse, and walked out. The bartender scowled at the back of her head. "Never mind."

A moment later, the guy from the corner table stood up and strode toward Bird. He was rail thin, thirty-ish, with a prominent nose and shaggy dark hair.

"You're that cop, right?"

"State police," Bird said. "Ian Bird."

The man hitched his too-large pants up over his bony hips and slid onto the bar stool to Bird's left.

"I'm Jake," he said, flashing his teeth. "Cutter. That's my last name. That's what people call me, mostly."

"Nice to meet you, Mr. Cutter."

"It's usually just 'Cutter.' No 'mister,'" Cutter said. He swiveled his head to glance behind him. A group of men at the table nearest the door appeared to be glaring at him.

"Okay," said Bird. "Cutter. I hear you knew Dwayne Cleaves?"

"You're looking for him, right?"

Bird cocked his head. "That's right. Have you seen him?"

"No," Cutter said quickly. "I mean, not since, you know. Not since you all have been looking. But I do see him, pretty regular. Usually in here."

"You're friends?"

Another nervous glance backward. "Sort of. More like acquaintances." Cutter paused, and Bird waited. After a couple fidgety seconds, he added, "I'm from Dexter; it's a little ways to the east."

"So you didn't know Dwayne growing up, then."

"No," he said. "I met him maybe four years ago? Five? Hard to say."

Bird fought back the urge to sigh. "Okay. So you saw Dwayne regularly. When did you see him last?"

"Oh. Uh, I'm not sure." Cutter bit his lip, looking confused, and Bird felt another surge of annoyance. As frustrating as it had been trying to squeeze information from the people of Copper Falls, their close-mouthedness had one upside, in that he hadn't yet had to deal with this sort of rubbernecking from people who wanted to treat the murder like a spectator sport. Still, Cutter had approached him on his own. Maybe he knew something, but something he was nervous to share. Bird decided to try another tack.

"How about Lizzie? Were you friendly with her?"

Cutter's lower lip slid out from between his teeth, his confused expression morphing into a smile.

"Nah," he said. "This isn't a bring-your-wife kind of place."

Bird blinked and gestured at the door that Cutter's dining partner had just walked out of. "Weren't you just—"

"Marie?" Cutter guffawed. "No. Hell no. I like to keep my options open."

"I see." Bird chewed a french fry, turning information over in his head. Snippets of prior conversations. Deborah Cleaves, snapping: *My son doesn't do drugs.* Earl Ouellette, describing how Lizzie had always kept to herself. But it was Jennifer Wellstood who loomed largest, particularly the way her eyes darted to the side when Bird asked if the couple's marriage had been in trouble.

He leaned in conspiratorially. "How about Dwayne? Did he keep his options open? You know what I mean."

It was a risk, but it paid off: the look on Cutter's face was an answer in and of itself. The smile turned into a smirk.

"That's one way to put it," he said.

Bird made a show of glancing around the bar. "Anyone in particular?"

Cutter guffawed again. "What, guys? Dwayne wasn't a fag, man. More like a hero. I'll tell you what, the chick he had was way above local grade."

The seed of an idea was taking root in Bird's head. "Not from around here, then."

"Nope," said Cutter. He shrugged. "I guess there's no harm in talking about it, it's not like he has to worry about the wife finding out." He snickered. "Ooooh. Bad joke. Sorry. Anyway, I don't remember the lady's name. Some rich bitch. She was staying out at the lake with her husband for, like, all of August. Except the husband was gone a lot. And left his hot wife at the house all alone." He paused. The smirk returned. "A lot."

Bird almost guffawed himself. There was only one person Cutter could be referring to. Bird tried to keep his expression neutral.

"The Richards woman?" Cutter blinked, and Bird pressed: "Are you trying to tell me that Dwayne Cleaves was sleeping with Ethan Richards's wife?"

Cutter sucked his teeth and dipped his chin—*affirmative*—and Bird snorted. An affair would have been a relevant lead, but this one smelled like bullshit.

"Come on, man. You know who her husband is? And she's a beauty queen, or was. Hard to believe a woman like that would bother with someone like your friend."

The snark had the desired effect; Cutter bristled. "Maybe Dwayne gave her what her husband couldn't," he said.

Bird smiled. "I'm sure that's what he told you."

"No, man," Cutter said, loudly enough that several heads swiveled in their direction. He cringed, then lowered his voice. "I saw fucking *pictures*. He had one of those shitty phones with the little, tiny screen, but you could see plenty. You could see her mouth just fine." He grinned again, sinking his teeth into his lower lip. "That girl was a freak."

"Hey," a voice said sharply, and both Bird and Cutter looked up—Cutter flashing the guilty grin of a kid caught talking during detention. The bartender was glaring, one balled fist resting on the bartop. He turned his attention to Bird. "You done with this asshole?"

Bird glanced at his watch. "I do have to go, yes. Let me get my check, and Cutter"—he shoved a pad and paper across the bar—"write down your name and number. Here's my card, too, if you think of anything else."

The bartender returned with the check. He pushed it toward Bird with a grunt, then turned.

"You. Either order a drink or get the hell out," he said to Cutter. Cutter flashed the guilty grin again, flipped a wave to Bird, and skipped out the door. Every pair of eyeballs in the room tracked his journey, and the door swung shut behind him with a squeak.

Bird turned back to find the bartender still there, still glaring.

"You want to tell me what that was about?" Bird said.

"He brings a bad element into my place of business," the other man said, and disappeared back into the kitchen.

Bird tossed back the last of his drink, tossed some cash and another business card on the bar, and left.

His phone started to buzz just as he slipped into the driver's seat. He fished it out of his pocket with one hand, using the other to twist the key in the ignition.

"Yes?"

"It's Ed." The voice was familiar, but Bird couldn't place it until it added, "Behind the bar. You're sitting in my parking lot."

"Oh," Bird said. "Hello. I didn't forget to tip, did I?"

There was a short bark of laughter. "That's not why I'm calling. That guy you were talking to—"

"The one you wanted me to arrest?"

Ed grunted. "Whatever. He's bad news and generally full of shit. He's also loud as hell. Some of the other folks couldn't help overhearing. You know, about Dwayne and that woman from the city."

"I'm listening," Bird said.

"Look, I don't know what Dwayne was up to, if he was up to anything. It's not my business, and I don't want to know. But I did see those city folks. Not in here, just coming and going. They had a big black SUV, real nice. Expensive. It was hard to miss." There was a pause. "One of my regulars, he don't want to give his name, but he says he saw it passing by the other night."

"Which night?"

There was a muffled sound in the receiver as Ed pressed a hand to the microphone; Bird could make out the cadence of a question. A moment later, Ed returned: "Last night, he says. Around midnight."

"Thank you, Ed."

Bird hung up the phone and smiled.

CHAPTER 13

THE CITY

"I'd like to liquidate my accounts."

The words sounded very loud and strange in the quiet of Adrienne's car. She cleared her throat, tried again, dropping her voice into a deeper register. The confident alto of an anchorwoman, or a CEO presenting an annual report. She couldn't sound like a scared little girl. Would she be able to say it when the time came? Could she say it without her voice shaking?

"I'd like to liquidate my accounts," she said softly. "I'd like to liquidate my accounts."

The traffic crawled along, the car crawling with it. It would be after dark by the time she got back. She had taken her time after the coffee shop, walking aimlessly through the streets, stepping in and out of stores. Not buying anything, just drifting, enjoying the sight of pretty things lined up on shelves or hanging on racks. Getting a little bit lost, ultimately, so that she lost track of where she'd parked the Lexus and walked two blocks in the wrong direction before she realized her mistake. She retrieved the car just in time to get caught in the snarl of the city's endless rush hour, but even that wasn't so bad. It was nice in here: the near-silent purr of the motor, the softness of the leather seats, the comforting sight of the gym bag resting on the passenger seat beside her, headlights and streetlights flicking on outside as the sky turned dusky. She was safe, cocooned. And alone. At last, alone. After all those hours of self-conscious performance, of giving her all to the one-woman show called *Nobody Is Dead and Everything Is Fine*, here at least was a place where she could scream, or cry, or slump, without worrying that someone was watching. Without having to manage her image. Without having to keep it together for his sake, knowing that she was the only thing keeping him from falling apart.

She bit her lip. The traffic oozed forward, unhurried as ever. But Adrienne's car didn't feel like an oasis anymore. For just a little while, she hadn't been thinking about her husband.

Now all she could think was that she had left him alone for much too long.

A phone began ringing from inside the house as she fumbled with her keys. There was no reason for the door to be locked, and as Adrienne's key finally slid home and unseated the dead bolt, she suddenly imagined—or was it something more, something like hope?—that she would find the place empty, her husband gone.

Instead, she pushed the door open and saw him standing motionless at the end of the hall. The ringing phone was on a table set against the wall, and he was standing in front of it, mouth open, watching it go off. She watched in slow motion as he extended a hand, took a step.

"Are you crazy?" she yelped, and he whirled around at the sound of her voice, stumbling backward as she rushed into the house. "What the hell are you doing?"

"It keeps ringing," he said. He sounded bewildered. "It rang before. I thought maybe . . . maybe it was you."

"Why the *fuck*," she said, and grabbed the receiver instead of finishing the sentence. She lifted a finger to her lips as she brought the phone to her ear. She was out of breath; her "hello" came out in a little gasp. She cleared her throat.

"Hello?" she said again, and then, "Is anyone there?" even as the bottom dropped out of her stomach and she understood that there would be no answer. The call disconnected with a soft click.

It was happening now, then.

She'd been foolish to imagine that they had more time.

She put the phone back on the table and turned to her husband, still standing beside her with the same confused, vacant expression on his face—waiting, like always, for her to tell him what to do. She fought back the urge to reach out and shake him.

"They're coming," she said. "The police."

He gaped. "What? How do you—"

"You have to leave. Now."

"Oh," he said, and though it was just one syllable, something about the way it slid out of his mouth made the hair on the back of her neck stand on end. She looked at him again, at his face, at the way he was standing, and felt a wave of disgust crawl over her.

"Oh my God. You're *high*."

He flinched, veering down the hall away from her.

"Don't yell at me," he moaned, and now she did take hold of him and shake him, hard, her nails digging into his shoulders.

"I thought you got rid of that shit. I told you to get rid of it. What were you thinking?! Of all the times—"

He wrenched away from her, his eyes wild. "I was freaking out in here!" he cried. "What was I supposed to do? You were gone for hours, and I was starting to—"

"Of course I was gone for hours!" she shouted. "Do you have any idea what I went through today? What I went through for you? All you had to do was sit still long enough for me to . . ." She cut herself off, shaking her head. "And where the fuck did you even . . . never mind. There's no time. Get your shit and get out. Now."

He glared at her and she glared back, and a terrible realization flashed unbidden into her mind: *We've been here before.*

Christ, it was true. So many times. How could they have come so far, only to end up like this? Last night, she had made a horrific choice that would change their lives forever—only nothing had changed at all.

His voice had the snap of a petulant child's. "Fine," he said. He pushed past her and disappeared into the bedroom. She called after him.

"Get your clothes from last night."

"There's still blood on them." He sounded scared, but she couldn't worry about that now.

"That's why I don't want them in the house when the cops come. There's still a suitcase in the Mercedes; you can wear what's in there if you need something. Take the car, drive out of town, find a place to spend the night. Not the Ritz. Someplace shitty. Pay with cash. Only cash. You understand? And get rid of that shit. I don't want it in the car, either."

There was the sound of a toilet flushing, of water running. He reappeared, still frowning, and muttered, "Yeah, okay. What are you going to do?"

"What we talked about. It's not me they're looking for. I'll take care of it, and then . . . and then we'll go."

"Where?"

"South, of course," she said, without missing a beat—and prayed he wouldn't hear the lie in her voice.

Because the truth was, she didn't know. Not just which direction to run, but whether she even believed anymore that there was a future for them outside that door. She'd told him she would take care of everything, and she'd meant it when she said it. In that moment, after the gun went off, she was sure there was a way out. But coming home to him, to this, to the same bullshit that had grown so very tiresome after ten long years, to a man whose greatest skill was creating burdens that she would have to shoulder . . . any woman would ask herself if more of the same was truly what she wanted. And there was still the question, too, of what *he* deserved. The marriage had never been a fairy tale. She had carried so much weight for so long. What was she doing here? What had she done?

But there was no going back. Her choices were finite: to give it all up, turn herself in, and him, too, and then it all really would be for nothing.

Or she could keep going.

It's not over for you, Adrienne, she thought—and unlike the vow to head south with her husband, this statement had the ring of truth. It was the beginning of a different story, one she had been telling herself all day without even realizing it. A story about a woman who woke up wondering about her future. Who took stock. Who started making plans.

Lizzie and Dwayne are dead, but we are alive.

I don't want to be the kind of woman who gets blindsided by life.

I'd like to liquidate my accounts.

She watched as he performed his pre-departure ritual: patting his pockets to feel the bulge of his wallet, turning back for a last look at the house to see if anything was being forgotten. His eyes were bright and glassy. Every motion was familiar, but in this moment, she suddenly felt as if she were seeing it all for the first time. Observing him the way she might watch a stray dog trotting toward her on the street, trying to discern its motives, to decide if it meant to bite.

For the first time, it occurred to her that she might not know him as well as she imagined.

"Hey."

He turned to look at her.

"Is there anything you haven't told me? About what happened. Between you and him." She paused. "Or you and . . . her."

Ethan's keys jangled as he moved them from one hand to the other.

"That's ridiculous," he said.

A moment later, he was gone.

CHAPTER 14

THE LAKE

The woman who answered the phone at Ethan Richards's home sounded out of breath, as though she'd had to run to pick up the receiver.

Or been caught right in the middle of a little down-and-dirty with her married, murdering, wanted boyfriend, Bird thought, an idea that seemed ludicrous even as he entertained it. But if Richards's car had been in Copper Falls last night, and Richards's wife was at home in Boston right now, then . . .

Then I have no idea. Even with an affair in the mix, there was no obvious explanation. A Bonnie-and-Clyde situation, with an "Uptown Girl" twist? Or was Ethan Richards involved, too, somehow, making this the world's most unlikely throuple?

Bird listened as the woman cleared her throat. "Hello?" she said again. "Is anyone there?"

Then he hung up. The only way to find out the truth was to follow the lead. He threw the car into gear and pulled out of the Strangler's parking lot, driving back the way he'd come. He passed the auto-body shop, the gas station, the grocery, the main street, where houses with warmly lit windows sat like beacons between the gray, overgrown properties where nobody lived. He continued through town until he reached its central intersection, where a single stoplight was strung above the darkened street. The county road veered left here, heading north into the wilderness. Bird turned right and drove south out of town. The state medical examiner and Lizzie Ouellette's to-be-autopsied body lay in this direction, seventy-five miles downstate in Augusta, but Bird wouldn't be stopping there. He punched in Brady's number at troop headquarters as the lights of Copper Falls disappeared behind him.

The supervisor answered on the first ring, grunting, "Brady."

"It's Bird, checking in."

"Hiya there, Bird," Brady said. It was a nice thing about the boss: no matter how shitty the case or how little you had to report, he always sounded happy to hear from you. "You wrap up with the locals? They'll be waiting on you to start the postmortem."

"Actually, that's why I'm calling," Bird said. "I've got a lead. Our guy, Cleaves, might've had a mistress. One of the renters at the lake house."

"You got a name?"

"You won't believe it. You know Ethan Richards? That finance guy who—"

"I know who he is," Brady interrupted.

"Well, it's his wife," Bird said, and was rewarded with the sound of Brady whistling under his breath.

"That's interesting," he said.

"It is," Bird said. "And apparently, she was in Copper Falls last night."

"*She* was?"

"Well, her vehicle. Their vehicle, I should say. It's registered to the husband. Mercedes GLE. Not something you see a lot around here, so people remember it."

Brady exhaled. "Well, that's something. And where's the vehicle now?"

"I don't know about the Mercedes, but the mistress is at home in Boston." Bird glanced at the dashboard. "I've gotta stop to fuel up, but I should be there in under four hours."

"Hmm," Brady said, and fell silent. Bird waited. He was used to these pauses; they meant Brady was thinking. On the other end of the line, Brady cleared his throat and asked, "You think she was an accomplice?"

"Maybe," Bird said, then quickly added, "I don't know. Really. I'm back and forth on it. If she wasn't in on it, it's a weird damn coincidence. Maybe she just drove the car?"

"What about a hostage situation? He tells her to pick him up, maybe he doesn't mention he killed his wife—"

"I don't think so," Bird said slowly. "She's at home now, she picked up the phone, and she sure didn't sound like she was doing it at gunpoint. But I don't know that she'd run away with him, either. Slumming it with the guy is one thing, but committing to him? Or helping him kill his wife? That's a whole other level."

"People do crazy shit for love," Brady said.

"Or for money," Bird replied, and found himself nodding along to his own words. "Yeah. If Cleaves is trying to run, he'll need cash, and he doesn't know many people who can get it to him. If he's with her now, or headed there—"

"Right, I'll call Boston PD," Brady said, picking up the thread. "Have them do a drive-by. If Cleaves is there, they'll grab him. If not, they can watch the place till you get there."

"And the autopsy—"

Brady jumped in. "Don't worry about it. Chase your lead. The local guy, what's his name? Ryan? He can send someone, or we will. I'll call him, too."

"Thanks, Brady," Bird said.

"That it?"

Bird thought for a moment. "One more thing. When you talk to Ryan, do me a favor: ask him about a guy named Jake Cutter."

"That's your source on the mistress?"

"Yeah," said Bird. "Twitchy little bastard. I'd like to know who he is, you know, locally speaking. And I'd like to know if there's a reason why Ed down at Strangler's wants him arrested."

Brady chuckled.

"I'll be in touch."

Bird hung up, tossed the phone aside, and let his foot come down heavy on the accelerator. Outside, the headlights flashed on two bright copper points by the side of the road, the eyes of a deer lifting its head to watch him pass. Bird flicked on the cruiser's rooftop strobe lights, even though there was no traffic ahead. Better for him and Bambi both if the wildlife saw him coming.

The exit for Augusta loomed ahead an hour later, white letters stark and reflective against the dark green of the interstate sign. Bird passed it at eighty miles per hour, sparing a thought for Lizzie's corpse and the impatient medical examiner, who would have to wait just a little while longer to put the scalpel to work. A few miles ahead was a service plaza, where he pulled up to the fueling area and set the nozzle to fill the cruiser's tank while he pulled out his phone. Before he showed up on her doorstep, he should get to know the woman he was on his way to see. Adrienne was probably best known for being the wife of one of the most despised men in America, but she was sort of interesting in her own right. She'd met Ethan Richards while doing an internship on Wall Street, then married him right out of college, a whirlwind affair—and a nasty surprise to Richards's first wife, who was left in the lurch. It was quite a strategic series of moves for a girl barely into her twenties; it made it that much harder to believe Adrienne had been unaware of what her husband was doing. Bird scrolled her Wikipedia page—apparently she'd been in the running for one of those *Real Housewives* reality series before the accounting scandal broke—and then clicked over to her Instagram account. There was one new photo at the top, posted earlier that day: Adrienne with wide eyes and pinkish hair posed alongside a pumpkin spice latte. Bird looked at the hashtags and scowled.

"'Fall hair don't care,'" he muttered. "Jesus fucking Christ." It was gratifying in a petty sort of way to see that the commenters on the picture largely agreed with him: Adrienne Richards was an asshole. The ridiculous hair, the latte, the idiotic hashtags; if she was trying to make people hate her, she was doing a good job. He scrolled down, past pictures of glossy manicures, expensive shoes, Adrienne in an evening gown at a fundraiser for a politician who was now on the verge of going to prison for fraud. Adrienne's face was everywhere, too, right up close, her big blue eyes framed by a row of impossibly thick lashes, probably fake. It all looked familiar in a generic girly sort of way, but eventually, he came to a view he recognized for certain: the lake, seen from the deck of Lizzie Ouellette's cabin, with Adrienne's pink polished toenails in the foreground. #LATERGRAM FROM XANADU, the caption read. It took Bird a minute, but then it clicked: with no cell service at Copperbrook Lake, Adrienne Richards could only document her vacation after the fact. Like a normal person. Which probably drove her crazy, he thought, chuckling.

It wasn't until he reached the next photo that the realization clicked. It was a shot of Adrienne with her back to the camera, hair tumbling over her shoulders, silhouetted against a peachy sunset. The light was low, the focus was soft; unless you knew to look for it, you wouldn't even recognize that one of her hands was resting on a long wooden railing, the one that wrapped around the deck of a house he'd been at just that morning. But the picture itself was one he'd seen before— gathered by Lizzie Ouellette into a photo album titled, *Dreams*.

As he scrolled farther back, he found others like it. Adrienne's outstretched hand with the fingernails painted cherry red. Adrienne's feet in a pair of expensive leather boots. Adrienne's martini, a sweating crystal glass on a dark wood bar. This was what passed for an ambitious fantasy in Lizzie Ouellette's world: a picture of another woman standing on the deck of the house that she owned.

And all that time Lizzie was idolizing Adrienne, wistfully saving pictures of her fingernails like they represented a life she could never have, Adrienne had been sneaking behind her back to suck her husband's dick.

He was wrong. Lizzie's dreams weren't banal. They were goddamn tragic. They were the saddest thing Bird had ever seen.

His thoughts were interrupted by the buzzing of the phone in his hand. He lifted it to his ear, tapping the screen to answer it.

"This is Bird," he said.

Brady didn't bother with formalities. "Boston PD says the lady is at home, evidently alone, drinking a glass of wine, and showing no signs of distress," he said.

A glass of wine, Bird thought bitterly. After what he'd just seen, the idea of Adrienne Richards blithely sitting around with a beverage, while Lizzie Ouellette was about to be dissected, was practically obscene.

"They know all that without knocking?" he asked.

"Apparently, there's a big glass window on the street side, second floor, with a good view in. She's sitting right up in it." Brady paused. "You know, I had a cat once who liked to do that."

"Great," Bird said.

"They've got one guy keeping an eye on the place until you show up. If Cleaves gets there first, they're prepared. I told them armed and dangerous, but it's only the shotgun that was missing, correct? No other weapons?"

"Not that we know of."

"All right. Good. A gun that big will be easy to spot, if he's dumb enough to walk around with it. And the other thing, your guy Cutter? You were right, he's a known entity. Heroin dealer."

"Huh," Bird said.

"You can't be surprised," Brady replied. He was right: heroin was having a boom in small-town New England, tearing its way through communities from Cape Cod to Bar Harbor and beyond. A frantic play by the cartels, who had flooded the region with cheap product in an attempt to recoup their losses from the slow state-by-state creep of legalized cannabis. Bird wondered if that was why the people he'd talked to today hadn't been more floored by Lizzie Ouellette's tragic death at the age of twenty-eight. The violence aside, dying young in Copper Falls just wasn't that unusual.

"Not surprised. It just hasn't come up," Bird said, and then instantly thought, *But that's not true.* There had been Deborah Cleaves's furious denial, *My son doesn't do drugs,* and then the follow-up question; it had seemed like nothing more than an angry retort at the time, but now . . .

"Actually, scratch that. It was suggested to me by Cleaves's mother that Lizzie Ouellette might be using," Bird added. "I thought she was being sarcastic, but maybe not."

"Well, we'll know soon enough," Brady said cheerfully. "If there was anything in her blood, the M.E. will find it. Let's check back in after you interview the mistress."

"Will do."

Bird hung up the phone, only to have it immediately buzz again against his hand. He glanced at the screen and saw a mobile area code. Not troop headquarters. He tapped the screen and the speaker came to life.

"This is Bird."

On the other end of the phone, a man's deep baritone replied, "Detective Bird? This is Jonathan Hurley."

The man's name rang a bell. A former teacher?

Hurley's voice came back again, answering the question for him. "I'm a veterinarian. Lizzie Ouellette was my employee, part-time."

That's it, Bird thought. Earl had told him that Lizzie worked as a veterinary assistant at Hurley's clinic, a job she was good at, according to her father. *Suited to it,* that was how he'd put it. Earl couldn't understand why she'd quit. Bird stepped out of the car, holding the phone to his ear as he replaced the fuel nozzle on the pump and twisted the cruiser's gas cap back into place. He was anxious to get on the road and had half a mind to tell Hurley he'd call back some other time, but the Boston PD was already watching the house. He could spare a few minutes for research.

"I'm sorry," Hurley was saying. "I was out toward Skowhegan with a sick horse, and I didn't find out what happened until—"

"That's all right," Bird said. "So Lizzie Ouellette worked for you. For how long?"

Bird could hear the veterinarian's breath: rapid, uncomfortable, like he was pacing back and forth.

"Two years. It was a while back. I think it's been maybe two or three years since we let her go."

Bird blinked. So Earl had misunderstood. "You fired her?"

"Listen," Hurley said, his tone becoming fretful. "I really agonized about this. I don't want to cause trouble for her family. I always liked Lizzie."

"Let's back up a minute. You hired her as an assistant? I thought you need schooling for that."

"I'd have to double-check my records, but I think she'd taken a couple classes at the community college," Hurley said. "For an assistant position, for what I needed, that was plenty. I only kept hours at the animal hospital a few days a week. My main business is large animals—you know, horses, cows."

"Where was the animal hospital?"

"Dexter," Hurley said, and Bird saw Cutter's face in his mind's eye. *A little ways to the east.* Was he lying? Had he known Lizzie after all?

"You know a guy named Cutter? Jake Cutter?"

"No," Hurley said. He sounded confused, the syllable coming out like a question.

"Never mind," Bird said. "So Lizzie was your assistant."

"Right. Yes. I was saying, I did like her. She was smart, a quick learner, and good with the animals. Some people come in thinking, *Oh, I'm an animal lover, I can do this job,* but when a dog comes in that's been run over by a snowmobile . . ." He sighed. "It's not easy. You've gotta be able to keep it together. It takes some nerve. Lizzie was good. She didn't balk at the sight of blood."

"Okay," Bird said. "So remind me, then—why'd you fire her, again?"

Hurley blew a frustrated exhalation into the receiver. "She really didn't give me a choice, man. I was sorry to lose her. That's why when I heard about what happened, I thought I should call."

"Sure, I hear you. Walk me through it."

"It was a bad situation. Basically, some medication went missing." The veterinarian's tone was perplexed, and Bird noted the phrasing: *went missing,* like the pills had wandered off on their own.

"Missing as in stolen?" he asked carefully.

"I still can't make sense of it," Hurley said. "Working around here, you know, you see a lot of that. You get to know people; you can tell who has a problem. Lizzie never seemed like the type. But only employees knew where we kept it, and whoever took it had a key. I knew it wasn't me, obviously, so . . ."

"Process of elimination," Bird said. "Right. What was the medication?"

Hurley's tone shifted; talking shop was more comfortable for him than calling a dead woman a thief. "Tramadol. It's an opiate, a painkiller. We give it to dogs, mostly, but it works on people."

"Tramadol. Got it. So what happened?"

"The whole thing was just so strange," he said, the regretful tone back in full force. "When I confronted her, she clammed up. Not even denying it—she just wouldn't say anything. At all. I really tried, Detective. I told her we could forget the whole thing, if she'd just return the meds. I meant it, too. The last thing I wanted was to let her go." He paused, sucking air through his teeth. "She didn't argue. She just took off her smock and handed it to me, and then she walked out the door."

"Did she say anything?" Bird asked.

"Yeah," Hurley replied. "I'll never forget it. She looked me dead in the eye and said, 'I really loved this. I should have known it couldn't last.'"

CHAPTER 15

LIZZIE

We're almost at the end now. The big bang, and everything after. Blood on the wall and soaked into the carpet; a body under a blanket; cops, picking up shattered teeth and bits of bone with tweezers and dumping them into a bucket marked OUELLETTE, ELIZABETH. I wonder what they'll do with the pieces, whether they'll be dumped down a sink somewhere or buried with the rest. I wonder what they'll put on my gravestone, if I have one. It's always someone else who decides how you'll be remembered. It's the name they called you that goes on the epitaph.

Daughter. Wife. Lover. Liar. Trash bag.

The only one I'm sure they won't use is "mother," because nobody ever called me that. He never got the chance.

My baby.

My perfect baby boy. It was the strangest thing, to see him. They gave him to me afterward, wrapped in a blanket, and you never would have known that he wasn't finished yet. His eyes were closed, his mouth was open, his tiny fists were lightly clenched around the air like he wanted to fight. There wasn't a single thing wrong with him, except that he wasn't breathing.

We never talked about the baby, Dwayne and I. We were such idiot kids, in over our heads, trying to fumble our way into a life that neither of us was ready for. Even the name was a choice we couldn't figure out how to make. I told Dwayne I wanted to wait, to see what he looked like when he came out. A James or a Hunter or a Brayden. I was sure I'd know right away, just as soon as I saw him, once I'd looked into his eyes. I used to look forward to meeting him, when he was still alive inside of me. But then he was born, and gone, and I was still drifting in the anesthetic twilight when they asked Dwayne what to put on the death certificate. I don't know why he said it—a sudden sense of paternal responsibility, or maybe he was just confused—but the name Dwayne blurted out wasn't any of the ones we'd ever talked about. It was his own. Dwayne Cleaves: that's what it says on the baby's grave, on the smallest stone in the cemetery beside the hilltop church. Like he only belonged to one of us. Like it was Dwayne's loss instead of ours. Instead of mine.

We never talked about that, either.

There was nothing to say. And as the years passed, there was nothing to remember him by. Not even a name of his own. With one Dwayne Cleaves walking around town alive, people seemed to forget about the other one, the one they'd never met, the one some people still tried to pretend had never existed at all.

But someone might remember my baby now. Now that it's convenient. Some uppity old bitch from that church on the hill might try it, spewing a stupid platitude as they pour dirt in the hole, about how the two of us are finally together in heaven.

If she does, I hope the words stick in her throat. I hope she chokes on them until she turns gray, just like he was when they put him in my arms.

It's a damn lie, anyway. The baby was blameless. He never did a single thing wrong, because he never did a single thing, period. Wherever he went, and I hope it's somewhere nice, there's no place there for the likes of me.

It should have been my last year in Copper Falls. It was a good one, as years go. Pop had won a contract to process the scrap from a state demolition project outside of town, on top of a nice side hustle dressing deer for some of the local hunters, work he passed over to me so that suddenly we had much more money than we'd ever had before. We didn't eat limb-chicken stew that year, except maybe once or twice by choice; I might as well tell you, I'd kind of developed a taste for it. The house at the lake was fully fixed up, too, though Pop kept to his word and only rented to locals; the fact that Teddy Reardon was six feet under by then didn't matter, he said. A promise was a promise.

And then there was me: seventeen, finally on the prettier side of that awkward, gangly divide that separates little girls and young women. I had already sketched a plan for after graduation: community college first, so I could be a vet assistant. That was the part I shared with the few people who asked, but there was more. My secret ambition, the part I didn't tell anyone because I didn't want to see them snicker when I said it. Once I had the certification, I'd be gone for good, to a city where I could work part-time and pay my own way through veterinary school. It would take time, but I didn't mind that. After seventeen years in Copper Falls, just the idea of being somewhere else was thrilling. It wasn't that things were bad; for a little while, actually, they were tolerable. The kids who'd messed with me growing up weren't doing it anymore, for no other reason than that it had gotten boring, for everyone. We'd all known each other too long. There was no satisfaction left to wring out of bullying me; they'd run out of barbs to throw, and I'd run out of retorts. All that was left was stale, tepid contempt, hardly worth scraping the barrel for. We left each other alone. When I passed them on the street or in the hallways at school, their eyes would skate right over me, like I was a boarded-up window, a doorknob, a weird stain on the sidewalk. Just part of the scenery.

That's why it was so incredible when Dwayne noticed me. Chose me. Growing up next to someone is funny that way, all the ways they change and all the ways they stay the same. He both was and wasn't the same boy who had killed Rags all those years ago, who pushed a toe into the junkyard dirt and told me he was sorry. He'd gotten tall by then, broad through the shoulders, with thick brown hair and a strong jaw that was starting to overtake the little-boy roundness of his face. His teeth had little gaps in between that would show when he smiled, which he did a lot; he had no reason not to. He was cocky the way that beautiful teenagers are, so sure that people would either love him or forgive him, depending on what he'd done. We'd barely spoken since that day in the junkyard, but sometimes I'd catch him looking at me, and it finally occurred to me that we shared a secret. Something special. Something he had with nobody else. I was sure he'd never told anyone about what he did to Rags, and I had nobody to tell even if I'd wanted to. I wondered how many other girls had ever seen that side of him. The downcast eyes, the naked regret on his face. The way he flinched at the sound of his daddy's voice. As far as I could tell, he kept it hidden, even from his closest friends. Maybe that's why he wanted me. Of all the girls in Copper Falls, I was the one who knew, and kept, his worst secret.

I was the only one who knew what Dwayne Cleaves looked like when he was afraid.

It was the end of junior year, the evenings finally warm enough for a T-shirt, the mood already cheerful in anticipation of summer. Dwayne was the starting pitcher for the high school's varsity baseball team, and he was good enough that people were starting to take notice. The word spread quicker after someone borrowed Sheriff Ryan's radar gun and clocked his fastball at eighty-seven miles per hour. Come June and the league playoffs, people from neighboring towns were showing up just to see him play. The last game, one man came alone, sitting off to the side, and by the end of the first inning a whisper was going around that he'd come all the way from Washington state to scout Dwayne for the Mariners. That was bullshit, of course. Actually, he was from the state university down in Orono, and the best he had to offer was an athletic scholarship—which was nothing to sniff at, either, but the prospect of a major-league baseball scout among us put magic in the air. Everyone felt it, including Dwayne. And, God, he gave them a show. I was there, too; the entire town was, I'd guess, so that a stranger happening onto Copper Falls would find the streets empty, all the doors locked, and think it had been abandoned. We watched from the bleachers as he fired off pitches. Strike after strike, strikeout after strikeout, until you couldn't even hear the umpire's calls because the sound of the ball whipping into the catcher's mitt alone would send up a frenzied cheer from the crowd. They stamped and yelled and went completely fucking nuts, and Dwayne stood there on the mound, grinning, ripping fastballs over the plate as the batters swung and caught nothing but air. Somewhere around the fifth inning, you could hear people muttering it under their breaths, low and careful like an incantation: *no-hitter.*

And then, in the top of the seventh, Dwayne threw a splitter that didn't break, and a big guy batting lefty got a chunk of it. The ball sailed high into right field. Knees went soft, cheers died in throats, and that was when it happened: Dwayne's shoulders slumped forward and he turned his head, and his eyes met mine. While everyone else watched the trajectory of the ball, we looked at each other. And although the sun was still up and the air was still gentle, a chill went down my spine.

And then Carson Fletcher, the right fielder who hadn't seen a single ball come his way since warm-ups, went charging into the backfield, leapt into the air, and came down on the other side of the outfield fence with the big lefty's almost-home-run nestled safely in his glove.

And if someone had been standing on Copper Falls's main drag at that moment, watching the sun creep toward the horizon and wondering where the heck everybody had gone, the sound of screaming coming from the ball field at that moment would've been his answer.

Dwayne did pitch a no-hitter that night, and didn't look at me again. When the game ended and he strode off the mound, it all felt so surreal that I thought I must have dreamed the whole thing: the way he'd looked at me, the way a jolt of *something* had seemed to pass between us. While everyone else stormed the field to celebrate, I walked back to my bike and started the journey home. Five dusty miles.

He caught me on that same stretch of road, grunting my way up the incline with my shirt sticking damply to my back. The same place where, five years earlier, I'd dropped my backpack by the side of the road and run from the boys who were chasing me. This time, I didn't run. I turned at the sound of tires coming up behind me. I stopped as his truck pulled alongside, slowed, stopped. I let him take my hand, and I looked at the back of his neck, his thick hair matted down with sweat above the collar of his uniform jersey, as he led me into the woods. The last thing I saw as I closed my eyes to kiss him was that same old hunting shack, the roof caved in, the walls buckled and slimy, finally reclaimed by rot.

We met in the woods until it got colder, and then it was a sleeping bag and the back of his truck—and then the front seat, when winter came. Fogged windows, our bodies slick with sweat and spit and sex, the heater on full blast and the radio turned down low. Always in deserted places. Nobody ever saw us together; nobody knew. It was another thing we shared—a secret, just for us. At least that's what I told myself. Even on the coldest night of the year, he would drop me at the end of the road instead of bringing me to my door. I was so drunk on the thrill of it, being wanted, it took me a long time to realize that Dwayne didn't see it the same way. That my exciting secret romance was his *nobody can ever know this* embarrassment. That for him, I was something shameful to be kept under wraps. The junkyard girl. A dirty little secret.

Until I wasn't. Until I made our little secret too big to hide. I didn't lie, exactly. I told him I was getting on the Pill, and I did, driving to the clinic in the next county and hiding the packs deep in my sock drawer at home. I took them like I was supposed to.

And then I stopped. I don't know why. It's so easy, to just not do something, and not tell anyone that you're not doing it. It's not like I didn't know what could happen. I'd been through sex ed like everyone else; I knew perfectly well how it worked. I knew. It's just that when you want something, what you know becomes irrelevant. And I did want it. Not the baby, but the acknowledgment. After all those nights trudging home in the dark, still raw between my legs, my nose red and running in the freezing air, I just wanted him to have to stand in the sun with me and say, *Yes, I'm with her.* I knew he liked me. I wanted him to do it where people could see.

I thought it was because I loved him. But it wasn't only that. It was the idea of him. Somewhere along the line, I started to play pretend again. I started telling myself stories on those walks back to the trailer, all of them with the sappiest, stupidest fairy-tale ending you ever saw. Because if I was Dwayne's girl, they'd have to see me. They'd have to admit that I wasn't trash, that they were wrong, that they'd been wrong to judge me. I was Dwayne's guilty secret, but here's my own: when you've been rejected all your life, the thing you want most in the world isn't to escape. It's to be let in. To have everyone embrace you as they welcome you to their special club, where there's a special seat waiting just for you. And did I dream of a happily-ever-after? Of us making a little life together, a little house with little lace curtains, a little wife with a little baby kissing her husband off to work? Did I imagine us showing up at a barbecue in the haziest part of August, where grinning schoolmates would hug me, and slap Dwayne on the back, and say *Good going, buddy* as they clucked over the baby?

Of course I did.

Because I'm a fucking idiot.

What actually happened was this: I told Dwayne I was pregnant, and watched all the blood drain from his face, and realized that I'd made a terrible mistake. That fantasy, the hazy summer afternoon and a baby in a little eyelet jumper, froze over and shattered with a snap, into a million glittering pieces. And by the time I got home, the news had gotten there ahead of me, and Pop was waiting with a look on his face that I'll never forget.

We said a lot of things to each other that night. Some of it, I still can't bear to think about. I'd been a lot of things to my father over the years: a help, a surprise, a responsibility. This was the first time I'd been a disappointment. The hurt in his voice was something I would've given anything to undo—only undoing it would have been even worse. When I said the word *abortion,* he reached out with both hands and laid them on the sides of my face.

"My Lizzie," he said. "Since the day you was born, there's nothing I wouldn't do for you. You hear? I would've killed for you. I'd have given my own life. But this . . ." He trailed off, pressing his lips together, gathering himself. "I can't condone it. It's an innocent life. So it's your choice, girl. I won't stop you. Even if I could, I wouldn't, because that's your body with the baby inside, and you got the right. But it's wrong, Lizzie. I know that much."

I think sometimes, about whether I would have done it. Even with Pop's words weighing heavy on me, I might have made that choice. But I didn't get to, because back at Dwayne's house, the same news was being reckoned with, and the preacher was doing what the preacher did. And in the end, it almost felt like it was meant to be. Like we were following a path laid out for us years before, by some puppet master with a taste for heavy-handed drama and a shitty sense of humor. It was early spring, not summer, and we weren't children anymore, but the rest of it was very much the same: the preacher's sedan pulled up, this time with Dwayne behind the wheel. He got out, he pushed a toe into the dirt, and he said the words his father had told him to say.

"I want to do right by you."

I looked at him, my arms folded protectively over my chest. It would be a while yet before I started to show.

"Do you?" I said.

The boy, my boy, lifted his eyes and met my gaze.

"Yeah," he said, and then, so quietly that I had to strain to hear him: "I want to marry you."

Maybe he meant it. I don't know. Maybe Dwayne had his own secret dreams about barbecues and babies, or maybe he just didn't want to walk the path laid out for him. In Copper Falls, he was our home-town hero, the golden boy who threw a no-hitter and was bound for a glorious future. At the state university, he would have been a small fish in a big pond, not even a starting pitcher despite the athletic scholarship. Maybe he was afraid of what it would be like, not to be special anymore. But as far as the town was concerned, Dwayne had been derailed, and I was the scheming jezebel bitch who'd blown up his future with just a twitch of my evil ovaries.

"He had his whole life ahead of him," they'd say. I mean, they did say it. At our wedding. Imagine hearing *that* on your way down the aisle, people talking about a guy marrying you like he'd been struck down in his prime by cancer. I was four months along then, still barely showing in my yellow dress, which only made it worse when I lost it. I know there are still people in town who think I made it all up, that I was never pregnant at all.

But I was. I made it all the way to November. It was wet and cold, colder than usual, and my belly was big enough by then to throw me off balance. I stepped out our door that morning and saw my breath, but not the ice. I went down hard, and they told me afterward that this was the beginning, the moment the placenta broke free, the moment my baby started dying. But I didn't know. I didn't know anything. I stood back up, hurting but not bleeding, and thought everything was fine. It wasn't until a week later that the nurse at the clinic went looking for a heartbeat and found only silence. They drugged me for the rest of it. I was grateful not to be awake for that part, and guilty for how grateful I felt.

And there it is. My sad story. There was more after that, of course, but it was just more of the same. Ten more years in Copper Falls. Ten years, which ended up being the rest of my life. And if you're wondering why I stayed, then you don't know what it's like—to be eighteen, with a mortgage and a husband and aching breasts that won't stop leaking for a baby who's not there. You've never built a life to hold a family, only to end up caught inside a cage for two. It's not what you imagined, but it's what you know. It's safe. You might as well live there. The truth is, Dwayne and I never even talked about splitting up, just like we never talked about the baby after he was gone. We were like two drowning people, alone in the middle of the ocean, clinging for dear life to the same shitty scrap of wood. Sure, you could always release your grip, let yourself sink all the way to the bottom. But if he's not letting go, are you going to be the first?

And maybe I didn't want to let go. Maybe I still loved him. I even imagined, back then, that Dwayne might have wanted the first pregnancy enough to want to try again. Everyone thought I'd trapped him, but there were plenty of things about our life, about me, that Dwayne liked—that any man could have liked. Growing up the way I did had taught me how to make the most of not-enough. I knew how to stretch a dollar. How to hunt and field dress a deer. How to make a house full of cheap secondhand shit look like something better than it was. I knew how to take care of a man who couldn't take care of himself. When Dwayne had his accident, it was me who convinced the doctors not to just take the whole foot. When the workmen's comp payout came, I was the one who negotiated a sweetheart deal for Doug Bwart's business. When the oxycontin ran out and my husband was writhing on the bed, sweating and screaming, with stumps where his toes used to be, I found a way to stop the pain—even though it meant losing the best thing I had, and even though I knew full well that I was only kicking a pile of misery down the line. I'd promised to love, honor, comfort, and keep. And like Pop said, a promise is a promise.

That's how it went. That's how ten years passed. And it wasn't as pathetic as you're probably imagining. Even after everything, I found ways to be happy. Eventually, I made it to the community college, for a few classes if not the certification I'd hoped for. I had the part-time gig at the vet, while it lasted. I had the lake house, with its untapped potential. And unlike Pop, I had no loyalty to Teddy Reardon or the insular, dumbass traditions of Copper Falls, the people who still called me "whore" and "trash" behind my back, and sometimes when they passed me in the street. Being the jezebel junkyard girl meant I had nothing to lose by breaking the rules—and even Dwayne stopped complaining about renting to outsiders once he saw how much money it brought in.

I had a life. I want you to understand that. It might not have been much to look at, but it was mine. If I'd had the choice, I would have kept living it.

CHAPTER 16

THE CITY

Adrienne wasn't much of a cook, and the pantry was largely empty except for spices, dried pasta, and a few cans of soup. But the wine rack: now, that was fully stocked. She pulled a bottle at random, barely glancing at the label, and rummaged through two drawers in search of an opener before she realized the bottle was the kind with a cap, not a cork. Somehow, it felt like just one more sign of how far they'd fallen. At the height of her fame and Ethan's success, Adrienne had been photographed by paparazzi in Ibiza, wearing a red bikini and sipping ice-cold gin on the deck of a yacht that belonged to an Academy Award–winning actor. It was a far cry from this moment, the privileged bitch alone in her town house, drinking twist-off Shiraz and waiting for a visit from the police, while her man cowered in a cheap motel somewhere outside the city. Her haters would be beside themselves if they could see her now, and she almost wanted them to. How perversely fun would it be to blow up her carefully cultivated brand with a single video: no cute camera angle, no flattering filter, just ten ugly seconds slugging wine straight from the bottle and then belching into the camera at the end. Maybe, for good measure, she'd film it sitting on the toilet. *How ya like me now, bitches?*

But then everyone would know that something was wrong.

She reached for a glass instead.

The wine was more purple than red, and she breathed deeply as she brought the glass to her lips. She caught a brief, vivid scent of dark fruit, blackberries heavy on the bush, so ripe and warm in the late summer sun that they'd paint your fingers with juice at the first touch. Then the wine was on her tongue, in her belly. The flavor wasn't familiar, not like blackberries at all, but the way the tension in her temples dissolved with the first swallow felt like home. She topped off the wine and walked to the big window, settling in next to it with her forehead resting against the glass. She would need to eat something, and to resist the urge to down that entire bottle while she was at it. It wouldn't do to be drunk when the cops showed up. Somewhere on the way, though, not sloppy but definitely not sober either—that might not be bad, she thought, and took another sip. Rich bitch, alone on a Tuesday night in her bajillion-dollar designer home, getting a little loose, maybe watching some shitty reality show: the more she leaned into the annoying stereotype, the less likely anyone was to look past the surface and see the disturbing truth beneath. Yes, she would drink.

But first, she needed to think. She gazed out at the dusky facade of the house across the way. An ivy plant was growing abundantly up one corner of the building and across its face, the vines like shadowy fingers gripping the brick, the leaves black and shiny in the streetlamp light. The windows were dimly lit rectangles, curtained to keep someone like Adrienne from looking in—or maybe to allow the neighbors to look out without being seen. She realized with a shiver how visible she would be right now, lit behind the glass like an animal in a terrarium. Was someone in the house across the street watching her? Was that a twitch, a tiny seam of light opening between the curtains as some unseen person peered out? Her husband had sworn up and down that he'd stayed out of sight while she was gone today, and she believed him—he didn't want to be caught any more than she did—but she'd have to remind him to be cautious, especially at night. If he passed too close to the window at the wrong moment, if he unthinkingly left a light on, there was no telling who might be lurking out there ready to notice. Even someone passing on the street below would be able to see in. Certainly they'd see her, here in her perch beside the window. She wondered what she looked like from outside. Was she only a shape, a woman's silhouette with a glass in hand? Could someone walking below discern the movement of her eyes, the twist of her mouth?

She lifted the glass, took another sip, and nearly choked on it as a car turned the corner and started driving slowly up the street. A Boston police car, blue and white, unmissable even without its strobes on. She held still as it passed in front of the house, and sighed with relief when it continued on down the street—but it didn't. She gripped the stem of the wineglass tightly, her breath shallow, her heart pounding, as the car turned and came halfway back, this time pulling to the side of the street in front of the next house down. She fought the urge to stand up, to move to another window for a better look. She'd thought there would be more time, but surely this was the moment: the car door would open, the officer would emerge, and shortly, there would be a knock at her door. No time to think, to plan; now it was time to lie.

The car was parked under a tree, shrouded in shadow. She could make out the dark shape of a man—or maybe a tall woman—behind the wheel, but nothing else. She waited for movement, the sound of the car door, a badge glinting as the officer emerged. Thirty seconds passed. A minute. Then, a flicker: from within the car came a soft glow as the man inside pulled a phone from his pocket.

She clenched her teeth. She wanted this to be over. Was he just going to sit there, watching? Waiting? For what?

A *warrant, maybe,* came the answer from inside her own head, and her skin rippled over with gooseflesh. It was a paranoid thought, the product of a guilty conscience—but what if it wasn't? If they were already suspicious enough to be filing paperwork to search the house, and if they already had enough evidence, enough to show whatever it took to have it approved . . .

"Fuck," she whispered aloud. She'd already done one quick and cursory sweep through the place, making the bed, scanning surfaces, satisfied that there were no obvious traces of her husband's recent presence, but if the house were swarmed over with cops, who knew what they might find? She would have to assume the worst, and make use of whatever time she had left.

She forced herself to take another few sips of wine—slowly, with long pauses between to scroll through strangers' photos on Insta. If the man in the cop car was watching, he'd see a bored housewife, glued to her phone; he might even see the quick movement of her thumb as she scrolled, tap-tapped, scrolled. Little hearts bloomed under the press of her thumb, but the images were a blur. The wine was tasteless on her tongue. Her focus was turned inward, sharpened by urgency and the knowledge that it was all up to her now. It was becoming a familiar feeling, the potent emotional cocktail of fear, exhilaration, determination. She already knew that she would do whatever had to be done. She would take steps to protect what was hers. Her husband. Her future. Her life. She had always been resourceful, but the past twenty-four hours had tapped into something deeper, darker, fiercer. There was another woman inside of her, one with steel nerves and sharp teeth, who had revealed herself at the crucial moment, and taken control. Cunning and vicious, careful and methodical, and ready to do anything—whatever it took—to survive. It was that woman who had been her guide last night, whispering in her ear as she pulled the trigger.

As she wielded the knife.

As she threw the mangled chunk of meat and cartilage into the garbage disposal and carefully flipped the switch with her elbow, on and off.

Afterward, it was the cold, cunning voice of her second self that advised her to step carefully, avoiding the blood, when she ran to the toilet to vomit.

Her thumb stopped moving over the phone's screen. The memory of last night, her bare feet racing back past the fat drops of blood that traced her path from the bedroom to the kitchen, had faded away; in its place was a more recent one, and the sense that an important detail was buried within. The late-morning light blazing through the windows, her husband stepping into the hallway with his hair freshly buzzed, bits of toilet paper stuck to his clean-shaven face. She understood in an instant, his words coming back to her at once.

"I cut myself." That's what he'd said. "It's going to bleed all day long."

Bits of bloody toilet paper in the bathroom trash, the stubble from a freshly shorn beard in the sink: this was what she'd overlooked, what would need her immediate attention. She would start in the bathroom, then. Flush what she could, and bury what she couldn't in the kitchen trash, under this morning's coffee grounds—and another image flashed through her mind, of two recently used coffee mugs sitting side by side in the sink. Hers could stay, but his would need to be washed, dried, put away. She would change the sheets they'd slept on last night, just to be safe. Polish the surfaces he might have touched. She would wipe away every visible trace of him, of the day's work, of last night's horrors. The only marks left would be the ones on her memory.

And a few other places, the voice inside her smirked, and for a moment her fingers unconsciously fluttered toward her chest. She balled her hand into a fist, hard enough to feel the bite of her own nails against her palm. She'd almost forgotten that part, had tried to forget it, and was amazed to realize that she'd very nearly been successful. The wound had bled, but only a little. It didn't even hurt anymore. Soon, it would heal. There would be a scab, and then a scar, and then, eventually, not even that. Like it had never happened at all.

If her body could forget, maybe she could, too.

A glance at the clock revealed that the pain wasn't the only thing her body had forgotten to feel. It was nearly eight P.M., and all she'd had to eat since that morning was the overly sweet pumpkin spice latte; she should have been hungry by now. She tapped at the phone again, opening the Grubhub app and then her order history. The last delivery had been a week ago from a Japanese place called Yin's; the app was already asking her if she wanted the same thing again, and she tapped the REORDER button without bothering to investigate what it was. Some decisions, at least, were easy. And she should eat, if only for the sake of sticking to something approaching a routine. It would be one less thing she'd have to lie about. *Today?* she could picture herself saying, her eyes wide with confusion and her head cocked inquiringly to one side. As a child, Adrienne had spoken with a light Southern accent that she still trotted out from time to time when she really wanted to put on a show of *Who, me?* innocence. *I got a blowout, had a meeting with our financial advisor, got a coffee, ordered some takeout, and watched TV. Just a normal day. Why, no, Ethan isn't here. Yes, I'm alone—of course, all night. The deliveryman saw me—ask him. Will that be all, Officer?*

She lifted her glass to her lips and drained the rest of the wine with one swallow. Outside, the street was quiet. In the building across the street, a shrouded window on the third floor brightened. Adrienne's neighbors were settling in for the night. The police car remained where it was, its lights off, its occupant waiting. Perhaps it was just a coincidence and he wasn't there for her at all. Or perhaps he was waiting for a warrant . . . or maybe a friend. It occurred to her for the first time that Copper Falls might send its own police officers to investigate the murder, a thought that filled her with sudden terror. Could she look into the faces of men who had known Lizzie Ouellette and Dwayne Cleaves, who had grown up alongside them, and lie so that they would believe her?

It was the voice of her inner survivor that answered back: *Yes, you can. You can, because you have to. You'll lie until you believe it yourself, if you have to, because you made this choice. Now you'll live with it.*

And there was no time to argue, either. She would need to work quickly, and not only that: there was still the other matter, the thing she'd been meaning to do, and who knew when she'd have another chance like this, without having to worry about her husband walking in. She wanted to be alone when she discovered what was inside Ethan's safe, the one built into the wall behind the desk in his home office. The combination was their wedding date, of course. So they'd both remember, even though Adrienne wasn't supposed to open it unless Ethan was around. But after everything else, snooping was the least of her sins. She'd earned the right to look, hadn't she? To know everything? God, what she'd done to earn it.

There had been so much blood.

Her bare feet thumped lightly against the polished floor as she stood and left the room, setting her wineglass on the counter beside the bottle as she passed, tucking her phone into her pocket. There were no windows in Ethan's office; to someone watching from outside, the woman in the window would have simply disappeared, leaving the lights on in an empty kitchen, clearly alone in an empty house.

In fact, the police officer in the cruiser was watching, but only barely. He flicked his eyes briefly toward the window, then returned his attention to the radio. It was game four of the ALDS, Sox already up two games to one on the Yankees, and Bucky Dent was about to throw out the ceremonial first pitch. The crowd in New York roared; the cop in Boston glanced at the clock. If the boys clinched tonight, the city would go apeshit, and he would probably end up standing out in the cold until three o'clock in the morning writing citations for disorderly conduct—but that would at least be less boring than sitting here on the swankiest street in the city, watching nothing happen, doing a courtesy stakeout for some out-of-state cop.

Inside the house, Adrienne's phone buzzed: the restaurant was busy and needed more time, but would deliver her order within forty minutes. On any other night, Adrienne would have pitched a fit about the wait, but this one felt like a sign from the universe, a gentle reminder that she shouldn't dally. She took a deep breath. It would be fine, she thought. She knew, better now than ever before, that a determined woman could get an awful lot done in forty minutes. She traversed the house with silent steps, a dark doorway opening up ahead of her. She crossed into the room, flicked the light, and knelt down in front of the safe. The keypad glowed green, inviting the code to unlock it. She didn't hesitate.

The door swung open, and her eyebrows arched skyward. So did the corners of her mouth.

"Well," she said quietly, allowing the debutante's drawl to creep into her voice. "I do declare."

CHAPTER 17

THE CITY

10:30 P.M.

Bird marked his southbound progress by the Red Sox radio broad-
cast, the roar of the crowd at Yankee Stadium fading into static as he
passed between counties, then states. Even if the GPS hadn't told him
he was getting close, he would have known from the sound of Joe
Castiglione's voice, coming through strong on WEEI out of Boston as
he neared the city limits. It was the top of the seventh, the Red Sox
holding on to a three-run lead, when he pulled onto the quiet street
in Beacon Hill where Ethan and Adrienne Richards lived. A Boston
police cruiser was parked underneath a tree on the even-numbered
side, and Bird muttered an oath under his breath; if the Richardses
were at home and even a little bit observant, they would have noticed
they were being watched. He pulled his own cruiser in several spaces
ahead of the blue-and-white, exited, and walked back with badge in
hand to tap the city cop's passenger-side window. It came down just
in time for him to hear the crack of a bat: two hundred miles away,

Xander Bogaerts grounded out to short, stranding the runner who could've opened up Boston's lead to a comfortable four runs.

"Evening, Officer," Bird said.

The man in the car extended his right hand. "Murray."

"Ian Bird. Thanks for holding it down."

Murray glanced at his watch. "Sure thing. You made good time."

"Anything happening in there?" Bird said.

"All quiet. Lady's still awake, I've seen her back and forth by the window a few times."

"Anyone else?"

"Like a six-foot bearded Mainer with a shotgun and a limp?" Murray said, cracking a smile. "Nope, no sign of your suspect. A couple folks walked by with dogs. The lady in seventeen had one visitor, food delivery guy. That was a couple hours back. Japanese, looked like."

"The guy or the food?" Bird asked, and Murray grinned again.

"Both. Dinner for one, going by the size of the bag. These rich chicks eat like fucking birds," he said, his accent coloring the words. *Fackin' bihds.* Bird stifled a laugh.

"Got it, thanks. Anything else?"

"I drove around the block when I got here, checked out the rear of the house. Everything looks normal. You know how these neighborhoods work? There's an alley behind the row here with back access. Seventeen has a little patio behind that they're using to park their cars. I heard you were looking for a Mercedes?"

Bird nodded. "GLE."

Murray guffawed. "Ridiculous fucking car," he said, and Bird smirked again at the accent: *Fackin' cahh.* "Some folks use a valet garage down the street, but there's a Lexus in the back and an empty spot next to it. Probably that's where your Mercedes would be. No sign of anyone trying to break in or anything. And no sign of the husband." Murray scowled, and Bird wondered if the other man had his own reasons to dislike Ethan Richards.

"Good," Bird said. "Thanks, Murray."

Murray nodded. "You got it." He put the blue-and-white into gear, then paused, sucking his teeth. "You said 'good.' So you're not here about the lady's husband?"

Bird grinned. "I'm here about the lady's boyfriend," he said, and Murray let out a short bark of satisfied laughter.

"That's rich," he said. "All right, you sure you don't need me to stick around?"

"Nah."

Murray nodded and gestured at the radio. "Then I'm gonna get my ass in front of a TV in time to see Judge break down crying like a little girl when the Sox clinch," he said, laughing. Bird grinned, tipped the Boston officer a mock salute, and watched as Murray drove off, disappearing down the street and around the corner. The wind rustled in the trees; a few dry leaves skittered over the curb and into the street, chasing one another past elegant homes with ivy crawling up their corners, stone steps leading up to their front doors, chrysanthemums planted in window boxes that hid the discreet wiring of high-end security systems. Bird started across the street, glancing up at the lit windows of number seventeen as he did so, and caught his breath. Adrienne Richards stood there, a dark silhouette against the glass, looking down at him as he looked up.

Bird was still considering whether or not to wave when she turned away. For a moment, he was overcome by the sense that she'd been watching for him, and waiting; he half expected her to appear at her front door, opening it before he could knock. But there was no further movement behind the windows as he crossed the street, no snap of a dead bolt drawing back in anticipation of his appearance. He mounted the stone steps to number seventeen, and pressed a finger against the bell.

Somewhere around the time he crossed the border from Maine to New Hampshire, on the heels of his conversation with Jonathan Hurley and his realization about the origins of the photos in Lizzie Ouellette's little album of "dreams," Bird had tapped into a profound and intense dislike for Adrienne Richards. By the time he arrived outside her door, he had decided that she was at least as bad as, if not worse than, her conniving fraud of a husband, and that she deserved to be dragged over the coals as hard as humanly possible for her involvement with Dwayne Cleaves—which made it jarring when the door opened and he found himself immediately apologizing.

"Adrienne Richards?" he said, and watched her nod, her eyes wide, as she peered out through the crack in the door. "I'm sorry to bother you so late. I'm Detective Bird, with the Maine State Police."

The door swung wider as he held his ID up for examination, and Bird looked at Adrienne as she looked at his badge. She was pretty in person, but not the way he'd expected. There was no sign of the pouting, posing, attention-seeking rich bitch he'd seen in pictures and read about in the news; unfiltered and in real life, Adrienne Richards had a haunted, vulnerable look, with a soft mouth and striking pale blue eyes that widened as they met his.

"The state police, you said?" She chewed her lip. "Why?"

"I have a few questions for you. Can we talk inside?"

She hesitated, then swung the door wide. He stepped in as she stepped aside, the scent of something light and citrusy trailing behind her. The events of that morning, the blood-soaked quilt being drawn away from Lizzie Ouellette's lifeless body to the angry buzzing of a hundred thirsty flies, seemed suddenly very far away.

"Were you expecting company tonight?" he asked.

Adrienne shut the door firmly and gave him an odd look. "What makes you say that?"

"I saw you at the window. I thought you might be watching for someone."

"I was just . . . sitting. It's a nice view," she said. A short set of stairs rose up behind her, and she turned, beckoning him to follow. "We can talk up here."

Bird watched her back as she ascended, taking in her outfit (bare feet, sweatpants that looked like they were made of silk, an artfully distressed gray sweater that probably cost a thousand bucks and came with its sleeves pre-frayed), her hair (twisted up on her head, that funny pinkish-copper color that Jennifer Wellstood had called "rose gold"), her posture (tense, but normal for a woman home alone getting an unexpected visit from the cops). There was a photograph on the wall where the landing turned a corner, Adrienne and Ethan posing on a hilltop terrace under a light pink sky. A sea of sun-bleached buildings were set into the hill behind them, with the real sea just beyond, stretching blue and endless to the horizon. She was blond and tanned and smiling; he was planting a kiss on the top of her head.

"Nice picture. Is that Greece?"

She turned, leaned in, squinted. "Yeees," she said slowly. "The islands. We honeymooned there."

"Looks beautiful."

"My husband isn't here," she said abruptly. She moved away, climbing the last three stairs to the second floor and then turning to look down at Bird where he still stood on the landing. She crossed her arms, shifting her weight. "I still don't know what this is about."

"You're alone here, then?"

"That's what I just said," she replied. "My husband isn't here. So whatever this is about—"

"Actually," he interrupted, "you're the one I wanted to talk to. And I think it's better that I speak to you first." He ascended the stairs, too, looking around again as he did. The stairs opened into a living area, the space marked by a deep sectional sofa, a plush chair, and a large wall-mounted television, turned on but with the sound muted. Beyond the living area was the kitchen—he could see the big bay window where Adrienne had been standing a moment before, and a half-empty bottle of wine perched on the countertop next to a half-poured glass of red.

"Is that yours?" He pointed to the wine.

"Yes," she said, and he thought he detected a note of exasperation underneath her politeness. "Like I said, it's just me here. You can look around if you don't believe me."

Bird plopped down on the couch instead.

"You want your wine?" She shook her head, and he shrugged. "All right. Please have a seat."

Adrienne shrugged back and walked to the other side of the room, scooping up a remote control from the arm of the couch as she passed; the TV went dark. She settled in the chair and drew her knees protectively toward her chest, then seemed to think better of it and allowed one leg to drop down, crossing it over the other. Bird waited, letting her discomfort percolate. When she stopped fidgeting, he leaned forward.

"Mrs. Richards, where were you last night?"

She blinked. "Me? I was here."

"Alone?"

"*Yes*. Officer, what *is* thi—"

"When was the last time you spoke to Dwayne Cleaves?" he shot back. If he hadn't been watching carefully, he would have missed the way her hands fluttered in her lap at the name, the flash of something—anger? fear?—that furrowed her brow before she regained her composure. Her pale blue eyes opened wider.

"Dwayne from . . . Copper Falls? The—what, the handyman? I don't—"

She was getting ready to lie; Bird pounced before she could go any further.

"Mrs. Richards, I know you and Dwayne Cleaves were having an affair."

This time, there was no need to watch carefully for a reaction: Adrienne Richards's mouth dropped open and all the color drained from her face. Her hands became claws, fingers digging into her knees.

"You know . . . about Dwayne . . . and"—she took a breath, swallowed hard—"and me. About us." Bird nodded. She shook her head slowly, staring at the floor. A long silence passed. When she spoke again, she kept her gaze fixed on a spot on the carpet just ahead of Bird's feet.

"Who told you?" she said quietly.

"Guy named Jake Cutter. You know him?" Adrienne shook her head again, *no,* her expression inscrutable. Bird pursed his lips. "Did you know Dwayne had taken pictures of you? In a, uh, compromising moment?"

"Oh my God." She buried her head in her hands. Bird watched her distress impassively, thinking, *She thought nobody knew.* She took a long breath, and finally lifted her gaze to meet his. "You saw the pictures?"

"No," Bird said. "Jake Cutter did. He may not be the only one. I get the sense that Dwayne wasn't exactly being discreet. Bragging, more like."

She pressed her lips together, then stood abruptly and crossed in front of him, headed for the kitchen. Bird swiveled his head, a hand flying automatically to his hip.

"Ma'am, what are you . . . oh," he said, as she reached the counter, grabbed the wineglass, and drained its contents in a single swallow. He waited as she poured herself another, the room silent except for the clink of the bottle against the rim of the glass and the sound of Adrienne's breathing, shallow and shaky like she was trying to keep herself from crying. She returned, glass in hand, but set it down instead of drinking it.

"I don't know what to say," she said.

"Does your husband know?"

She shook her head furiously. "No, no."

"When was the last time you saw Dwayne?"

"I . . . I don't know. Six weeks ago?"

"In Copper Falls?" She nodded. "Not here at your place? You ever bring him back here?"

The woman actually had the nerve to look indignant. "Of course not," she snapped.

"What about your husband? Did he have a relationship with Dwayne? Were they in contact?"

Adrienne's voice grew shrill. "No! I mean, I don't know who Ethan talks to, but I don't know why—how would I—"

"How about Dwayne's wife? You talk to her lately?"

"Lizzie?" She was wild-eyed now, twisting her hands in her lap. "What does that have to do with anything? Oh God, does *she* know? I don't understand what's happening. Why are you asking me all this? Why are you here?!"

Bird allowed the question to hang in the air. He couldn't shake the sense that she was hiding something, but it was only a sense, as ephemeral as the scent of her perfume hanging in the air. Apart from the moment where she'd tried to lie about the affair, there was no one thing he could point to, no one answer that stood out as an obvious lie—and maybe he was just mistaking embarrassment for evasiveness, because she certainly wasn't faking her shock and distress at being found out as a cheater. The reaction when he'd told her about the photograph: that was real. Even now, she looked like she might burst into tears at any moment.

As if to prove his point, Adrienne sniffled loudly and wiped her nose on the sleeve of her expensive sweater. Bird grimaced. If she thought this was bad, he'd give her something to really cry about.

"Mrs. Richards, Lizzie Ouellette is dead."

She gasped. "What? When? How?"

"We're still figuring that out, but she was found at the lake house this morning. She was shot." He paused for impact. "And Dwayne Cleaves is missing."

"Missing," she said, and pressed a hand to her chest. "Oh God. Then that's why—but you couldn't possibly think that I—I mean, I hardly knew Lizzie. I just rented her house."

"And slept with her husband," Bird said mildly, and she flinched as though he'd slapped her. "Did Dwayne ever say anything to you about wanting out of his marriage? Or maybe you said something to him? Made him think he had a chance with you if the wife was out of the picture?"

Adrienne glared at him, an expression of pure disgust on her face. "You can't believe that."

Bird shrugged, and said, "In my line of work, we can believe just about anything. Don't get me wrong, I'm sure you never meant for him to kill her. But maybe you said something offhand." He batted his eyelashes, and his voice became light and breathy, a cruelly accurate imitation of Adrienne's speaking style: "Oh, Dwayne, we could spend so much more time together if your wife weren't always in the way."

In the course of their short conversation, Bird had seen Adrienne Richards wounded, frightened, cornered—but always in control. Now she exploded.

"As if I would ever say that," she snapped. "I would *never*. Are you kidding me? What would someone like me want with someone like that? Someone like him? You think I want Dwayne fucking Cleaves in my life? This life? My *real* life? Do you think I'd want him here, in this house? Scratching his balls and spilling beer on my five-thousand-dollar sofa? Pissing in my kitchen sink because he woke up drunk and couldn't find the bathroom? We could never be a couple. We're hardly even the same species. And if he didn't understand that, if he thought there was any kind of future for him here, then he's even stupider than I thought. You want to know why I fucked him? Because I was bored and he was there, that's why."

The last sentence was practically a shout, and Bird blinked with surprise—as did Adrienne, who looked like she'd swallowed a bee. *That was the truth,* he thought. *That, right there.* This woman would never risk her own future to help Dwayne Cleaves.

The only question remaining was whether Dwayne knew that.

"All right," he said finally. "When was your last contact with Dwayne?"

She sighed. "We rented the house this summer. Same as last year, except we stayed a little longer this time. We came back toward the end of August. I don't remember the exact date, but I didn't see or talk to Dwayne after that," she said.

"What about Lizzie? I heard she spent a lot of time at the house while you were there. Some people even seemed to think you two were pretty friendly." He paused, then added, "Of course, they might think differently if they knew the real story."

Adrienne looked at him coolly, not taking the bait, and Bird shrugged. Even if he couldn't provoke her into another outburst, the dig was too good to resist.

"I don't particularly care what people in Copper Falls think of me," she said matter-of-factly. "Lizzie and I got along fine. We were friendly. I'm truly sorry to hear that she's dead. But 'friendly' isn't 'friends.' She spent extra time at the house because I paid her to. And I didn't keep in touch with her year-round. The last time I heard from her . . ." She trailed off, thinking. "It was maybe a month ago. She sent me a message saying we could rent the house for another week before they shut it for the winter. I don't know why. I guess maybe I said something once about wanting to see the lake in the fall, but I didn't really mean it. I was just making conversation. I told her I'd get back to her, and I really meant to, honestly, but then things got busy . . ."

Bird sat up a little straighter as the notation on Lizzie's calendar came into focus in his mind's eye. *AR-7.* Not a gun, but a guest: Adrienne Richards, seven days.

"You would have arrived last night," he said.

"Yes, but like I said, I never confirmed."

"What about your husband?"

"What about him? He's away."

"Could he have been in Copper Falls last night?"

"No," she said immediately, then frowned. "I mean, I don't know. Jesus. What are you saying? What does Ethan have to do with this?"

Bird looked grave. "Mrs. Richards, do you own a black Mercedes? A big SUV?"

"Yes."

"Where is it?"

"My husband took it."

"Okay. And where is he?"

Adrienne began shaking her head, blinking rapidly. "I . . . I don't remember. Or maybe he didn't tell me. He doesn't always tell me. He said it was a business trip, just a day or two, and he'd call when he could."

Bird scrutinized her face. Was she lying?

"Has he called?"

"No," she said quietly.

"And when did he leave?"

Adrienne bit her lip. Her voice dropped to just above a whisper. "Yesterday."

"You haven't tried to call him?"

"Ethan is an important man," she said, and her tone turned pleading. "He doesn't like for me to bother him when he's working."

Bird suppressed the urge to roll his eyes. "Okay," he said, softening his tone. "I'd like you to call him, please. Would you do that for me?"

Adrienne nodded and retrieved her phone, tapping at the screen. She looked at him anxiously as she lifted the phone to her ear, then frowned again.

"Straight to voice mail," she said, tapping the speaker icon; an electronic voice filled the room, midsentence: ". . . is not available. At the tone, please record a voice message."

"Do you want me to leave a message?" she asked, and at the same time, Bird's phone began to buzz. He fished it out of his pocket and glanced at the screen. Sheriff Ryan, calling from Copper Falls. Probably something about the autopsy; Bird could ring him back when he was done here.

"Hang up, please," he said to Adrienne. She did, but looked bewildered.

"You're scaring me," she said, then again, more urgently: "You're *scaring* me. I thought you wanted to talk to me. Why are you asking about Ethan?"

As Bird weighed how much to tell her, the phone buzzed again in his hand. He looked at the screen, frowning: Ryan had not only left a voice mail, but also followed it immediately with a text. He tapped the message, and froze.

CLEAVES VEHICLE FOUND. BODY INSIDE. CALL ASAP.

"Sorry, ma'am," Bird said. "We'll have to end this here for now." He stood, fishing out a business card. "If your husband calls, have him call me."

Adrienne took the card with a look of horror on her face. Bird wondered why, then remembered: *She thought nobody knew.* The stricken expression wasn't concern for her husband. She was just worried he'd find out she'd been screwing around.

"I'll be discreet," he said, knowing even as the words passed his lips that he would break this promise if he had the chance, if only to see the look on Ethan Richards's face when he found out his wife had been giving it up to a redneck dirtbag with only one and a half feet.

But Adrienne didn't need to know that.

He left the way he'd come, past the photograph of a newlywed Adrienne and Ethan in happier times. He could feel Adrienne's eyes on him as he descended the stairs. As he reached the door, she called after him.

"Detective Bird," she said. "Am I in danger?"

He paused in the doorway, looking back at her.

"I hope not, ma'am," he said.

As he turned his back on Adrienne Richards and stepped into the night, he was surprised to realize that he almost meant it.

CHAPTER 18

THE CITY

She stood in the doorway to watch him go, hugging herself to stop her body from trembling. It was a beautiful night, unseasonably mild, the air soft against her skin. She shivered anyway. She couldn't stop thinking about the way Ian Bird had looked at her when he said, "I know you and Dwayne Cleaves were having an affair," the way his mouth tweaked at the corners as he described the photograph of Adrienne in what he called "a compromising moment." The smug loathing in his eyes. He hadn't even tried to hide the enjoyment he got from humiliating her.

Imagine how he'd have looked at me, if he knew the truth.

She shuddered again, digging her fingers into her upper arms. Inside, the calculating survivor's voice suggested that she should be grateful, that the detective's prejudice against Adrienne had worked in her favor, particularly in the moments where she'd lost control, said too much, allowed her emotions to get the better of her. *Be glad,* said the voice, *that he thinks he already knows who you are. He thinks he under-stands.* And because he thought he understood, Ian Bird assumed that what he'd seen upstairs was embarrassment, the entitled rich girl cry-ing because she'd gotten caught with her hand in the cookie jar. But it wasn't tears she'd been holding back; it was a howl of rage. Thank God she'd managed to clamp it down. If she had let loose, started screaming, she would never have been able to stop.

It was true: she should be glad it ended this way, with the cop walking away from her, fumbling his phone from his pocket, tapping at the screen. He didn't glance back, and she thought that this, too, was a good sign. When Bird arrived, he was focused on Adrienne; now it seemed like he'd forgotten all about her. She watched the cruiser pull away from the curb and down the street, disappearing around the corner, and then watched the gentle movement of the trees in the lamplight as silence descended. She held her breath. A moment later, the quiet was broken by the ambient sounds of city life: the electric buzz of the streetlights, the far-off wail of a siren. But the street stayed empty, and the breath she was holding came out in a satisfied *whoosh*. She supposed he might be trying to fool her, hiding around the corner or a few streets down, but she didn't think so. For now, at least, it seemed that Ian Bird had decided to leave her alone. And by the time he sought her out again . . . well, things would have changed.

It helped, she thought, that she hadn't lied to him about every-thing. My husband is away: True. He took the Mercedes: True. That Adrienne had once said she wanted to see Copperbrook in the fall, and Lizzie, seeing an opportunity, had offered her the week in peak leaf-peeping season: This, too, was true.

But Adrienne hadn't forgotten. Christ, she wished she had. It could so easily have been the truth: that Adrienne had ignored Lizzie's offer and then simply forgotten all about it. It was exactly the kind of thing she *would* do. But no: she'd told Lizzie to go ahead and hold the week for them, and she and Ethan had arrived in Copper Falls the previous night, right on schedule. Right on time for everything to go utterly, irretrievably wrong. And what a relief it had been, when Bird finally said the words—*Lizzie Ouellette is dead*—and she could stop pretending not to know, pretending she hadn't been there. It had taken every ounce of restraint she had, to keep from leaping around like a lunatic and screaming the truth aloud: *Dead, she's dead, and he's dead, too.*

I don't know where Ethan is.

Another lie.

She locked the door. She climbed the stairs, ignoring the picture that had caught Bird's attention, turning left at the top of the landing, moving purposefully. She walked to the bedroom, to the bed, freshly made with clean sheets only an hour before, back when she'd still imagined that there was some kind of happily-ever-after at the end of all this. Gently, she lifted a pillow from the bed.

Then she pressed her face into it and screamed.

All day long, she'd been practicing her lines, telling herself a story, repeating the words until they felt true. This was who she was: a woman who woke up thinking about possibilities. Who realized she needed to take control. A woman who spent the day making plans to secure her future. *I don't want to be one of those women who gets blindsided by life.*

And after all that, she almost had been.

Almost.

But now she could see with the most incredible clarity. She knew how things had to be—because she was out of options, a realization that should have been terrifying, but instead felt like freedom. Every door had shut, every exit closed off, save one. Just one. One chance to make it through this, if she was strong enough to take it.

Though she had no way of knowing it, her instincts were correct. By the time the clock struck two A.M., Bird was nearly two hundred miles away; he wasn't there to see the big, black Mercedes roll down the alley behind the Richardses' home, easing into the courtyard alongside the smaller Lexus. He wasn't there to see the tall man with a buzz cut and day-old stubble who got out, glancing cautiously at the dark windows of the row homes to either side of number seventeen, and fumbled with a set of keys until he found the one that unlocked the back door. She had told him to stay away until morning, but of course he hadn't listened.

He never fucking listened.

She heard the creak of the door and his heavy tread on the stairs, halting and uneven, the brush of his fingertips against the wall as he reached out to steady himself. There was a thump as one foot hit the landing, and then she saw him, a shadow, lurching past the honeymoon photo and emerging into the living room. He was breathing hard, and sweating; she could smell it, rank and sour, an early warning of the withdrawal to come. Soon he'd be saturated in it, his hair damp, his armpits soaked, shaking and moaning with pain. She waited patiently as he moved toward the bedroom, not noticing the shape of her melting out of the shadows and following behind. He bumped against the wall as he stepped halfway through the bedroom door, peering in the direction of the bed.

"Fuck," he muttered. Then a loud whisper: "Hello? Are you here?"

"Hi," she said, behind him, and he yelped and whirled to face her.

"Jesus! What the fuck? I thought you would be asleep. You scared the shit out of me."

"You were supposed to wait until morning," she said. "Didn't I tell you that?"

He shifted uncomfortably. "I didn't know where to go. I was afraid I'd get lost, and then . . . and I don't feel good, anyway. I didn't want to spend all night puking in some shitty motel." He squinted into the dark. "I can hardly see you. What happened? With the police? Did they, I mean, do they . . ."

"The detective came. We talked. I didn't tell them anything."

He leaned against the wall, a slump of relief.

"Come on," she said, beckoning. "I want to show you something."

With a groan, he followed. Away from the bedroom, farther down the hall. Into the office. She brushed her fingers over the desk lamp, and a soft glow filled the room. He leaned against the doorway, bringing a hand to his face to massage his temples.

"I feel like shit."

"This won't take long." She knelt behind the desk, out of sight. Her fingers touched the keypad.

He cleared his throat. "So, the detective. Was it like you thought? He was looking for Ethan?"

"No," she said without turning around. "He was looking for you."

Dwayne Cleaves, sweating and sick and still wearing Ethan Richards's too-small college sweatshirt, which he'd put on that morning, dropped his hand from his forehead and gaped at her.

"See, he thought you'd come here." She took a long breath, then turned, glaring. "Because you just couldn't help yourself, could you? You had to go telling your idiot friends, including that fucking dipshit drug dealer, that you'd been fucking the rich city bitch who was renting your lake house. That's what the police officer told me." She kept her eyes on him as he stared back at her. In her left hand, the latch on the safe opened with a barely perceptible click. Her voice became a singsong drawl. "Dwayne and Adrienne, sitting in a tree, F-U-C-K-I-N-G. The cop told me you were bragging about it. He said you were showing people pictures. Is that true? You took *pictures?*"

"Listen," he said, his voice panicked. He took a hurried step forward. "Look, just let me expla—"

She turned to face him then, and he stopped talking. Froze in place. His eyes, glazed and huge in the dimly lit room, were fixed on what was in her hands. Dark and sleek and fully loaded.

Well, I do declare.

"Wait," he said.

She cocked the hammer.

"*Lizzie,*" he said.

She shook her head.

"Not anymore," she said, and pulled the trigger.

PART 2

CHAPTER 19

LIZZIE

I told you death has a way of making you honest.

And I told you the truth.

I just didn't tell you everything. An incomplete truth is still the truth, and so I left out a few details. Not just about that terrible day at the lake, but about what came before. I never told you about how a carelessly secured log rolled off a truck and over my husband, crushing his bones to a pulp, and as I drove to the hospital—the same one where, two years before, I'd cradled the corpse of my stillborn son—I felt a brief, fierce flush of satisfaction at the idea that now Dwayne would know how it felt to lose a piece of himself.

I never told you about the first time I found him passed out on our bed with the rubber tubing still wrapped around his upper arm, or about the wave of visceral disgust and contempt that surged through me as I leaned in to see if he was breathing or not. I never told you how I put a finger under his nostrils, and when I felt the damp heat of his shallow breath, I briefly wondered how hard it would be to clamp a hand over his mouth, pinch his nose shut, and hold him down while he smothered.

I never told you how, in that moment, I hated him. Hated him for every broken thing he'd stamped on, for every broken promise, for our broken stupid life, which he could escape at the tip of a needle while I was left here, living it. I hated him more than I'd ever hated anything, a loathing so fierce that it felt like something with a thousand legs crawling around alive in my belly, and I never told you how I bent close to his ear and whispered, "I hope you die," so quietly that I could barely hear the words myself, so quietly that there was no way he could possibly hear me, and I nearly screamed when his eyelids fluttered and he muttered back, "I hope we both die."

And then he turned to his side, puked on the pillow, and passed out, and I stood there with my mouth open, feeling like I'd just lost the only intellectual debate we'd ever had.

I never told you how staying with him started to feel like a competition, each of us daring the other to blink first. How it became almost a point of pride, the way we hurt each other and kept hanging on. How it was like drinking poison, year over year, until you can't remember what it was like to drink anything else, and you've even started to like the taste.

I never asked, but I thought there probably were other women, or had been, over the years. Everything changed after the miscarriage, the sex most of all. At first he'd only touch me if he was drunk, coming home from Strangler's with beer on his breath, dirt under his fingernails, coming up behind me where I stood at the sink with a dishcloth in my hand. Jamming a knee between my legs to spread them, bending me over where I stood. I knew I was being hate-fucked; the sad thing is that I actually missed it later, when he wouldn't touch me at all, no matter how drunk he was. That electricity I used to feel when I'd look up to see him coming toward me with angry lust in his eyes—it was gone. At first I thought it was because of the accident, after the doctor warned us that there might be problems—he called

it "sexual side effects of traumatic injury," a whole lot of fancy words
to describe your basic case of limp dick. But then, a few months later
at somebody's backyard barbecue, I went to use the bathroom and
walked in on Dwayne with Jennifer Wellstood. He was sitting on
the toilet with his pants around his ankles, and she was tugging on
that thing with both hands, and from what I saw before she started
screaming and I slammed the door, it was standing up on its own just
fine.

But I hadn't known he was cheating with *her*. Not until Ian Bird
showed up to thrust it in my face, thinking he was humiliating Adrienne, when what he really did was make me look at what I'd been
working so hard not to see. Maybe I should have figured it out. Maybe
I just didn't want to. Looking back, the signs were everywhere. The
trailing scent of her perfume, so strong that it couldn't possibly have
been coming off her hand-me-downs, buried in my closet. Those long,
long hairs—reddish like mine, but brittle, and with a half inch of
mousy root at the base. Clogging the drain at the lake house, clinging
all over the furniture in every place she'd laid down her stupid head.
They'd weave themselves into the fabric, somehow, so that not even
the vacuum could pull them free, and I had to draw them out one
by one, pinching them between my fingers. When I found them on
Dwayne's clothing and in Dwayne's truck and even stuck to the elastic
waistband of Dwayne's underwear, I told myself they'd probably just
traveled with me. On me. I was the one spending so much time with
her, after all. And the alternative was unfathomable.

My husband fucking Adrienne; Adrienne fucking my husband.

It still sounds impossible. Ridiculous. It sounds like a sick goddamn joke.

But I should've known. I could have known. You could always tell
where she'd been.

And I know how it looks: like we planned it, Dwayne and I, to kill
the rich couple and run away with their money. It looks like I got

close to Adrienne, pretending to be her friend, learning her tics and her accent and her smartphone pass code, just so that I could steal her identity after I shot her in the face. I even figured out how to make myself look more like her, mimicking the way she styled her hair and overlined her lips to make them look bigger. But Christ, it's not because I wanted her dead. It's because I wanted her *life*. And didn't I tell you I was always good at pretending? It was so easy to imagine myself slipping out of my sad little existence and into hers. I could see so clearly how it was possible. Have you ever seen one of those movies where the grubby girl takes off her glasses, and plucks her eyebrows, and poof, she's magically transformed from a mousy nobody into somebody worth looking at? That was us, me and Adrienne. She was the after; I was the before.

Dwayne laughed in my face the first time I said it, in an unguarded moment during that first summer, after I'd delivered their first round of groceries. The words just came out of my mouth—"Don't you think we look a little bit alike?"—and he laughed so hard that he started to choke, while I stared at the floor and felt my cheeks flush crimson.

"In your dreams," he said. "Maybe after a million bucks of plastic surgery."

But it didn't take a million. Not even close. I know the exact dollar amount it took to erase the one significant difference between me and Adrienne Richards: five hundred. That was the cost of the injection that filled in the hollows under my eyes, the lines on my forehead, and the funniest part is that she's the one who told me I should do it. I can still hear her voice, never more syrupy sweet than when she was insulting you in the guise of a compliment: *Girl, I've been getting preventative Botox for ages. I wish I could be more like you, and just not care what I look like. Those under-eye bags would drive me crazy. They can fix that, you know.*

I did it just after Christmas, while Dwayne was making his one and only half-assed attempt at getting clean. He'd found a short-term facility in Bangor, a five-day detox; he told people he was going away on a hunting trip so that his mom wouldn't find out the truth. I did my part, following him in my car to the rehab, staying long enough to make sure he went in. But instead of turning around and going home, I kept on driving, down the coast, until I found a chic little town I'd read about on some travel website, where rich lady tourists would go with their friends for "girls' weekends"—strolling galleries, tasting wines, and pumping their faces full of filler before sleeping it all off at a seaside bed-and-breakfast. I spent the night there in the only place that stayed open during the off-season, walking along the sweet little streets where most of the shops and galleries were closed for the winter, pretending to be someone else. And the next morning, before I left, I used some of the money I'd made from renting to Adrienne Richards to make myself look just a little more like her. The way I might have looked if I had been born a few hundred miles away, if I'd been someone else's daughter. The way I might have looked if I weren't married to a junkie—who, by the way, had already bailed out of rehab after less than twenty-four hours, and was at that very moment cruising through a strange city, looking for a needle of his own. If I'd known that Dwayne had already relapsed, I might have told the guy with the syringe to forget it. But I didn't, and I'm glad. The injections erased a decade of worry, pain, and bad decisions from my face overnight. Botox in the angry frown line between my eyebrows, filler in the bags beneath. The guy was a dentist, of all things. I didn't care; he was cheaper than the fancy medical spas, set up in a little strip mall on the outskirts of town. He even bleached my teeth after, for free.

Nobody ever noticed, of course. When you see the same faces every day, year in, year out, there comes a point where it's all so familiar that you stop noticing what they look like. Like a long-married couple who are so close, for so long, that they never notice all the ways that time is slowly leaving its mark on the other person's face. Certainly nobody was looking at me closely enough to notice anything different—except Jennifer, and only because she saw the bruises a day later, when she showed up hovering outside my door with the roasting pan I'd forgotten I let her borrow. We never had it out or even talked about that little incident at the barbecue, and she was always nervous around me, like she thought I might start screaming or hitting her or both. I never bothered to explain to her that I didn't have the energy to stay angry. Catching my husband getting jerked off on the toilet by the local hairdresser seemed almost poetic, just another little reminder from fate or God or whoever that things could, and would, always get worse. And I'll tell you what: I'll bet she feels bad now. She probably thought Dwayne was hitting me. Isn't that rich? I almost wish he had. Not because I deserved it, but because maybe if he did, I would have left.

The truth is, I never meant to kill her. You probably don't believe me, and I probably wouldn't believe me, either. But the kind of coveting I did, it wasn't about her at all. It was about me, about the crazy fantasy of disentangling myself from my shitty marriage, my shitty everything, a lifetime of false starts and missed chances and squandered potential, never amounting to anything but a cautionary tale. I didn't want to kill Adrienne. What would I have done without her? How could I live a better life if she wasn't there to show me what "better" looked like? She inspired me. Every time I looked at her, it became a little bit more possible to imagine that it wasn't too late after all, that I could still become someone else. I imagined myself speeding out of town in a big, black car with a driver up front, sipping champagne in the back seat—or maybe driving myself, in a cream-colored convertible with the top down. I imagined torching the junkyard as I left, a Molotov cocktail tossed out the window as I sped by, blowing a kiss to the spreading flames as they grew bigger and brighter in my rearview mirror. Destroying my father's last tie to this piece-of-shit town, in the hopes that he'd finally leave, too. I paid that dentist with the needle to show me a glimpse of another life, to make me look the way I might've looked if I'd made different goddamn choices. If I'd married rich, into the kind of money that forms a cushiony layer between you and the world, so soft and thick that nothing can touch you hard enough to leave a mark. Adrienne was five years older than me, but I was the one with the tired eyes and two unhappy furrows already beginning to form between my brows.

I'd whisper it back—*hi, y'all*—and imagine myself in all the places she'd been. A big stone town house in the city, with white marble countertops and a pool underground; a broad porch somewhere below the Mason-Dixon line, sipping sweet tea in the shade of a grand live oak strung with lacy Spanish moss. I'd imagine holding out my hand to admire my beautifully manicured fingers, my soft skin. I'd imagine sleeping in her bed, eating her food, petting her cat.

I'd imagine living her life.

That's why, in my dreams, Adrienne was never dead. She couldn't be. I needed her to show me how to live, how to be. I needed her to step lightly ahead of me, leaving pretty little footprints that I could match with my own. She was the architect of my fantasy—and the fantasy never included killing her. I want you to know that. I want you to believe me. I didn't know I would, didn't know I could.

I didn't know, until the gun was in my hands.

I didn't know until I pulled the trigger.

And I never would have done it if there had been another way.

Of course, I know now that the beautiful life Adrienne seemed to live, those pretty little footsteps I fantasized about following in, was nothing but smoke and mirrors. I had to literally spend a day walking around in her shoes—shoes that, ironically, are half a size too small for my feet—to understand what a vampire she was. A succubus. A black hole that sucked in attention, energy, love, and spat it back out as a filtered, hashtagged advertisement for a life she didn't even appreciate. Imagine having all that, having so much, and doing so little with it. Imagine having all that, and still taking, taking, taking. Even when the thing you wanted belonged to someone else. Imagine being so sure that what you wanted was all that mattered, that the rules didn't apply to you. Imagine getting away with it for your whole entire life. That day at the lake, she threatened to take everything from me.

Imagine how surprised she was when a redneck bitch like me took her entire fucking head off.

You want honesty? Here it is: now that it's done, and there's no going back, I'm not exactly sorry.

I told you that Lizzie Ouellette was dead, and she is. I ended her. She's gone, in every sense of the word that matters. And she's not the only one. Four lives ended that day at the lake, in one way or another.

But there was one survivor. A woman with two names, or no name, depending on how you look at it. I'm still figuring out who she is. So this is her story. My story. A true story.

And it's not finished. Not even close.

CHAPTER 20

LIZZIE

THE LAKE

All I knew at first was that my husband was screaming. I could hear it from the moment I picked up the phone, not angry shouting but a sobbing, moaning, stream-of-consciousness babbling—*Lizzieareyou thereohfuckohfuckyouneedtocomerightnowpleasefuckfuckingfuck*—that made every hair on my body stand on end, even though I could only pick out my name and one other word. It was the "please" that did it. It wasn't a word Dwayne used, especially not with me, and especially not like that. The last time I'd heard it, he was screaming in the background, his foot crushed to a pulp, while one of his work buddies yelled into the receiver that I needed to meet them at the hospital.

The "please" is what I remember. It scared the shit out of me.

Maybe that's why I grabbed the gun.

Sometimes, it felt like my purpose in life was to build little castles, plant little gardens, just so that Dwayne could come clomping through and knock it all down. Not even on purpose or out of meanness; it was just how he was, a clumsy, selfish, idiot animal who couldn't understand that every action had consequences. Who never considered how one little act of cruelty or kindness could reverberate down the line, bigger, louder, until it broke everything apart. But who am I to judge? I never understood, either. Not until it was much too late. Dwayne didn't play ball at State because he stayed in Copper Falls and married me. He lost half his foot at that logging job, the job he took because he had a pregnant wife and bills to pay and no college degree. He got hooked on the pills because of the accident. He turned to dope when the pills ran out.

And Adrienne—that rich, entitled, privileged bitch who was so desperate that she'd do anything, even heroin, to escape the terrible boredom of being herself—she knew Dwayne was a guy who could get dope for her, because I told her all about it. I sat there with her, drinking chardonnay, and I blabbed my stupid face off. Everything that happened, the endless saga of deferred dreams, ruined bodies, pills and needles and pain, was like a little mechanical theater, just clicking along. And if you pulled back the curtain, there I was. Every time. All of the times. All the way back, to the very first moment where everything began to go wrong.

It only made sense that I was there at the end. That it was me, not Dwayne, holding the gun. Pulling the strings. Making the choice, like I had so many times, to clean up the mess that my man had made. I'd already lied for him, stolen for him. Maybe it was inevitable that eventually I'd kill for him, too.

I don't remember pulling the shotgun down from the wall before I left. I don't remember loading it. But as I pulled up to the lake house, I looked over, and there it was. Sitting on the passenger seat. Just along for the ride. Dwayne was waiting for me outside, pacing, his eyes wild. I felt a flare of anger, then fear: the Richardses' big, black SUV was parked neatly in the carport. Our guests had arrived. And if Dwayne wasn't sick or injured, that meant the frantic phone call must have been about something—someone—else.

The gun was in my hands as I stepped out of the car. I don't remember what I said to him; I do remember that he pointed toward the house and said, "She's in the bedroom," and I went running through the open door not knowing what waited for me inside. Knowing only that it must be bad, beyond bad, for my husband to admit that he needed me.

Adrienne was curled up on the edge of the bed with both feet still on the floor, so slow and sleepy that I knew right away she was stoned. An overdose, I thought. Had she found Dwayne's drugs? Had he given them to her? Why else would he be so panicked—and how could he be so stupid? I put the gun aside and screamed for him, demanding to know how much she'd taken, how much he'd given her, whether he'd called an ambulance. If they got here in time, they could hit her with Narcan. I knelt down, grabbed her by the shoulder, and shook her, hard. She gazed back at me with slack lips, her pupils huge and dark. There was a smudge of dried blood in the pit of her elbow, deep red and perfectly round, and a length of rubber tubing lying on the floor at her feet. Her eyes were glassy.

"Hey!" I yelled in her face. "Stay with me! Stay awake!"

She flinched at that. Her big blue eyes opened wide as she looked over my shoulder, focusing on Dwayne.

"I," she said, and took a deep breath before letting out the rest of the sentence as a long, slow sigh, "am soooooo fuuuuuuuucked."

Her eyes flicked in the direction of the deck outside. I stood and turned to look at Dwayne, who was bent at the waist with his hands braced against his knees, breathing hard.

"Dwayne?" I said. "I don't understand, is she—did you—what the fuck is happening?"

Adrienne took another deep breath, exhaled again with a soft whisper.

"He's outside," she said. Her breath smelled sour; I wondered if she was going to vomit, or already had.

"Dwayne's right here," I said, and both she and Dwayne shook their heads in unison. He stood and gestured at me to follow.

"Not me," he said. "Him. The husband."

Adrienne pressed her hands against the bed—already made up with the high thread-count sheets I'd ordered just for her, after she complained that the linens at the lake house were too scratchy—and sat up with a grunt. Her lips peeled back from her teeth as she turned her head to look out the window, grimacing with the effort.

"Ethan," she said. She blinked, so slowly that it took several seconds for the movement to complete: heavy lashes descending downward, then opening only to half-mast. She pursed her lips, and her tone turned hopeful. "Maybe he's not dead anymore."

Ethan Richards was halfway down the long stairs that started at the deck, descending steeply down the wooded coastline to the lake. He'd fallen headfirst, and while there was no blood, the utter stillness of his body against the busy landscape, the movement of the water and the trees gently creaking in the breeze, left no room for doubt. One of his legs was bent unnaturally beneath him, and there was a dark splotch on the front of his pants where his bladder had let go. His head was the worst part: it was hanging over the edge of one step at a hideous angle, dangling, as though his neck bones had shattered so completely that only his skin was still keeping it attached. His eyes were open, unseeing, facing the lake. The last thing he would have seen, if he was still alive when he landed, was the fiery blush of the changing trees on the opposite bank and the bright ripples of sunlight on the cold, dark water.

Even with a dead body sprawled awkwardly in the foreground, it was beautiful. Breathtaking. It was true, what I'd told Adrienne: this was my favorite time of year.

I had a creeping feeling that this was the last time I would ever enjoy it.

"How did it happen?" I said quietly. I was still praying even then that maybe it had been an accident, even though every instinct I had was telling me it was something so much worse. Adrienne was a mess—she would need several hours and a nap before I could expect any answers from her—but Dwayne wasn't stoned at all, and the expression on his face was pure horror: a grown-up version of the way he'd looked all those years ago, on the day he killed Rags. He kept flicking his eyes toward the bedroom, and it occurred to me that he must have helped Adrienne inject the drugs before preparing his own. *Ladies first.*

"I fucked up," he said. His eyes were red, and he kept pushing his hands into his hair, gripping the sides of his skull like he was trying to keep it from coming apart. I stepped forward to peer more closely at Ethan's body. Even from high above, twenty feet away, I could see a discoloration on the curve of his jaw, the barest beginnings of a bruise. There was a matching one on Dwayne's cheek.

"He hit me first," Dwayne said. I whirled to face him.

"So you pushed him down the fucking stairs?"

"No, I—" he began, then shook his head furiously. "I didn't mean it. I was defending myself. I just wanted him to back off. I didn't think he'd *die.*"

"But why? Why were you fighting in the first place?"

Dwayne's eyes slid sideways, and Adrienne's syrupy voice answered instead.

"Ethan doesn't like it when I try new things," she cooed. She'd managed to get off the bed and was leaning against the frame of the sliding door that opened onto the deck, one bare knee tucked behind the other. "He wasn't supposed to know. He was supposed to be in the boat. He likes the boat." She lifted a hand in slow motion, raised a finger to point at Dwayne, the most languid of accusations. "You said he was in the boat."

"He was," Dwayne said, and looked at me helplessly. "I was splitting wood when they got here. I let them in like you asked, and he said to bring in the suitcases because he wanted to go out in the kayak right away, while it was still sunny. I saw him putting it in, but I guess . . . he changed his mind, maybe. He walked in right when— but she *wanted* to. It was her idea!"

Adrienne's eyelids were drooping again.

"I need to lie down," she said. "I don't feel right. It feels different this time. My arms are so *heavy*."

I stared at Dwayne. "This time?" I said through gritted teeth. "How many times has she done this?"

"I don't know. A few." He was whining now.

"Since when?"

"This summer," he said. "She *asked*."

"She asks for lots of things," I hissed.

Adrienne made a croaking noise, somewhere between a retch and a belch. I turned just in time to see her cheeks bulge, then hollow out as she swallowed her own vomit. She grimaced and took a few tentative steps out, bracing two hands against the railing to gaze down at the body on the stairs below. The trees creaked. The lake glimmered. Ethan Richards stayed dead.

"You killed him," she said, in the same slow, sleepy voice. And then, almost as an afterthought: "Wow."

It was the "wow" that did it. I crammed my own fist into my mouth to stifle the shriek of hysterical laughter. My father had built those stairs with his bare hands. Now Ethan Richards was sprawled out on them with a broken neck, and his wife was too stoned to do anything but barf in her own mouth and say "wow."

Adrienne stumbled back inside.

"We need to call the police," I said.

Dwayne blanched. "But—"

"We have to. Right now. It already looks bad that you didn't call them right away, and when she comes down, she's going to figure that out. If she's not calling them herself—"

"She was already nodding off when it happened," he interrupted. "You saw her. She's gonna be in and out like that for another hour at least. And anyway, I unplugged the phone after I called you. Just in case."

I stared at him in disbelief. He sounded almost proud of himself, but the worse part was the expression on his face: haunted, scared, and guilty, yes, but also hopeful. My husband had called me and then unplugged the phone, knowing that I would come running, so sure that I'd fix what couldn't be undone. I wanted to hit him. I wanted to scream. Why had he had to bring his addiction here—to Adrienne, to the lake, to the house that I'd actually thought could be a path to a better life? The house my father had deeded to me, to me alone, so that no matter what else happened, I would have at least one thing, one place, that was mine.

It wouldn't be mine anymore. Not when this was all over. Dwayne had made sure of that. I had read the fine print on the rental agreements, the ones that outlined what you could and couldn't be sued for if someone got hurt on your property. Accidents were covered. Your junkie husband pushing a billionaire down the stairs was not. He would probably go to prison, probably for a long time, but I'd be handed my own life sentence. Everything I'd worked for, the life and the future I'd finally started to build here in a place where both were so hard to come by, was about to go up in flames.

I sat down heavily in one of the deck chairs, and put my head in my hands. Dwayne squatted beside me.

"We just have to get our story straight," he said. "So they understand it was an accident."

"An accident?" I snapped. "You pushed him down the stairs and he broke his neck. How is that an accident?!"

Dwayne grabbed my hand and peered urgently into my face. "But it wasn't like that! I didn't push him down the stairs. I hit him, and he kind of reeled backward, and then he fell down the stairs. Doesn't that mean it was an accident? Like, legally?"

"No," I said. "Jesus Christ. Legally, you fucking killed someone. And what about the drugs? Are we going to tell the cops how that was just an accident, too? You were running through the house with a syringe full of dope and you tripped and fell on top of Adrienne and whoopsie, the needle went in?"

"That's not funny, Lizzie."

"I'm not laughing, Dwayne. What did you think would happen when I got here?"

"I don't know! I thought you'd have an idea! You're so fucking smart, right? You always act like it, like you're so much smarter than me!" He was shouting now, flecks of spittle flying off his lips and landing in his beard. He stood, started pacing, and his voice grew hoarse. "I'm not a bad person. I'm not a bad person! I just made a mistake! They can't put me in jail for one mistake!"

"Oh, DJ," I said, and my voice broke. It had been years since I'd called him by the nickname. "Of course they can. And you know what's great? You called me, and now I'm involved. That's what it looks like now, like I was part of it. So probably, we both go to prison. You've fucked me over, too."

Dwayne sucked his teeth, sighed, and eased into the deck chair beside me.

"I guess that's how it is, huh?" he said matter-of-factly. He looked over at me, a funny little smile playing at the corners of his mouth. "I fuck you over. You fuck me over. And on and on. That's just our whole fucking life, isn't it? That's just what we do." He sighed. "So fine. You want to call the cops?"

I looked out at the lake. The sun was dipping lower, casting long, deep shadows across the water. Somewhere on the opposite bank, a loon began its loopy call, laughing hysterically all alone. We sat, listening, and then both jumped when another, closer bird suddenly screamed in response. Calling across the water to its mate. They shrieked together as the breeze grew stronger, as the trees creaked and groaned above. From the bedroom behind us came the light rattle of Adrienne, snoring. I wondered briefly if I could somehow pin the entire thing on her. That we'd shown up to welcome them to the house and found them just like this: one stoned and sleeping, one stone dead. The police might believe that, I thought . . . for five seconds, until Adrienne woke up and spilled her guts.

I sighed.

"Shut up and let me think," I said.

He did.

It was two hours later, close to sunset, when Adrienne woke up. I stood in the doorway, watching her. She struggled to a seated position, but there was no grogginess or confusion in her expression as she gazed back at me. I shifted uneasily. Her eyes narrowed, and she cleared her throat.

"I thought the police would be here by now," she said. "My husband is dead, isn't he? I know he is. Dwayne killed him. I saw it. Why aren't they here?"

I stepped into the room. "We were waiting for you to wake up. We need to talk."

"Talk about what?" she spat back, rubbing her eyes. "Jesus, what time is it? And where's Ethan? Has he been just . . . just lying out there? You just left him there?!"

"That's what we want to talk to you about," I said, and looked over my shoulder at the hallway behind me. This was Dwayne's cue: I beckoned and he stepped into the room, taking a few steps toward Adrienne before he seemed to think better of it and came to an awkward, hovering stop, halfway between us. He looked from me to her and back again.

"Listen," he said. "We're all in this together now."

Adrienne blinked at him. "Excuse me?"

I took a step toward her, too, and said, "What Dwayne means is, we need to figure out what to tell the police. Given the situation. I know you asked him to hook you up with heroin——"

"Oh, is that what you told her?" she said, looking at Dwayne with a smirk. Her tone had changed, that Southern drawl creeping in around the edges of her words.

I held up my hands. "I'm saying, it makes this complicated. For all of us. If you hadn't been shooting up, none of this would have happened."

Adrienne cocked her head, folded her arms, and pressed her lips together. Long seconds ticked by while I waited for her to reply. Dwayne was pushing his hands into his hair again.

"So," she said finally. "Blackmail. Is that what you think we're doing? I pretend Ethan pushed himself down the stairs, and you won't tell them that I was experimenting with illicit substances. Do I have that right?"

"Nobody said anything about blackmail," I said hurriedly, even as a sardonic inner voice added the subtext: *Not out loud, anyway.* "I'm just saying, there were . . . extenuating circumstances. A lot happened here."

The smirk played on her lips again. "Extenuating. You don't know the half of it."

"So help me understand, then," I said. "When I got here, you were—"

"I was high on the dope your husband pushed on me," she said, glaring at Dwayne, whose mouth dropped open.

"Because you asked for it!" he said. "As soon as Ethan walked away, you asked if I had any!"

"Did I?" Adrienne said. "I'm not sure I remember it that way."

"Adrienne, please," I said, desperation creeping into my voice. "We need to think clearly about this. It's not just about Dwayne. If the police think you were involved, you'll be in just as much trouble as any of us."

In fact, I had no idea if this was true. But Ethan's body had been there for hours now, the telltale bruise from Dwayne's fist discoloring its jaw, and Adrienne had been here when it happened. This was the best I could come up with, the plan that hours of sitting and thinking had yielded: to talk to Adrienne and try to convince her that it was in all of our best interests to say that Ethan's death had been an accident. I thought she might take some convincing, some coaxing, but this—the strange little smile, the narrowed eyes, the teasing tone, and the way she kept looking at Dwayne—was unsettling and not at all what I'd expected. I wondered, briefly, fleetingly, if there was something she wasn't telling me. Something everyone else in the room knew that I didn't.

I should have wondered harder. I should have asked.

But I didn't.

Because that was when Adrienne stood up, jabbing a finger at me, and said, "Let me explain this to you, Lizzie. Both of you. I'm the victim. I'm the survivor. You think the police are going to believe you over me? Your redneck junkie husband shot me up with dope and murdered Ethan, and you—for all I know, you were in on it. You probably planned it! Was I even supposed to wake up?"

It was my turn to stare. "Excuse me?" I said. Even then, I was already unwittingly starting to mimic her, using the same words Adrienne herself had used only moments ago.

Adrienne whirled, facing Dwayne. "That needle. It felt different this time. Didn't I say that? What did you give me?"

He gaped at her. "Nothing. I mean, nothing different." He looked at me with wide eyes. "Honestly. I swear. I wouldn't—"

"What?" Adrienne shrieked. "You wouldn't what? Kill someone? Should we ask my husband what he thinks about that?"

I took a deep breath. My ears felt like they were on fire, and a rapid pulse was pounding behind my eyes. I could still fix this, couldn't I? I had to.

"Adrienne, that was an accident. Nobody tried to kill you," I said.

"I don't believe you!" she screamed. She looked wildly from me to Dwayne, and then, suddenly, she let loose a short bark of laughter. Shaking her head, she said, "Oh God, and it doesn't even matter. Look at the two of you. Look at me, and look at you. You're a pair of fuck-ing trash bags. When I tell people what you did, nobody will believe you when you say you didn't. If I say that you lured us out here to the middle of nowhere so that you could kill us and rape us and rob us, they'll believe me." She was talking faster now, her hands fluttering, her voice creeping up in pitch. "The police, the press. Holy shit, what a story. People will go crazy for it. I'll probably get a book deal. I mean. I mean, Lizzie. Just look. Look at me, and look at you."

Adrienne was breathing hard, and so was I. I could hear Dwayne babbling in the background, but I ignored him. I focused. Because something important was happening: I was doing what Adrienne wanted.

I was looking at her. I was looking at her very carefully.

Her hair was a mess, her makeup smeared. She was wearing her favorite outfit, the red bikini and the striped slub tee, clothes I'd bought for myself but given to her before I ever got to wear them, because there was so much dirt and tar at the lake and she was worried about staining her dry-clean-only wardrobe. Her skin was splotchy. Her lips were cracked. She even had a bruise on one knee.

We looked more alike than ever.

Adrienne smiled triumphantly.

I reached for the gun.

When I was a little girl, and Pop was first teaching me how to shoot a rifle, he told me that the most important thing about hunting was waiting for the right moment. After the buck wandered into your sights, but before he caught your scent and bolted. He taught me that being a good shot wasn't worth shit unless you could also be patient. He told me that pulling the trigger was mostly about *not* pulling the trigger. You had to wait. You had to know. You had to see when the time was right—but then, you couldn't hesitate. When the moment came, you got one breath to do what had to be done.

Inhale.

Exhale.

Squeeze.

And you had to be ready. Not just for the crack of the bullet and the jolt of the kickback, but for what came after. The dying gasp. The final twitch. The creature that had been moving a moment ago, gone forever and irretrievably still.

He told me that taking a life, even an animal's life, is something you can never take back. But if you have the patience, if you have the strength, if you choose your moment: you can do what has to be done. And you can know, in your heart, that you made the right choice.

I was making the right choice. Even Adrienne was always telling me I deserved a better life. I don't think she really meant it. I don't think she thought about me much at all. But I guess, somewhere along the way, I must have started to believe her.

Adrienne was standing very still, staring at the shotgun.

"Dwayne," I said. "Step back."

"What are you doing?" he said, sounding bewildered. But for once, he did what I asked. He stepped back.

I racked a bullet.

Adrienne lifted one hand, her index finger extended. I'll never know what she meant to do, accuse me or ask for time.

"You crazy bitch," she said, and then swiveled her head to look at my husband. "Dwayne," she said, through gritted teeth. "Dwayne! Tell her to stop! Do something!"

I took a breath. The light in the room shifted from golden to pink, as the sun dipped behind the treeline. *Inhale. Exhale.*

"I don't know why you're looking at him," I said. Already, my voice didn't sound like my own.

Squeeze.

The shotgun kicked against my shoulder.

Outside, a loon screamed on the empty lake.

Next to me, my husband whispered another woman's name.

There was so much blood.

CHAPTER 21

LIZZIE

THE LAKE

I tried to think of what was in front of me as meat. Nothing more. Like the squirrels we snared and skinned for stew. Like the bucks I dressed to make extra cash. How many times had I pulled a bandana over my mouth and nose and gone to work cutting a body apart? Coring the anus, removing the entrails, stringing it up to let the blood drain out. Filleting out the tenderloin, slicing the flanks. Packaging it neatly in plastic wrap, all sanitary, all squeaky clean. Like something you'd find in a grocery store.

Meat.

After I pulled the trigger, after Dwayne said Adrienne's name and then didn't say anything else, we stood in silence for what felt like ages. I should have been panicking, but I wasn't. The sound of the gun had been monstrously loud, but there was nobody around to hear it. Only the loons, and all they did was laugh and laugh, their cries echoing across the water as the sky turned from pink to purple. We were alone. What was done was done. And inside my head, a cool, reasonable voice spoke up: *You know what you have to do.*

Dwayne shifted his weight beside me. He'd been closer to Adrienne than I was when the gun went off, and there were little flecks of blood scattered like freckles across his forehead.

"Don't touch her," I started to say, but he wasn't moving toward Adrienne. He was backing away, staring at me with huge, frightened eyes.

"You shot her," he said. "Holy shit. Why did you shoot her?"

I looked at the bed, where Adrienne, or what was left of her, had pitched back with the force of the bullet and landed in a sideways sprawl. There was a spray of blood on the wall behind her, and a spreading stain underneath, soaking into the linens. I felt my gorge rise, and swallowed hard.

"You heard her," I said quietly. "You heard what she was going to do."

"Yeah, but—"

I turned, thrusting the gun at him with both hands. He flinched away from it like he thought it might bite him. "Take this," I said. "Put it in the truck. Then get his body off the stairs and put it in the passenger seat. He's not a big guy. You should be able to carry him up on your own. If there's blood, don't step in it. Be careful."

"But," he said again, and I stepped forward and shoved the gun roughly into his chest. "Take. It. You wanted me to have an idea? This is it. This is my idea. I'll explain the rest to you later. Right now, we need to get this part done while there's still some light left. Put the gun and the body in your truck. Wait for me outside. Where's your buck knife?"

"In my pocket."

"Give it to me."

Wordlessly, he did. I clutched the knife against my chest.

"Do what I said, and then stay outside. I don't want you coming back in here."

I thought he might argue, but he didn't. If anything, he looked relieved, casting a final, sidelong glance at the body on the bed before he turned away, the gun in his hands. A lover's last look, I would realize later. I wonder what he was thinking, whether it was something tender. I wonder if he even really liked her.

I waited until I heard the screen door slam and his footsteps crunching across the driveway. I didn't want Dwayne there for what I was about to do, but even once he was gone, I hesitated. The voice in my head was urging me on, but a part of me still understood, in that moment, that I didn't have to listen. That there were other ways for this to end, including a version of the story where I plugged the phone back in, called the police, and let them arrive just in time to catch my blood-spattered husband stuffing Ethan Richards's body into the passenger seat of his truck, right next to a recently fired shotgun. A version in which I told everyone that Dwayne had killed them both, and I was either too late or too frightened to stop him. It would be my word against his, but I thought I could make them believe me. If I had to. If I wanted to. Certainly, the odds of that were better than the odds of pulling off my other plan, which wasn't even fully thought through yet and only seemed like it might work because it was so utterly, bat-shit crazy: the way that Adrienne, in those last moments, had looked for all the world like a fun-house-mirror reflection of myself.

The truth is, I didn't rush into it. I imagined it the other way, all the way through. I thought about how it might end: with Dwayne in prison, or maybe even dead, if the police arrived at the wrong moment or if he was stupid enough to reach for the gun. With me, standing alone in our dingy little house, looking at the long dent on the couch where the man I'd promised to comfort and keep, for better or for worse, used to sprawl out at the end of the day. I imagined the looks, the whispers, the anger, if he went away and I went free. They'd say I drove him to it. They'd say he should have killed me, too. The police might believe me, even a jury might, but my neighbors? Never.

Could I possibly stay in Copper Falls, after that? And if I left, where could I go? I imagined trying to start over, broke and uneducated and almost thirty, in a place where nobody knew my name—and then realized that after what had happened here, that place wouldn't exist. No matter where I went, there I'd be. The junkyard jezebel. The redneck bitch. The one who got off scot-free after her husband killed two people. Adrienne was right: it was a hell of a story. Only unlike her, I wouldn't be getting the survivor's book deal, making the talk-show rounds. I wasn't that kind of girl. I could still hear her words, the truth of them, echoing in my head.

Look at me, she'd said. *Look at me, and look at you.*

I took the knife and went to work.

Dwayne kept his blade sharp. The mole under my breast came off with a zing of pain so fierce and fine that it made me gasp. One moment, it was part of me; the next, it was just a small, black nub, caught between my thumb and forefinger, nothing left but a dull throb in the place where it had been attached. I'd been worried about blood, but there was hardly any. I kept a bottle of Gorilla Glue in one of the kitchen drawers; I'd used it earlier that summer to mend a broken handle on Adrienne's favorite coffee mug. A tiny dab was all it took to make the mole stick—well, that and a lifetime's worth of rumors. I thought of the boys who'd chased me into the woods all those years ago, who'd pulled my shirt over my head and told everyone what they found underneath. The humiliation of that moment had followed me all my life, but now I was grateful for it: it made it absurdly easy to pass off someone else's body as my own. I slipped the diamond ring off her blood-greased finger, and slid my plain gold band on in its place. I stepped back, closed my eyes, took a breath. My heart was pounding, but my thoughts were eerily calm. I reached behind me for the light switch. For this next part, I'd need to see clearly.

Look at me, and look at you.

I turned on the light, and I looked.

The reddish shade of her hair would easily pass for mine. Her body wasn't quite the same, her torso a little bit longer and her breasts rounder, but it hardly mattered when nobody but Dwayne had seen me undressed in years. Her toes were polished in a shade I couldn't remember if I owned, but who would bother to check? Especially not if they were sure it was me, and I felt certain that they would. The mole was right. The clothes were right. She was fair-skinned, like me. Eyes blue, like mine. Below that, the gunshot had done too much damage for it to matter. Although her nose . . . I squinted. It was close. Maybe a little bit snubbier. A subtle difference. You had to really be looking for it. I was almost positive nobody would notice.

"Almost" isn't worth the risk.

I grimaced. Hesitated.

Meat, I thought. *It's just meat.*

When I was done, I threw the quilt over her, taking care not to smudge the blood around, mindful of every step. Listening to the calculating voice inside that told me to be quick, thorough, careful.

I hit the switch on the garbage disposal with my elbow: no fingerprints.

I made sure to lift the toilet seat before I threw up.

I double flushed with a capful of Clorox, just in case.

When I turned around, I saw a long-sleeved shift dress hanging on the back of the bathroom door, and a pair of riding boots set neatly on the floor next to Adrienne's overnight bag: the clothes she'd been wearing when she got here. I put on everything, including the underwear that were crammed into a side pocket of the bag. Only the boots were tight; her lace thong sat neatly across my hipbones, my breasts snugged into the cups of her bra. The dress zipped smoothly and fell into place, the hem brushing lightly against my bare thighs. I tossed my own clothes into the hamper, so that anyone who looked would assume I'd done what she had: arrived at the house on a warm fall afternoon and changed into a swimsuit to lounge in what was left of the afternoon sunshine. Every trace of Adrienne went into her bag. I would leave my own in its place.

When I turned to check my reflection in the mirror, I found a stranger staring back. A woman who looked a little like me, but more like *her,* as though I'd started to transform into a more polished self but popped out of the chrysalis before the process was done. My mirror image stood tall with her shoulders back, held her chin at a confident tilt, pursed her lips just so. I rummaged in Adrienne's bag for a lipstick and swiped it across my own lips, rubbing the color into the corners with my finger like I'd seen her do. I lifted the corners of my mouth.

There you are.

Adrienne Richards smirked back at me. I cocked my head; so did she. I placed a hand on my hip, and she did the same.

Then a muffled thump came from the other side of the wall, and it was me again in the mirror: frozen, one hand to my heart, my mouth open in a little O.

Something was moving in the bedroom.

I peered around the door, and let out the breath I'd been holding. It was only Dwayne. I'd told him to stay outside, but of course he hadn't listened. Not only that, but he was leaning toward the coverlet, reaching for it, ready to lift a corner to peer underneath. I stepped out of the bathroom and cleared my throat.

Dwayne looked up—and if I hadn't been confident already that I could play my part in what was to come, his reaction would have been all the convincing I needed. He stumbled back with a shout, holding his hands out in front of him as if to ward me off.

"Fuck!" he yelled. He caught himself against the edge of the dresser, breathing hard, peering at me across the room. I brought a hand to my hip.

"I told you to wait outside," I said.

"Jesus fucking Christ," he said. "I thought you were her. You scared the shit out of me. Honest to God, you look just like . . . Wait. Are those her clothes?"

"Yes."

"Why?"

"Let's talk outside." He hesitated, glancing again at the bed, the motionless shape under the bloodstained blankets. I stepped forward. I held out the buck knife, wiped clean, and he took it from me with a questioning look.

"Trust me," I said. "You don't want to see what's under there."

After that moment in the bedroom, it wasn't hard to make Dwayne understand how it was supposed to work. How it would work, if we were lucky. Over the course of two summers, many conversations, and a few dozen bottles of wine, Adrienne had unwittingly given me— given *us*—all the information we needed to drain her accounts and disappear. Once, when she was really drunk, she'd confessed that she and Ethan had been prepared to flee the country when it looked like he might actually be charged for his crimes. I didn't even have to pretend to be shocked, and the more I stared openmouthed, the more she talked.

"Girl, you should see your face," she said, laughing and refilling her glass. "You're so naive. It's adorable. Oooh, I'd be in so much trouble if Ethan heard me talking about this, but I don't care. Who are you going to tell, right?" She giggled, took a long swallow. "Ethan was never going to prison. He's got *connections*. It all would have been taken care of." She shrugged. "But then the case fell apart, so we got to stay put. Just as well. I fucking hate Moscow."

"They have cash stashed everywhere," I said to Dwayne. We were leaning back against his truck, smoking cigarettes from a pack that he'd had to reach past Ethan Richards's stiffening body to retrieve from his glove compartment. "Maybe even passports, I don't know. Plus whatever she's got in her accounts—if I get my hands on that, we'd be golden."

Dwayne frowned. "Do you know her ATM code or something?"

"Dwayne. People like this don't use ATMs. They have financial advisors. If I go there, tell him I need to liquidate some assets . . ."

"Don't you think he'll notice that you're not her?"

I pressed my lips together. "No. No, I don't. He's only met her a couple times, and I don't think it was recently. If Adrienne Richards makes an appointment at his office, and then a woman shows up driving Adrienne's car, wearing Adrienne's clothes, walking and talking like Adrienne . . . I think he'll see what he's expecting to see. I looked enough like her to make you look twice, didn't I? And you knew she was dead."

He took a drag on his cigarette. "How much money are we talking about?"

"A lot. Maybe even enough to last us the rest of our lives, if we plan it right." My voice was getting animated, my heart beginning to pound. After the horrors of the day, all the things we had both done that couldn't be taken back, the thought of escape was enough to make me giddy. There was a dead body in the truck behind me and another cooling on the bedroom floor, but I was alive, and so was my husband. Maybe it wasn't too late for us. Maybe we could begin again, and this time, we'd do it right.

"We could go anywhere, Dwayne," I said. "We'd have to be careful, stay off the grid for a while. Maybe a year. We'd have to be smart. But we could start over. You can get sober"—he looked sharply at me, and I grabbed his hand again—"You *can*. I know you can. I'll help you."

He took a last drag on the cigarette before dropping it and stubbing it out in the dirt. I bent to pick it up, marveling at how quickly my brain had adjusted to the idea that we should be leaving no trace. I stubbed out my own cigarette and pitched both butts into the bed of the truck. Dwayne chewed his lip.

"Do you really think you could do that?" he said. "I mean, get that extra money."

"Yes," I said. I sounded more confident than I felt. The truth was, I didn't know for sure. But having begun to imagine what might be possible, how much *more* was possible if I just played my part correctly, it seemed foolish not to try. We were already running. I was taking a risk regardless. Why not take the slightly bigger risk for the far greater reward?

"Florida," Dwayne said suddenly, and I snapped back to reality.

"What?"

"We could go to Florida. There was a guy at the logging camp back in the day, he said that you can hunt wild pigs down there in the swamps." He shrugged. "I don't know. You said off the grid, so—"

"Yeah, of course," I said quickly, ignoring the fact that the idea of Florida made my skin crawl. Mosquitoes, alligators, cockroaches the size of a fucking shoe, the endless and inescapable heat. But I needed Dwayne on board, and if the prospect of hunting wild swamp pigs would get him there . . . I smiled. "Florida. Perfect."

Dwayne nodded. "Yeah. They wouldn't think to look for us there."

"Well, if we're lucky, they won't look for us anywhere."

He gave me a quizzical look. "They won't?"

"Nobody comes looking if they think you're already dead."

It was just after midnight when we left, pitch black and breezy. My last glimpse of the lake house was in my rearview mirror, nothing but a dark shape surrounded by the swaying, creaking pines. I drove Dwayne's truck, my fingers wrapped tightly around the wheel, carefully chauffeuring Ethan Richards's lifeless body to its final resting place. I'd buckled him in—the last thing I wanted was to take a turn too fast and end up with a dead man facedown in my lap—but there was nothing I could do about his head, which lolled grotesquely back and forth every time a stray rock or pothole jolted the cab. I could just make out the lights of the Mercedes far behind me on the straightaways, Dwayne behind the wheel and following at a distance. There was no need to caravan; we both knew the way.

The junkyard was silent, the heaps rising like jagged peaks against the midnight sky. The truck's headlights illuminated my path, although I could have driven it blind. After all these years, I still knew this place, its twists and turns permanently etched in my memory. The trailer sat dark and shuttered at the end nearest the road, empty, as I knew it would be. Pop would be at Strangler's by now, drinking until two o'clock in the morning and sleeping it off in his pickup until dawn. By the time he came back, the whole place would be up in flames.

I had started telling a story back at the lake house, and this was the last chapter. It went like this: Once upon a time, after ten unhappy years together, Dwayne Cleaves killed his wife and then himself, coming full circle to end his life back in the junkyard where they first met. Throwing a flare before he pulled the trigger. Burning it all down to ash. It was the kind of story people would believe, I thought. Not because Dwayne and I had been especially miserable, but because we hadn't—and don't those couples always seem happy enough, right up until the first body hits the floor?

I would set the stage, light the fire, and say goodbye forever to Lizzie Ouellette. To the town where she never belonged. To the junkyard she used to call home. As I did, I'd blow a kiss to the man who made me, raised me, gave me the best life he could. Who once told me he would have killed for me, and meant it.

I held the flare in my hand. Lit it. Inhaled, exhaled.

I liked to think that Pop, of all people, would understand the choices I'd made tonight. Not condone them, but understand them. This would be my last gift to him. I knew, at least, that he would be taken care of. Even after I married and moved into town, I'd still helped out here and there with the upkeep of the yard—including making sure the insurance policy stayed up to date. Pop always said we should get a cheaper one; I always insisted on full coverage. How many times had my father joked about it, how he'd make twice as much if the place caught fire as he ever would selling it? I hoped that was true. I hoped he took the payout, packed his bags, and never looked back.

Maybe I shouldn't have. Maybe destroying everything that tied us to this town was my dream, not his.

But the fire was already lit.

The flames flickered in Ethan Richards's open eyes, then rose to engulf him. I backed away, watching as the fire filled the cab, waiting until the nearest pile of scrap began to burn, too, before I turned my back and ran. I darted back down the corridor for the last time, wind in my ears, eyes streaming, looking above the heaps to a sky filled with millions of glittering stars. Running so fast it felt like I was flying. Not knowing what came next, and in that moment, not caring at all. Behind me, the flames began to lick higher. In front of me, nothing but the wide-open night.

CHAPTER 22

LIZZIE

THE CITY

Dwayne flinched as the gun went off, then staggered forward, swaying, his feet braced like a boxer's. His mouth dropped open, and for a single horrifying moment I thought he might speak, that I'd somehow missed the mark and might have to pull the trigger again. I wasn't sure I could do it. Worse, I suddenly wasn't sure I wanted to. My husband stood in front of me, a tiny hole in the front of his shirt where I'd shot him. The edges of the hole were starting to turn red, and all I could think of was what he'd said to me all those years ago, the day he'd killed Rags.

I wish I hadn't done it. I wished it right away.

But it wasn't like that for me. Whatever I felt about what I'd done, it wasn't anything as pure or straightforward as regret. I didn't wish I hadn't done it. I didn't want to unmake my choice. I just didn't want to make it twice.

And then I didn't have to. Dwayne's legs buckled and he went down in a graceless heap, pitching forward, crashing face-first into the corner of Ethan Richards's fancy mahogany desk. There was a wet crunch as his nose broke on impact, and a second, sickening thud as he crumpled the rest of the way onto the carpet. His arms, dangling useless at his sides, never lifted to break the fall. I think he was dead before he hit the floor.

I hope that's how it was. I hope it was quick. As angry as I was at Dwayne, who'd fucked up my life so thoroughly that he almost managed to fuck up my death in the bargain, I never wanted him to suffer. It wasn't about desire at all. It was about survival, the realization that I couldn't save us both, because I couldn't save my husband from himself. The drugs, the lies, the goddamn grainy cell-phone photo of Adrienne that he couldn't stop himself from flashing around but also couldn't bring himself to tell me about: he would have kept on like that, until he made a mistake I couldn't fix, one that would destroy us both. Dwayne would have fucked up and gotten caught, eventually. And if I hadn't found the courage now to take a different path, I would have been dragged along with him, still clutching his hand as we both went down.

Letting go was the only choice.

I stood where I was for a full minute after he fell, the gun hanging limply from my hand, watching as Dwayne didn't move, didn't breathe. Even as the seconds ticked by, I knew I didn't need them. After ten years of sharing a home, a bed, a life, you can tell the difference between your husband and the empty shell where he used to live. He was gone.

It was time to start telling a new story.

The buck knife was still in his pocket. I set the gun aside while I tugged it loose, clutching it to my chest.

He was there when I woke up. He had a knife.

He said he'd killed my husband.
He said he wanted money.
He didn't know we kept a gun in the safe.

My back bumped against the wall, and I leaned into it. Let myself slide down. Watching for another minute to see if he moved—not because I thought he would, but because that's what she would do. Inside my head, the calculating survivor's voice continued describing an alternate, plausible version of events:

I shot him. I took the knife. I thought he might still come after me.

I took a deep breath. Then another. Gulping air, my heart starting to race, silver stars dancing and wriggling at the fringes of my vision.

I waited. When I was sure he was dead, I ran.

I ran.

I used Adrienne's phone to call 911. I told them the address and that I needed an ambulance.

Then I hung up, cutting off the operator as she told me to stay on the line, and called a lawyer.

Not just because that's what Adrienne would do, but because I'm not a fucking idiot.

The attorney's name was Kurt Geller. I could have remembered it from the news stories about Ethan Richards's almost-trial, but I didn't have to. Adrienne kept notes for all her contacts—*housekeeper, makeup, trainer.* Earlier that day, I'd looked up Anna, the SoulCycle blonde; her note said, *dumb bitch from SC but is Lulu ambassador.* Typical of Adrienne; she didn't have friends, just people she loathed but kept around because they might be useful to her. My own entry said, simply, *lake house,* and Dwayne's number wasn't saved at all, which confused me until I realized that she'd never needed it: she had me. All those stupid jobs she kept finding for him to do, all the times she'd asked me to send him over, and I'd nodded along like the world's biggest asshole. She should have added a second note to my name: *pimp.*

Geller was listed as *Ethan's lawyer,* with multiple phone numbers: office, assistant, emergencies. I called the last one and listened as it rang. He answered on the second ring, his voice gravelly.

"This is Kurt Geller."

I took a deep, shaky breath, and let my voice pitch higher.

"Mr. Geller, this is Adrienne Richards. I'm sorry if I woke you. I didn't know who else to call."

"Adrienne," he said. In the background, a muffled female voice said, *Who?* Geller cleared his throat. "Of course, Ethan's wife. But why—"

"Ethan's dead," I said. "And I just shot the man who killed him."

I don't know what I expected. A gasp of shock, maybe, or stunned silence. Instead, I found out why Kurt Geller was the kind of attorney who gave his clients a special phone number for midnight legal emergencies.

"All right," he said smoothly. "Did you call 911?"

"Yes."

"Good. Anyone else?"

"Just you."

"Good," he said again. "We're going to keep this brief. The first thing they'll look at is your phone records. Here's what you need to do."

I sat heavily on the living room sofa and listened to Geller's instructions. I tried not to think about Dwayne, facedown and dead in the room down the hall. The hand not holding the phone was starting to shake. Not at the violence, or the loss, but at the realization that I was alone. Truly. For the first time since everything had been set in motion, maybe even for the first time in my life. Strangest of all, the self I was left to rely on was someone I barely even knew. I had stepped into Adrienne's life, a performance that was only meant to last a few days but was now extended indefinitely, and for a much bigger audience. For a moment, I imagined hanging up, grabbing whatever I could carry, and running. I had killed Lizzie; I could let Adrienne go, too. And maybe I should. I could be reborn somewhere out there in the world, choose a new name, create a new self. I could be nobody at all. The gym bag with the cash, the diamonds, was sitting in a closet just a few feet away. Less than three minutes had passed since I'd dialed 911. I could still be gone before they got here.

Something was moving in the hallway, just beyond the faint rectangle of light spilling through the open office door. My breath caught in my throat, then came out in a little whimper as the cat appeared, padding silently out of the dark and across the floor toward me.

"Adrienne?" Kurt Geller's voice was sharp. "We should end this call now."

The cat hopped into my lap, purring, and stretched up to rub his face against my chin. I drew another breath. Slow, steady, even.

I wasn't going anywhere.

"I understand."

I don't know how long I sat there, petting the purring cat, listening for the sound of sirens or pounding on the door. I was on my own tonight, but I would meet Kurt Geller tomorrow, and I wondered how much contact he'd had with Adrienne, how long it had been since he'd seen her. If he knew her well enough to notice that something seemed off. I tried to imagine what she would say. *You'd seem different, too, if you'd just been attacked by a maniac in the middle of the night.*

Eventually, I stood, clutching the cat in my arms, and walked back to the office. I stood in the doorway, in the same spot Dwayne had been in the moments before I shot him. The last thing he ever said, the last word that passed his lips, was my name.

I tried not to think about that, either.

I told you I never wanted to kill Adrienne, that I never thought about it even once, and that was true. But I promised to be honest, and honestly, I thought about Dwayne dying. I did. I thought about it all the time. There was the time I imagined pinching his nose shut and letting his drugged-out sleep turn into something more permanent, but it didn't stop there. His death was a constant what-if thrumming away in the back of my mind. It didn't have to be that I killed him myself. Sometimes, I imagined standing on our doorstep while a police officer approached with his jaw set and his hat in his hand, the surest sign of bad news. I thought about hunting accidents. Overdoses. A brake failure on the same icy stretch where my mother spun out and crashed. I imagined myself putting a hand on the doorjamb to steady myself, as the officer asked if there was someone I could call. *You shouldn't be alone at a time like this*, he'd say, because that's what they always say.

Nobody ever stops to think that "alone" can also mean "free."

And free was what I felt. All those years I had drifted along with Dwayne, the two of us clinging to our shitty life like it was the only thing to stop us from drowning. There was nothing left to cling to now. I was unanchored, already moving much faster than I ever had before, carried away by an unseen current. Alone, but afloat.

Free.

Downstairs, someone began pounding on the door. There were shouts—"Police!"—and the cat startled, leaping out of my arms and darting away, disappearing into the darkness of the house. I turned.

"I'm here!" I shouted. "I'm coming out."

I've never been a sentimental person. I felt no desire to pause for last looks, or plant a kiss on his cooling temple. I would leave him behind the way I'd left everything else: without saying goodbye. I was grateful that he'd died facedown, so that his eyes wouldn't follow me when I left. So that I wouldn't have to see the permanent surprise etched on his face. Except for the awkward slump of his body against the floor, he could have been asleep. There was hardly any blood at all.

That's what happens when you hit your target in the heart.

CHAPTER 23

BIRD

Bird had gotten back on the road just shy of eleven o'clock, and just in time to hear the Sox nearly blow a four-to-one lead in the ninth inning. He white-knuckled the steering wheel, the lights of the city fading behind him, the smooth, dark highway opening up ahead. In New York, a sold-out crowd roared their approval as the Yankees closed in.

He was only a few miles up the interstate when Kimbrel, who was supposed to *close*, for fuck's sake, clocked a batter with the bases loaded and forced in a run. He wondered if the Sox would somehow manage to lose in spite of themselves, clutching defeat from the jaws of victory—and when the Yanks scored again, bringing the lead to a single run, he allowed himself to briefly consider that a loss might be some sort of bad omen. Not just for the Sox, but for him, personally. Speeding back to Copper Falls with his tail between his legs, cursing the waste of time that the long drive to Boston had been. Adrienne

Richards: a promising lead—turned—wild-goose chase in the span of a single text message.

Bird grimaced. He should have known. The fire at the junkyard was just too weird to be a coincidence, and yet he'd almost come around to accepting that a weird coincidence was all it was. Junkyards burned down all the time, after all. It was just his luck that Earl Ouellette, surveilling the wreckage with a flashlight in hand, had spotted Dwayne Cleaves's truck partially buried by a pile of scrap. The truck was a burned-out husk, practically unrecognizable unless you knew, as Earl did, that he'd never had a pickup parked in that particular part of the yard. The driver's-side door had fallen open, and the high-pressure blast of the fire hoses had washed out what was in the cab, including a piece of the charred body that had been perched inside. When Earl walked up to investigate, something crunched in the ashes under his feet; he told the police he thought it was glass, only all the glass had melted, and when he turned the flashlight toward the sound, he found himself standing on the snapped pieces of a human femur.

How the fuck do you like that? Bird thought. He'd spent a full day of hunting for Lizzie Ouellette's murderer, conducted dozens of interviews, logged hundreds of miles on his vehicle, and was fast approaching the halfway point of what was shaping up to be a solid forty-eight hours without sleep. And all that time, it appeared that the son of a bitch had been sitting pretty right there in Copper Falls, already dead, transformed by his own hand into a fully crisped hunk of human barbecue. Just waiting to be skewered. It was a lucky break; if not for Earl choosing that particular moment to explore the ruins of his livelihood, it might have been months before they found the body.

And then Gleyber Torres grounded out, stranding the winning runs on base, and all Bird's worries about baseball and bad omens were drowned out by the outraged groans of the New York crowd and the sporadic, courageous cheering of the Boston fans in attendance. Alone in his car, illuminated by the glow of the dashboard lights, Bird pumped a fist and pressed the accelerator. The cruiser soared into the night.

By the time the Sox finished soaking their locker room in champagne, the start of a celebration that would rage until dawn, Bird was crossing the Maine state line and feeling ready for what came next. Dwayne Cleaves's death meant closure, if not justice. Cops tended to prefer the latter, but families often felt differently, and Bird thought that Earl Ouellette might be happier with this outcome. A trial had its downsides. Plea bargains, parole, the specter of a killer someday being forgiven and set free, not to mention having to hear in graphic detail just how badly and brutally your loved one's life had ended. Lizzie's father didn't need to sit in a courtroom, to hear a forensic expert describe the mess that Cleaves and a shotgun had made of his daughter's face. And even if suicide was a better, cleaner fate than the fucker deserved, at least Earl could take comfort that he no longer had to share a world with his daughter's killer.

It was three o'clock in the morning, the cruiser eating up the last few miles of county road en route to Copper Falls, when Bird's phone began to buzz.

"This is Bird."

"Hiya there, Bird," said Brady. "Still on the road?"

"Nearly there." Bird stifled a yawn.

"You might want to pull over."

"Nah, I'm good. I just want to get there. Check out the scene while it's still fresh."

"I'm not talking about taking a nap," said Brady drily, and Bird felt a familiar tickle of foreboding at the back of his neck. He'd experienced the same sensation hours earlier, as he drove away from his unproductive interview with Adrienne Richards, but he thought he'd left it behind. Now it was back, stronger than ever. It was something about Brady's voice; he sounded almost apologetic.

"What, then?"

"I just got off the phone with Boston PD," Brady said. "An Officer Murray?"

Bird instinctively lifted his foot from the accelerator. The cruiser began to coast.

"Tell me," he said.

"There's been a shooting at the Richards residence. One deceased at the scene. Murray says it's our suspect."

Bird hit the brakes and pulled the car to a stop, parking it at a half straddle across the faded white line where shoulder met road, its headlights beaming into the empty night.

"Cleaves?"

"That's what they tell me."

"You've got to be kidding me. How?"

"No further details, Detective. Sorry. You might want to count yourself lucky that they got in touch at all."

"Are they sure?"

"I'd guess so."

Bird dropped the phone into his lap and tented his fingertips over the bridge of his nose. His face suddenly felt like not enough skin stretched over too much bone, and his eyes had started to ache. Gritty feeling around the edges, like the lids were made of sandpaper. He groaned. Brady's tinny voice floated up from the phone in his lap.

"Bird? You there?"

He lifted the phone to his ear.

"Yeah. Sorry. Just . . ." He trailed off. Thinking. He shook his head. "Then who the fuck is dead in Cleaves's vehicle at the Copper Falls junkyard?"—only even as the words crossed his lips, he realized he knew the answer.

Just a few hours ago, he'd entertained himself with the idea of being the one to tell Ethan Richards about his wife's affair. Now he was pretty sure he'd missed his chance.

Not just because Richards already knew, but because Richards was already dead.

Bird sighed. "Never mind."

Brady sounded amused. "Really? Just like that, you got it all fig-ured out?"

"Probably," said Bird. "Maybe." He paused, and then thumped his hand against the steering wheel. Once. Twice. Hard.

"Bird?"

"I'm here." He took a deep breath, and sighed it out noisily through pursed lips. "Goddammit."

A few moments later, the cruiser pulled back onto the road and drove on. Toward Copper Falls, the junkyard, toward Dwayne Cleaves's aban-doned truck and the charred human remains sitting in it. Remains that would not turn out to be Cleaves, after all—couldn't be, because Cleaves had just been shot to death by his mistress two hundred miles away. Bird shook his head. There was no point in turning around, even if he'd wanted to; Boston PD had been accommodating enough about surveilling the Richards house, but they wouldn't welcome an out-of-state cop pushing in on a homicide while the body was still warm. Instead, he'd finish this journey right back where he'd started, watch the day break over a new crime scene, and hopefully end it with the case wrapped, or close enough. Full circle. There was something right about it.

It was nice, at least, to know that his instincts were on point. He must have just missed Cleaves in Boston, the two of them passing like ships in the night as Bird drove back out of town. Another weird coincidence—or maybe Cleaves had been lurking just out of sight, watching, waiting for the police to come and go before he made his move. Something about that felt correct, too, except that it would mean Cleaves must be much smarter than given credit for, which didn't feel right at all.

Bird sighed, wishing he'd stopped for coffee before getting off the interstate. He had the frustrating sense of having almost figured out something interesting, a dangling thread worth pulling on, but his thoughts were all out of focus and then interrupted by a massive yawn. He rubbed again at his eyes—and then yelped and slammed the brakes as a shape loomed out of the darkness ahead, frozen in the glare of his oncoming headlights. The cruiser screeched to a stop. Bird peered through the windshield at the deer, which stared back at him, pale and unmoving in the middle of the road. It was a doe, and he instinctively looked toward the dark behind her, expecting to see fawns or friends, but she was alone. Bird tapped the horn, annoyed, but the deer only swiveled her head, looking back where she'd come from. He hit the horn again, harder.

"C'mon, girl. Make a decision," he said, and then chuckled a little as the deer swiveled her head again, her eyes glinting amber as the headlights hit them. Like she'd heard him, and was considering her options. For a moment, she stayed like that, unmoving. Then with a single, graceful leap, she cleared the center line and ran ahead, tail high, and disappeared into the dark.

CHAPTER 24

LIZZIE

"It was self-defense."

I held the words in my mind because I wanted to be ready to say them. Knowing that this is what I would say, the only thing I'd say, when they asked. But for the longest time, nobody asked me anything at all. An EMT had checked my vitals, asking if I was injured and then nodding in agreement when I said, "I'm okay." He told me to stay where I was, and I did. Perched on the curb on the dark street, a still little island amid the electric red-blue strobing of the police cruisers and the busy movements of the cops, swarming in and out of the house, stepping around me like I was a bush or a fire hydrant. Just part of the landscape. Some of them glanced at me, but nobody really *looked*. I couldn't blame them. I was the least interesting thing around, a silent lump covered in a blanket; it was the dead man in-side the house who everyone was there to see. I watched an officer walk up and down the street, up and down the short stone stairs that led to the neighbors' fancy front doors, the entryways decorated with grapevine wreaths or flashy chrysanthemums in pretty pots. He was methodical, going house by house, knocking and then waiting, looking up at the windows to see if any lights came on. Once, a door was cracked open and someone inside peered out, while the cop gestured toward the house behind me and spoke rapidly. Asking if they'd seen or heard anything, probably, but the door closed again too quickly for the answer to have been anything but "no." I'd worried that a gaggle of curious neighbors would come out to see what was happening, craning their necks for a glimpse of something gossip-worthy, but everyone stayed inside. Watching from the comfort of their homes if they were watching at all, taking care not to make the curtains twitch. But maybe they'd all come out to talk about it after the police had left—after they took me away. Maybe they'd say that they always knew there was something strange about that woman, that couple. Something dark and wrong, something that told you it was only a matter of time until things ended, and badly.

Maybe the city was more like Copper Falls than I had ever imagined.

The knocking officer reached the end of the street and turned back, stopping to talk to another cop just a few feet away. He gestured at the adjacent houses, shook his head, and shrugged. I shifted my weight on the curb, trying to wiggle my toes inside the pair of shoes that someone had brought me from inside after they noticed my feet were bare. I hadn't noticed.

But, of course, I was in shock. I knew this, because Kurt Geller had told me so.

"Tell them it was self-defense, and you want to speak to your attorney before making a statement," he'd said. "They'll try to persuade you to talk. Don't. You can't do that tonight."

"I can't?" I asked, and Geller's voice took on a grandfatherly tone.

"Nobody in your position is capable of having that conversation, Adrienne. Not right away. You've lost your husband, and you just killed a man. You're traumatized, whether you feel it or not. When they tell you you're free to go, leave."

In truth, I didn't feel it. I didn't feel anything, except tired, in the bone-deep way that you get when you've spent all day using your body to push things around. The kind of tired I would get from clearing brush, scouring rust, digging the car out of a hard-packed pile of snow and ice after Dwayne had stupidly plowed it in and buried it for the third time that winter. Slinging the shovel like a sledgehammer to break up the crust of filthy ice, all mixed together with dirt and gravel so that it was damned near impossible to chip away. I'd work until my hands ached and my armpits were soaked with sweat inside my winter coat. I would dig and dig, the whole world reduced to the motion of the shovel and the harsh huffing of my own breath, lost in the job until the job was done. And then the exhaustion would be on me, so heavy that it pinned me where I sat as soon as I stopped moving. So that I couldn't do a single thing more, not even bend at the waist to unlace my boots or lift a hand to unzip my jacket.

My twenty-four hours as Adrienne Richards hadn't required shoveling or scouring—she had people to do that for her; hell, even the cat had a fucking robot litter box that self-cleaned every time he took a shit—but the exhaustion was the same. I'd been walking around all day wearing another woman's identity like a second skin, and it was heavy. All I wanted was to go back into the house, slide between the impossibly silky sheets, and close my eyes on the world. To spend the night as my naked self. Just Lizzie, living dead girl, unburdened by the weight of Adrienne Richards for a few short hours before I woke up to put her on again.

But I couldn't shed her. Not now, not yet. Maybe not for a long time, and the exhaustion sank deeper still as I realized that there was nothing to do but keep plodding forward.

Geller's words echoed again in my head: *You're traumatized, whether you feel it or not.* In my previous life, I would have wanted to slap the man who said that to me. But now I was grateful for it, condescending as it was, or maybe *because* it was. It made things easier. Adrienne didn't have any friends, but she did have people like Kurt Geller or

Rick Politano, people who were only too happy to instruct her on the details of who she was, how she felt. It made me think of a scary story I'd read growing up, the one where a woman wakes up in the middle of the night to her husband gently undressing her, reaches for the bedside lamp only to have him pull her hand away. There's something not quite right, not quite familiar, but she's too sleepy to wonder about it; it's a little bit sexy, even. They make love in the dark—and then she wakes up the next morning to find her husband sprawled dead on the bedroom floor, dead for hours and hours. Her body is covered with bloody fingerprints, and there's a message scrawled across the bathroom mirror: *AREN'T YOU GLAD YOU DIDN'T TURN ON THE LIGHT?*

Adrienne had always had people there to hold her hand, to guide her through the dark, to make sure she did what was expected of her. Now they were holding mine. If I wanted to know how to be her, all I had to do was ask—and unlike the woman in the story, I doubted they'd ever know the difference.

"Mrs. Richards?"

I looked up. A man was standing in front of me. I saw his shoes first, brown and scuffed, then lifted my chin to look at his face. He had tired eyes in a middle-aged face, and a raggedy blond beard that made me feel a little bit sorry for him, not just because the beard was terrible, but because there was apparently nobody in his life who loved him enough to tell him that it wasn't working. He wasn't wearing a wedding ring, but there was a gold badge hanging around his neck that said DETECTIVE. I stared up at him and nodded, wondering if I should try to look scared, then realizing that I didn't have to look like anything. Geller's instructions were a stroke of genius; I was traumatized, whether I felt it or not, which meant that trauma could look any way I wanted it to. If I screamed and tore my hair out, that was trauma. If I seemed too calm, that was trauma, too. Trauma had seared every detail of tonight's terrible ordeal in my mind, unless of course there were inconsistencies in my story, in which case it had fragmented my memories. Trauma explained everything. Trauma was my new religion.

"Mrs. Richards, I'm Detective Fuller," the man said. He extended a hand and I reached out my own, but instead of shaking it, he pulled me to my feet. The blanket fell off my shoulders as I stood, and I shivered, hugging myself. From behind me came the sound of wheels on stone: I turned just in time to see them bringing out a gurney through the front door, with a black rubber bag strapped to the top. Someone had already zipped it up, and Dwayne was nothing but a lump inside. I couldn't even tell for sure which end was his head. *No last looks*, I thought. And no goodbyes, either: the gurney disappeared into the back of a van, and one of the cops slammed the door shut.

I turned back to see the detective watching me, his eyebrows raised.

"It was self-defense," I said.

"We'll cover all of that, Mrs. Richards. But we'd like to talk to you down at the station."

"Shouldn't I have a lawyer with me?"

"This is just a casual chat. You don't have to make a statement. But CSI will be inside your house for a while yet, so come on. Let's go somewhere more comfortable, yeah? You can ride with me."

He gestured, and I followed, shuffling in Adrienne's too-tight shoes. I left the blanket where it had fallen, even though the night was cold and I already missed its weight over my shoulders. I wondered if Geller would want me to be so cooperative, but it was too late to ask. If I called him again tonight, it would be because I'd been arrested.

The police station was only a short drive away, but I was disoriented within a few blocks as we left Adrienne's neighborhood behind. I craned my neck in search of a landmark but saw nothing, and a claustrophobic knot formed in my gut. In the sunshine, surrounded by other people, the anonymity of the city had felt like freedom; now the miles of empty streets made me feel trapped and exposed, lost in a sea of samey brick and shuttered storefronts, empty lobbies behind plateglass windows that glowed pale below the streetlights. Then the road curved, and a crop of taller buildings came into view.

"Here we are," said Fuller, and I said, "Mmm," because I didn't know which of the buildings in front of us was "here," and maybe I was supposed to. The station was massive, a fat brick box with a single row of narrow windows slotted into the side. It looked more like a fortress than a jail, designed to keep people out rather than in. Fuller led me through the doors, past a security desk with a yawning officer sitting behind it, into an elevator where he pressed a button and we rode in silence to the sixth floor. When the doors opened, we exited and turned right down a long corridor where doors opened on either side into empty rooms.

"We're a little short-staffed tonight," Fuller said conversationally. "Every time we beat out the Yanks for a championship, some folks get a little too excited and try to burn the city down."

"Oh," I said.

"Not a baseball fan, huh?"

"Oh," I said again. "Baseball. No. Not really." The truth for Adrienne, a lie for me. Watching baseball was one of the few things Dwayne and I had always done together, and still did; he hadn't thrown a ball in years, but he liked yelling at the TV, particularly when one of the umps was being stingy about the strike zone. If not for the events of the past couple days, we would have been watching the game tonight, and it was strange to realize that I'd missed it. That the world had continued on as usual while I was burning it all down.

"Can I get you a coffee?" Fuller asked.

"No, thank you."

I wanted one more than anything, not for the caffeine but for the warmth of the cup, the familiar, comforting bitterness of that first sip. Coffee was coffee, no matter how far you'd traveled, no matter who you were. But I'd seen a movie once where they tricked someone that way, took the cup and used it to analyze his DNA. I didn't know if it was real, or even what they'd do with my DNA if they had it, but that survivor's voice inside my head—a voice that was starting to sound more and more like Adrienne herself with every passing minute—told me I was better safe than sorry.

"If you change your mind," Fuller said, and then turned away without finishing the sentence. He pointed down the hall to a line of chairs. "Sit tight for just a second, Mrs. Richards. I appreciate your patience."

I cleared my throat.

"Adrienne," I said. "Please call me Adrienne."

It's what she would have said.

I didn't have to wait long before Fuller returned with another officer, this one in uniform and looking like he might have graduated high school sometime last week. He looked at me, and I felt the hairs on my neck stand on end. There was a strange expression on his face, expectant, like maybe we were supposed to know each other. A ripple of panic ran up my spine: Did Adrienne have friends in the Boston police department? Or worse, more than friends? It suddenly occurred to me that Dwayne might not have been the only side dish on Adrienne's plate; for all I knew, she'd fucked this baby-faced beat cop and all his friends.

"Officer Murray is going to join us," Fuller said.

"Hi," I said.

"Nice to meet you," said Murray, and I felt my whole body relax: *He doesn't know her.* The emotion must have shown on my face because the younger cop shook his head, chagrined. "I mean, not *nice*; I didn't intend—"

"Never mind, Officer," Fuller said. He pointed, and we filed into a room that seemed designed to make people want to tell the cops what they wanted to hear, just so they could leave. It was bare and much too bright, with a smeary window that looked out on the hallway. The only furniture was a metal table and chairs, and there was a camera mounted high in one corner. Adrienne's voice piped up in my head again: *Nobody looks good from that angle.*

I shuddered.

"All right, Mrs. Richards," Fuller said, and sat down in one of the chairs. Murray, either very polite or just pretending to be, pulled out a chair across the table from Fuller and motioned to me to sit. I did.

Fuller smiled. He had nice teeth; it was a shame about the horrible beard.

"You are absolutely free to go," he said, and I thought of Geller's instructions. This was the moment I'd been waiting for. *He said it. I can leave.* But could I stand up now, when I'd only just sat down? Would Adrienne, traumatized and terrified and waiting to find out that her husband was dead, be so eager to go back to the empty house where she'd just shot her lover? I was sure she wouldn't. Not now. Not yet.

"Okay," he said. "I know it's late and we all want to go home, so we'll try to make this quick. But it'll be best for everyone if we can get your side of the story right away, while it's still fresh."

"It was self-defense," I said, again. This was all I was supposed to say, but both men watched me, waiting for more, and the silence stretched long and uncomfortable. It was self-defense; what else was there? I swallowed hard, clutching my own crossed arms. Maybe I should ask a question of my own.

"He killed—he said he killed my husband. Have you found him? Have you found Ethan?" I asked.

Fuller and Murray exchanged looks.

"We're working on that," Fuller said. "But there's no reason to necessarily believe, you know—"

"But he *said*!" I cried, and incredibly, maybe just from sheer exhaustion, I felt my eyes start to well with tears. I sniffled and swiped at them, remembering as I did the way that Adrienne used to press a finger into her lower lid and draw it outward, because rubbing her eye like a normal person would make her mascara smudge. Fuller leaned in.

"Listen, try not to worry about that for right now. We're going to find your husband. I promise. Let's back up, okay? Why don't we get a little background, a little more about you. No pressure. You're from the South, yeah?"

I sniffled again.

"North Carolina."

"Good," Fuller said. "That's good. Raleigh?"

"No," I said, and heard Adrienne's voice. First in my head, and then coming out of my mouth. "West. Near the Blue Ridge Mountains."

"Country roads, take me home," Fuller suddenly warbled, in a gruff but surprisingly tuneful voice, then smiled. "Sorry, couldn't help myself. That's a nice spot. You get back there much?"

I stared at him. "No."

He nodded. "Your folks still there?"

"Just my mother." I paused to think. I knew a good amount about this; Adrienne had been candid with me about her mother's condition, how she felt about it, how little she cared. But would she talk about that with this man? No. Never. "She's . . . in a home. Alzheimer's."

"You don't visit?"

I shook my head and sniffled again for good measure. "She's in pretty bad shape. It would just upset her."

"Sure, sure," said Fuller. "So, no other family? How about around here?"

"Just my husband."

He cocked his head. "You been married long?"

"Ten years."

"Long time," he said. "I never made it that far myself. You got any tips?"

I almost answered. The question was so casual, so conversational, that I almost didn't notice how we were sliding sidelong toward Adrienne's marriage, Adrienne's happiness, Adrienne's relationship with Dwayne—which they knew about, didn't they? They had to. I glanced from Fuller to Murray, wondering if the other cop might jump in, but he didn't seem to have any lines. Fuller cleared his throat, opened his mouth to ask another question—and then someone rapped on the window, and he blinked with annoyance. Outside, another man in plain clothes was holding up a hand with the thumb and pinky extended, the universal symbol for *phone call*.

"Excuse me," Fuller said. "This should just take a second."

Fuller left, pulling the door closed behind him. In the fraction of a second before he did, I heard him growl at the interrupter: "This better b—" he started to say, and then the latch clicked and silence descended. I was alone with Murray, who was now looking at me with equal parts nervousness and contempt, like I was a pile of vomit on a carpet that he was afraid he'd be tapped to clean up. He glanced up at the camera, then back at me. The hallway outside the window was empty, both Fuller and the interrupting cop no longer in view. Long seconds passed without anyone speaking. I hugged my arms tighter across my chest.

"Are you cold?" Murray asked.

"A little."

"Mmm," he said. He flicked his eyes toward the door and then the hallway behind the window—still empty—and shifted in his chair. His Adam's apple kept bobbing like he was getting ready to say something, then deciding better of it. I wondered if he'd been instructed not to talk to me, and if so, I wondered why.

"You know," he said finally, "I was outside your house earlier. Sat there for a while, actually."

I tried to keep my face neutral.

"Oh? I didn't see you."

"Well, I saw you," he said. He smirked at me. "How was your dinner? What'd you get, Japanese?"

I was starting to sweat. How long had he been there, watching?

"Yeah. It was fine." A lie: I thought Japanese food would be something like Chinese food, greasy and salty, but of course Adrienne didn't eat that stuff. Her dinner order turned out to be one little tray full of raw fish and a second one full of something slimy, probably seaweed. I'd choked it down out of desperation. Murray was still smirking.

"Not your first time talking to a police officer today, is it?"

My stomach lurched; the seaweed was threatening to come back up. "What?" I said.

"The trooper. What, you thought we didn't know about that? He thought this guy Cleaves might be coming around your place to visit. Guess he was right."

"I wouldn't call someone breaking into my house in the middle of the night a *visit*," I snapped, and Murray's eyebrows went up.

"The report said he had a key."

"He must have stolen it."

"You didn't give him one? I heard you were involved."

"What are you"—I began to say, realizing even as I did that I was taking the bait, that I should shut up, and then the handle on the door turned and both our heads swiveled to see Fuller reentering the room. He had a strange expression on his face and a notepad in his hand. He closed the door and then leaned back against it instead of sitting down.

"Mrs. Richards," he said. "That was the Maine State Police on the phone."

I blinked. "Okay," I said slowly.

"I had hoped to discuss this with you." He sounded tired. "It's my understanding that before you shot Dwayne Cleaves, a police officer came to your house looking for him, and that you and Cleaves had been having an affair. Were you planning to share that with us?"

"I thought . . ." I trailed off. Shook my head. Now would have been a good time to start crying again, but my eyes were suddenly, infuriatingly dry. "I don't remember what I said or didn't say," I whimpered. "I've been through a lot tonight."

"Of course," Fuller said. But as he looked at me, his lips pursed, I thought, *Yeah, there it is*. I'd seen that expression before. Only a few hours ago, in fact, on the face of Ian Bird. It was the smug irritation of a man who thinks he knows exactly who you are, who's absolutely sure that he's the smartest guy in the room. Well, good. I hoped Fuller thought Adrienne was an idiot. The less he thought of her—of *me*—the less he'd waste his time wondering what I was capable of.

Fuller sighed. "All right, Mrs. Richards. I'm sorry, there's no easy way to say this. The police in, uh"—he glanced at the pad in his hand—"in Copper Falls have found Dwayne Cleaves's truck, and some, ah, human remains."

I allowed my mouth to drop open and thought, *Dammit*. I'd allowed for this possibility, the slim chance that an insurance adjuster might stumble across the body, but I thought it would take weeks. Plenty of time for Dwayne and I to disappear. I thought I was being so smart: knowing how things worked in Copper Falls, it would never occur to anyone that it might not be Dwayne in the truck. His mother would push to have the body released, so she could bury him in their family plot behind the hilltop church before the first freeze—and the local cops would push along with her, anxious to get the whole sordid mess behind them. There would be a bunch of blather about not dragging things out, so the community could begin to heal. There would certainly be no reason to connect a murder-suicide in rural small-town Maine with the disappearance of a shady billionaire and his wife in a city hundreds of miles away. And with any luck, I thought, that's where it would end: with Adrienne and Ethan buried in graves with our names on them, and Dwayne and I sitting on a pile of cash in some swamp, eating feral pig jerky and figuring out what came next.

That plan was shot to hell, for a million reasons. But it was lucky for me that it was: this had to be why Ian Bird had left in such a hurry, and why he wasn't lurking around the house when Dwayne came back in the middle of the night.

Fuller and Murray were both staring at me, and I clutched my hands to my heart, trying to look stricken.

"Human remains?" I said. "Oh God. You mean . . . Ethan? Is it Ethan?"

"We can't know for sure, ma'am. There was a fire, and the remains . . . well, they may take some time to identify. But under the circumstances, and given what you say Cleaves told you . . ." He paused, nodding, pressing his lips together. "We think it may be your husband, yes."

I buried my face in my hands. Still no tears. Everything was moving much too fast. I should have left the moment they told me I could; the next-best thing was to go now. Right now.

I dropped my hands and glared at Fuller.

"Did you say I was free to go?"

He looked startled. "Yes, ma'am, but—"

"I can't do this. It's too much. I need to sleep, and I need to speak to my attorney before I give you a statement, and I need to go home."

"Ma'am, if I could just ask you," Fuller started to say, and finally, *finally*, my eyes started to leak again. It was because the last thing I'd said was the truth: I did need to go home. Desperately. Only when I said the word "home," the image that flashed through my mind wasn't the row house across town where Adrienne Richards lived, or even the dingy little cape where I'd made a life with Dwayne. It was the junkyard, our little trailer standing guard with the heaps rising behind, Pops inside and kicked back in front of the TV. Napping in the ridiculous way he always did in the evenings, with a can of beer in hand and a bowl of peanuts balanced on top of his stomach. A home that didn't even exist anymore, because I'd burned it to ash.

"Please," I said, and as if on cue, like something out of a goddamn movie, both my eyes hit overload at the same time and spilled two perfect tears down my cheeks. Both men winced, and I knew I'd won.

Adrienne had an app on her phone that could summon a car for you. I thought it might be complicated, but by the time the elevator dinged at the ground floor, Adrienne's phone had flashed a message, *Where do you want to go?* and I simply tapped the topmost option. An honest answer, even if it meant something different to the phone than it did to me. The little gray car on-screen tracked my path across the city, retracing my earlier route. Where did I want to go?

Home.

Whatever that meant.

I was afraid that the street would be blocked off, but it was quiet and nearly deserted. The coroner's van and all the cop cars were gone. Only a single SUV remained, and a man and a woman in blue CSI jackets were leaning against it. She was smoking; he was laughing. They both looked at me curiously as I got out of the car. I brandished my keys.

"It's my house."

"Oh," the woman said. "Yeah, okay. We're done. You can go on in."

"Okay," I said. In my hand, the phone vibrated, inviting me to review my ride. Pushy. It made me think of the cops, needling me to talk before Dwayne's corpse was even cold. *It'll be best for everyone if we can get your side of the story right away, while it's still fresh.* I started up the front steps, fitting the key into the lock.

"Hey," the man in the CSI jacket said. "You know how it's gonna be in there, right?"

I turned, just in time to see the woman throw an elbow into his ribs and hiss at him to shush. The man winced.

"What?" I said warily.

"I mean," the man said, stepping away to avoid a repeat elbow, "we just bag stuff. You know. We don't clean."

"Oh." I nodded like I understood, and twisted the key. The door swung open, then shut behind me. I watched through the glass as the woman stubbed her cigarette out and the two climbed into the SUV, started the motor, pulled away. I climbed the stairs in the dark.

It wasn't until a few minutes later, pausing in the doorway to Ethan Richards's office, that I realized what the CSI tech meant. The body was gone, of course—I'd watched them wheeling it out—but there were still bits of Dwayne here in the room. A smear on the corner of the mahogany desk, a small, almost perfectly circular spot of red on the carpeted floor. The cat padded out of the dark and began twining around my legs as I stood there, looking at all that was left of my husband. Blood drying to a rust-colored stain on the carpet. The last mess he ever made.

Of course I would have to be the one to clean it up.

Or maybe—Adrienne's voice yawned in my head—*you'll pay someone to do the scrubbing for you. Or burn it. Toss it. Whatever. I always said that wall-to-wall was tacky, anyway.*

At my feet, the cat rose up on his hind legs, meowing, begging for attention. I bent, scooped him into my arms, snuggled him close, and pulled the office door shut. The sun would be coming up in only a few hours, and when it did, I would have work to do. But down the hall, in that dark blue bedroom, there was nothing to do but sleep, and I did. Deeply. Dreamless. Dead.

CHAPTER 25

BIRD

The fire had consumed the man in the way that fires did: from the outside in, starting at the extremities. The smallest bits were always the first to go, swallowed whole by the flames. Ears, nose, toes, fingers. All of them, gone. The body in Dwayne Cleaves's truck had burned uninterrupted for a long time, and had no feet, no hands, and most unsettling of all, no face, just a featureless mass of charcoal with two slight indentations where the eyes had been. By the time the sun crept over the tops of the pines at the junkyard's eastern border, there was nothing left for the techs to do but stir the ashes around in search of any pieces they might have missed, their fingers numb with cold. Mostly, they found nothing. Just ashes on top of ashes, everything sodden and stinking of smoke, tar, melted rubber. The state's forensic team kept their eyes on their work; the local cops glanced their side-long discomfort at each other over the tops of the masks they'd been told to wear to keep toxic particles out of their lungs. The mood at the lake the previous morning had been practically jovial by comparison, that blond jackass all but snickering about the mole and how they all knew about it, about what a tramp poor, dead Lizzie Ouellette had been. That same man was here now; Bird could recognize him by his beady eyes alone, and the little slice of his face visible above his mask and below the brim of his hat looked pale and sweaty. *Not laughing now, eh, chief?*

It was hard to know what was making the locals more uncomfortable: the fact that the body wasn't one of their own, or the fact that their good friend Dwayne Cleaves was officially a multiple murderer, and now lying dead in a city morgue. Bird had told Sheriff Ryan, Ryan had told the rest, and the news had gone over like a sack of bricks as the cops of Copper Falls realized what it meant, and what was still to come. The press hadn't gotten wind of it yet, but it was only a matter of time. When they did, they'd descend on Copper Falls like vultures, scrapping and snarling until they'd plucked the last scrap of meat off the bones of the town's tragedy. The coroner told Bird that there might be some teeth still left for an ID, clenched shut behind the mottled black mask that used to be a man's face. The medical examiner would need to get his hands on dental records, but as far as Bird was concerned, it was just a formality. The folks in Augusta would only confirm what he already knew: this charred body, its handless arms curled up in death like it was still trying to ward off the oncoming flames, was Ethan Richards.

Sheriff Ryan, red around the eyes and looking fifteen years older than he had the previous morning, pulled down his mask and rubbed a hand over the graying stubble on his chin.

"Hell of a thing," said Ryan. "I know folks always say this, but goddamn, I knew Dwayne Cleaves a long time. We all did. Hard to believe he'd shoot his wife. Harder to believe he'd do a thing like this. Burning a man to death. Jesus."

"Well, most likely he was dead before the fire started," Bird said. "Or unconscious, maybe. But I take your point."

"They say they're about finished here. Debbie Cleaves is an early riser. I'd like to get over there and knock on her door, before someone else does. She's going to have a real bad day ahead of her." He shook his head. "Boston. Shit. They're sure it's him?"

"Seems that way," Bird said. "She'll have to drive down there to ID him, of course."

"Of course."

Bird watched the sun rise red above the treetops and climb until the light spilled over, illuminating the stinking, blackened ruins of the junkyard, burning away the last tendrils of creeping morning mist. He watched the team pack up, the local cops exchanging awkward shrugs as they rubbed their cold hands together and avoided eye contact. Myles Johnson wasn't among them, and Bird wondered if he knew what was happening. What had happened. He and Dwayne Cleaves wouldn't be taking any more hunting trips together—but after the past few days, maybe Johnson wouldn't be so keen on killing things for sport anymore. Bird shrugged to himself. Either way, it was none of his business. If he had his way, he'd be gone from Copper Falls by sundown. He waited until the last of the cars pulled away, then climbed into his cruiser and followed them into town, where he pulled into a space at the far end of the municipal building that held the local law enforcement offices. He kept the motor running, turned up the heat, and closed his eyes. Later, Dwayne Cleaves's friends and family would need to be re-interviewed, and paperwork would need to be filed, and coffee would need to be acquired urgently and first thing. But for at least the next blessed hour, there was nothing to do but nap.

The buzzing of his phone awakened him some time later—not enough time, Bird thought, and looked at the clock to discover that only twenty-five minutes had passed. It was an email: the preliminary autopsy report on Lizzie Ouellette was complete. He scrolled it quickly on the tiny screen. Mostly, it was a restatement of things he'd either known or guessed already. *CAUSE OF DEATH: GUNSHOT WOUND, HEAD.*

MANNER OF DEATH: HOMICIDE.

The information he was looking for was toward the end of the report, and he frowned as he read it.

There is a puncture wound on the inner left forearm consistent with injection.

Track marks. So Lizzie was using, then. Her and Dwayne both, probably—that was usually how it worked—but it made him unhappy to see it there on paper, made him feel almost disappointed in her. He tried to picture it: Lizzie in the bedroom, a needle in her arm. Dwayne, standing by the bed with a gun. And then, stumbling into the tableau like a human non sequitur, Ethan Richards. Bird groaned, rubbing his eyes. He still needed coffee, but he also didn't need a coffee to know that once he had one, the story this case seemed to tell would still make no damn sense at all. He opened the car door and gave his thighs a couple thumps to get the blood moving, then walked stiffly into the municipal building. He found the men's room first, taking a piss next to two men he recognized from the junkyard scene and who studiously avoided looking at or speaking to him as they zipped up and left the room. He followed them a moment later, finding the station quieter than he'd expected. Some of the guys had gone home to change, maybe, or wash off the stink from all those hours wading through the ashes. There was a pot of freshly brewed coffee in the break room, and he filled a cup to the brim. Then he returned to his car and called Brady. His gravelly voice came on the line after three rings.

"Hiya there, Bird."

"Hey, boss. What were you, sleeping?"

"I'd never do a thing like that," Brady said. "Just one second." There was a clatter as the phone was put down, and Bird heard a toilet flush.

"You know there's a mute button for moments like this," he said when Brady picked up again.

Brady snorted. "Noted. What've you got?"

Bird gave him the rundown: the facts as they stood, his frustrated sense that he was missing something. He waited while the older man read through the forwarded M.E.'s report. He thought again about Lizzie, needle marks on her pale, dead arm, the baffled regret in her former boss's voice as he said, "She didn't seem like the type."

The type, Bird thought. There was something to that, the idea of categories, what kind of woman Lizzie was, what kind of wife, what kind of victim. And then:

"Oh," Bird said. "That's it."

"What's it?" Brady sounded distracted. "In the report? I don't see—"

"No, no. I just realized, I've still been approaching this like a domestic incident."

"Well, sure," Brady said. "Dead wife, missing husband. Makes sense."

"If it were just the two of them involved, yeah. But if that's Ethan Richards in the truck, and I'm pretty confident it is, then I've been looking at this wrong."

"I'm not following."

Bird set his coffee down, thinking hard. "Adrienne Richards said her husband didn't know about the affair. I'm thinking, what if she was wrong about that? What if Richards knew, and he wanted to do something about it? Maybe this whole thing kicked off because he caught wind his wife was cheating, and came out here to confront Cleaves himself."

"Huh," Brady said. "Wasn't this guy a banker or something? Seems a little in-your-face."

"As someone recently reminded me, people do crazy shit for love," Bird said, and Brady chuckled.

"Right. Or for money. There was a photograph of the wife somewhere, right? Nudie pic? Could be a blackmail thing. You go to the husband, say, give us a million bucks or we'll send this naughty nudie picture of your wife to . . . uh . . ."

"TMZ?" Bird offered.

"Yeah, sure. Whatever. So Richards goes up there alone to handle things, shit gets out of hand."

Bird nodded, the phone pressed to his ear. "That makes sense. But then . . . you think Lizzie was in on it, too."

"Don't sound so disappointed, Bird. No perfect victims, right? But no, not necessarily. Maybe she wandered into it. You saw the part in the M.E.'s report, about the track marks?"

"Yep."

"So maybe she goes out there to shoot up, not realizing her husband is meeting Richards out there. Maybe she finds out then about the affair. There's an argument, it gets heated—"

"And Cleaves has the shotgun," Bird interjected.

"Right. Hell, maybe he always planned to kill her, take Richards's money, and run."

"That's a pretty stupid plan," Bird said.

"Correct," Brady said. "But it's the kind of stupid plan that a stupid person thinks is smart."

"All right, yeah," Bird said. "If Cleaves wanted out of his life, and the opportunity presented itself . . . and don't forget the nose. Whoever did that, it was personal."

"True," said Brady. "But if he hated his wife enough to kill her . . ."

A few moments passed, Bird sipping coffee in silence, thinking. On the other end of the line, Brady stayed quiet. When Bird spoke again, his tone was contemplative.

"Man, the nose. I guess there's no way to know—"

"If it was postmortem or not?" Brady finished for him. "Nope. Especially with the overall damage to the face. But for her sake, let's hope it happened after." He paused. "Actually, hang on. I just realized . . ."

There was a clatter again as the phone was set down. Bird heard the scrape of a drawer opening, the rustle of paper, and then Brady was back.

"Initial report from Boston PD says they found a hunting knife at the scene. The Richards woman said Cleaves threatened her with it."

"Oh," Bird said. "If it's the same one he used to . . ."

"Yeah, exactly," Brady said. "I'll put in the request. Maybe they'll even test it for us, save us a little money on labs. Bet you anything they pull some blood off it that matches our deceased. Between that and the shotgun in Cleaves's truck, I'd say you have all your weapons. You can clear this; no loose ends. Congrats, Detective."

"Yeah. That was fast." Bird sighed. "I'll tell you, though, I'd still like to know what exactly happened out there. Cleaves kills two people, then Cleaves's mistress shoots him, and now it's all tied up, nice and neat. And she's the only one left."

"The cheese stands alone," Brady said, with mock solemnity.

"And speaking of cheese," Bird said, sitting up straighter, "how much do you think she inherits now that the husband is out of the picture?"

Brady guffawed. "This took a turn. What, you think *she* planned it somehow?"

"No," said Bird. Then: "Maybe. I don't know." The catnap hadn't been long enough, and the caffeine wasn't working to sharpen his thoughts.

"I'm just trying to put it together. Say you're Adrienne Richards. You want your husband dead. So you fuck the handyman at your vacation house, and then once you've got your hooks in, you ask him to kill your husband. Maybe you promise to run away together when it's done. Then when the deed is done, you welsh on the deal, and shoot him to death instead, and you're left all alone with a giant pile of money." Brady paused. "I mean, sure. I guess? Pretty cold."

"Yeah," said Bird, but his mind was already several steps ahead, saying, *Yeah, but no.* Brady was right: it was pretty cold. It was also pretty stupid—to trust someone like Cleaves with a job that could go wrong in so many ways. And Adrienne Richards, annoying and conniving as she might be, was definitely not a stupid person.

"Okay," Bird said, "so hearing you say it out loud like that, it doesn't really sound that plausible."

Brady laughed and said, "Look, I understand. Loose ends are part of the job, but that doesn't mean they're not gonna nag at you. If you really think there's something here to pursue, you've got my support."

"But," Bird said.

"But," Brady said, "sometimes knowing the who, what, and when is as good as it gets, and it doesn't make sense to get hung up on the why. Not to mention, the people who care about clearance rates are gonna wonder why you're looking a gift horse in the mouth on this, when you could put a bow on it right now and be done. There's not exactly a shortage of work here, you know. I was waiting to mention it until you were out of the weeds on this case, but you got a callback day before last on one of your cold cases. That witness you were looking for on the Richter thing? Pullman or some such?"

Bird perked up. "Pullen," he said, as his mind's eye conjured the image of the grainy newspaper photograph from the case file. It was the only photo anyone had of George Pullen, and he was almost out of frame; the only reason you'd notice him at all was that he was the only one looking at the camera, a moon-faced man in late middle age, standing in a group of onlookers who had gathered to watch the police dredge a quarry for the body of a missing woman named Laurie Richter. George Pullen had called the police twice, claiming he might know something about the case, but was inexplicably never interviewed. He fell through the cracks in 1983; by 1985, he'd fallen off the radar entirely. It was the kind of mistake you hated to see; by the time Bird started looking for Pullen, it was with the understanding that the likeliest place to find the man was in a graveyard. But now—

"Pullen," Brady repeated. "Right, that's it. You'll love this: he's a local celebrity down east. The oldest resident of the senior home in Stonington."

"No kidding," Bird said. "He's been in state all this time."

"Yep, and if you want to interview him, you might want to get down there sooner rather than later. You know what they say about people who hold the record for seniority."

"They never hold it very long," Bird replied, chuckling. "Yeah. Good point. I'll get down there."

"I think that's a good plan," Brady said. "And look, not for nothing, unless you turn up something ironclad—and I mean *ironclad*—we'd probably have a hell of a time convincing a judge to let us go on a fishing expedition to build a case against Adrienne Richards. She's loaded; she's connected. People are paying attention to this one, and one of our state troopers harassing a grieving widow who just survived a home invasion? That's what they call 'bad optics.'"

Bird sighed. "Understood. Just out of curiosity, when you say 'ironclad' . . ."

"You didn't happen to pull a severed dick and balls out of her garbage disposal, by any chance?"

Bird laughed, hard, and then felt bad for laughing even as he struggled to stop. Poor Lizzie. Dead, disfigured, and now a punch line for the kinds of jokes you know you shouldn't make, let alone laugh at—the kinds of jokes cops tell because sometimes it's the only way to keep yourself getting up and doing the job, staring into the hellmouth of humanity's worst, day in and day out. She deserved better.

But it was too late for Lizzie. She was dead, and for better or worse, so was the man who killed her. The man who'd killed Laurie Richter, on the other hand—he might still be out there. After forty years, at that, and this too seemed too poetic to be a coincidence. Back in 1983, the Richter case stank of the same small-town New England bullshit that hung over this one: locals who knew something but wouldn't talk, or lied to cover up secrets of their own. There were whispers about a boyfriend, or maybe multiple boyfriends, phantom leads that went poof and vanished every time someone tried to examine them. Rumors that Laurie's car was sunk in a quarry somewhere up near Greenville, the Forks, maybe even as far west as Rangeley; the dredging that George Pullen had attended was one of several that took place the summer she vanished. But back then, there were too many quarries and too many rumors, too many closed mouths and closed doors. To know now that justice might be served, and relief brought to a family who had been waiting far too long for answers . . .

He lifted a thumb and forefinger to either side of his nose, massaging his sinuses. Down east, then. If he worked efficiently, he could be on his way to the coast by the day after next. He'd see if George Pullen still remembered what he'd wanted to tell the cops back in 1983. Maybe stop outside Bucksport on the way back. There was a place he used to go with his folks back in the day. They had good seafood that was always best in the off-season, the tourists long gone and never knowing what they were missing. The lobsters were so much sweeter in the winter.

On the other end of the line, Brady finished chuckling at his own terrible joke. There was a long, comfortable pause. Then Brady coughed.

"Oh, Jesus Christ," he said.

"What?"

"That Richards woman," Brady said. "How much you want to bet she ends up writing a fucking book?"

CHAPTER 26

LIZZIE

All this time, I thought I knew Adrienne Richards pretty well. Well enough to anticipate her needs, well enough to covet her life for myself. Well enough, obviously, to step into that life and walk around in it like it belonged to me. And I thought, I *thought,* that I knew about the bad as well as the good. The loneliness. The resentment. The yearning—for attention, acceptance, security. For a baby that her husband admitted too late they would never have.

I didn't know the half of it.

I woke at noon to the sound of Adrienne's phone clattering to the floor. I bolted upright, my head aching, heart pounding, guts coiling with instant and instinctive dread. The cat, who had been asleep in the crook between my thighs and my belly, leapt off the bed and streaked out of the room with an indignant *meow.* For the second day in a row I was waking up in this room, *her* room, but if anything I felt even more anxious and out of place than I had yesterday. That first morning, Dwayne had been sleeping beside me, and we were still us, and I was still me. Not now. Not anymore. The whole room seemed like a minefield: the dresser alone was covered with photographs of places I'd never been to, jewelry I'd never worn, mementos of a life I hadn't lived. I stared at it, my skin crawling. There were five perfumes in heavy glass bottles collected on a little tray, and I felt an absurd but all-consuming panic at the realization that I had no idea what they smelled like. It seemed impossible that only two days had passed since I'd pointed a shotgun at Adrienne Richards as she pointed a finger at me. Since the blood, the fire, the long and silent drive south, with Copper Falls lost in the dark behind us.

I swung my legs over the side of the bed and breathed deeply, trying to calm down, but every breath only filled my nose with scents that didn't belong to me. The sheets, the clothes I was wearing, even my own hair; I smelled like the salon where I'd had it dyed to look more like Adrienne's, where the stylist had frowned and asked me if I was sure, was I really, when my natural color was so pretty. I pulled my T-shirt up over my nose and took another deep breath, then sighed it out with relief. I fucking stank, but in a way that was fully familiar, yeasty and a little sour, like something inside me had gone slightly off and was starting to leak out of my pores. My armpits still knew who they belonged to, at least.

The phone had fallen into the slim opening between the bed and the wall, and when I crawled under the bed to retrieve it I understood why: it was lighting up with alerts, and the incessant vibrating had buzzed it closer and closer to the edge of the nightstand until it had gone over the side. *It committed suicide,* I thought, out of nowhere—which made me want to laugh until the phone lit up again, a new missive coming in.

It said, in all caps, KILL YOURSELF.

"What the fuck?" I said, aloud, but of course there was no answer. I was alone in Adrienne's house, and the only one here to receive whatever messages the world wanted to send her. I stared around the room again, looking at all the things in it that didn't belong to me, that were now mine anyway. My hand with the phone in it dangled at my side, periodically buzzing. I stepped into the hallway and began walking toward the front of the house.

There was something happening outside. I could hear it as soon as I got near the kitchen, the murmur of voices rising from the sidewalk below. I walked to the window and looked out; below, a gaggle of reporters was clustered out front, jostling for position near the door. One of them was looking up as I looked down, and he shouted and gestured, a dozen heads swiveling to look in the direction of his pointing finger. Looking at me. I darted backward, but it was too late. They'd seen me. So that was it: while I was sleeping, someone must have leaked the story about Dwayne to the press. I dismissed the scroll of messages and opened the phone's browser. It wasn't hard to find the story, blasted out overnight. COPS RUSH TO ETHAN RICHARDS'S HOME AFTER 911 SHOOTING CALL. Someone, a neighbor maybe, had snapped a picture of me sitting on the curb in the middle of the night, hunched in a blanket while police swarmed all around. It was a low-quality photograph, taken from a distance; you couldn't see anything except my hair, falling in a coppery sheet on either side of my face. The caption called me "Ethan's wife, Adrienne," which was a relief even as I knew Adrienne would have been infuriated by it: after all this time, her husband's infamy was still the most interesting thing about her.

"And now he's dead," I murmured. The news was vague on that count: whoever had taken the picture knew about the body, but not whose it was, and the reporter had been careful to use words like "allegedly" in describing what might have happened. The commenters on the story, though—they weren't being careful at all. They were absolutely sure that Adrienne Richards had killed her husband, and more than a few of them seemed to be annoyed that she hadn't offed herself, too. *That bitch was just as guilty as he was.*

I wondered if things would get better or worse once the truth came out. Not the actual truth, of course, but the "true story," about a sordid affair between a socialite and a redneck that ended with a series of bangs. Worse, probably. Adrienne had been right about one thing: this was a hell of a story. But the way she'd imagined it, she was going to be the victim. The survivor. The hero.

Maybe she would have been. Maybe the real Adrienne would have found a way to make herself sympathetic to all the people who wanted to see her suffer. But as her phone buzzed in my hand, as I scrolled the messages that kept rolling in like an unstoppable tide of malice, I thought she must have been fooling herself. No wonder she was fucking Dwayne and doing drugs; no wonder she never complained that the lake house had no cell service, no Wi-Fi. It must have been the only place where she could escape from herself—or the self other people imagined for her, grotesque and hideous and with only the barest resemblance to the real Adrienne. A woman so vile that you, a stranger, wouldn't think twice about telling her to kill herself. I found myself shaking my head. Adrienne Richards was a privileged bitch, but fuck, she wasn't a *monster*. I watched the messages lighting up her phone like you might watch someone else's house burning down, except that I didn't have the luxury of just watching. I was the one inside the blazing building. It was my face feeling the terrible heat, my skin starting to blister.

In my hand, the phone began vibrating urgently, and I almost pitched it across the room before I realized that it was ringing: Kurt Geller's name appeared on the screen. I sat heavily on the floor and tapped the screen.

"Hello?"

Geller's voice was annoyed. "Adrienne, are you all right? I've left you several messages."

"I'm sorry," I said, my voice tremulous. "I . . . I didn't see. Someone took a picture last night while I was outside with the police and now it's on the internet. My phone—it's horrible, what people have been sending me."

"Ah," Geller said, his tone softening. "I'm sorry to hear that. It was bound to happen, unfortunately. You remember how it was with Ethan."

I had no fucking idea how it was with Ethan.

"I've tried to forget," I said cautiously, and Geller chuckled a little.

"Well, we'll handle it the same way. I'll send someone for you; he'll escort you from your door. Can you come to the office this afternoon, three o'clock? I spent some time this morning on the phone with a friend in the district attorney's office. We have things to discuss, but I'm optimistic."

"Okay," I said. "The press—"

"Don't talk to them," Geller said. "Don't talk to anyone. I'll draft any statements on your behalf after we meet."

After I hung up, I stayed where I was, watching helplessly as notifications kept lighting up the phone's screen. The phone on the table rang once and I scrambled to my knees to pick it up, listened as a woman's voice said, "Mrs. Richards? This is Rachel Lawrence. I'm a reporter with—"

I hung up. Then I unplugged the phone.

As I scrolled back through Adrienne's messages, it suddenly occurred to me how strange it was that her cell phone wasn't ringing off the hook. She had hundreds of contacts saved, but apart from three missed calls and two voice mails from Kurt Geller, not a single person with a direct line to Adrienne had tried to call or text her. Instead, she was inundated with messages from strangers. The picture I'd posted to Adrienne's account yesterday was racking up dozens of comments. She had more than a hundred unread emails, the most recent crop mainly from reporters or television producers hoping to get an interview. The police didn't seem to be saying anything for the moment—every story I read said only that an unidentified male had been pronounced dead at the scene—but that would only last so long. As bad as things were now, I realized, they were only going to get worse. After all those years in Copper Falls, I thought I knew how it felt to be hated. But this . . .

Surprise, said Adrienne's voice in my head. *You should see your face right now.*

Kurt Geller's car arrived promptly at quarter to three, nosing up to the curb as the gaggle of reporters jostled for position. I was ready, showered and dressed, wearing a broad-brimmed felt hat and a pair of oversized sunglasses that I'd found in Adrienne's closet. They were the same ones she'd been wearing several years previous, when she and Ethan were photographed leaving their home at the height of Ethan's financial scandal, which I knew because I'd looked up the picture online just an hour before. It was like a costume on top of a costume: me, dressed up as Adrienne Richards, dressed up as nobody at all. I looked ridiculous, but then again, so had she. Neither one of us looked good in hats, and I would probably have to wear this one for weeks. This particular hat, every time I left the house, for as long as the press wanted to camp out on my doorstep.

In that years-old picture, Adrienne and Ethan were being partially shielded from the cameras by a huge, broad-shouldered man with dark brown skin and close-cropped hair. As I peered out the window, I saw the same man, now a little grayer around the temples and thicker through the waist, climb out from behind the wheel of the town car that was idling at the curb. He shouldered his way easily through the crowd and up to the front door. My phone began to ring again. I answered it, looking down from the window. He was on the stoop, holding his own phone to his ear, looking up at me. His mouth formed the words as I heard them in the receiver.

"Mrs. Richards? It's Benny. Your driver."

"I'm ready."

"Come on down, and I'll escort you to the car."

I took the stairs carefully, holding tight to the railing, my gait unnatural in Adrienne's heels. I had been feeling proud of myself for thinking ahead, trying every pair of her shoes to find one that fit well enough, but I'd forgotten the part where I would have to walk in them. It was a struggle not to stagger. Outside, I leaned on Benny as heavily as I dared, shaking my head as reporters thronged around us, shouting questions, thrusting voice recorders in front of my face. All around me, the rapid-fire shutter sound of cameras going off. I kept my head down, eyes on my feet and my heart in my throat as we reached the bottom of the stone steps and crossed the sidewalk. I saw the car door in front of me and unthinkingly reached for the handle.

"Ma'am?"

I looked up: Benny was standing to my left, holding the door that he'd opened for me. There was a strange look on his face.

"Oh. Right. Thank you," I said, and he blinked, his eyebrows knitting together like I'd said the wrong thing, because of course I had. Of course Adrienne wouldn't say thank you. I could hear her voice in my head right now, incredulous: *Since when do you tell people "thank you" for doing their job? That's what the money is for.* But the awkward moment was only a moment, and Benny stepped aside. I practically dove past him into the back seat, yanking my throbbing feet in behind me. The door closed. I was safe once again, invisible behind dark-tinted windows. In front, the driver's-side door opened and then closed again.

"Hey," Benny said. I looked up, meeting his gaze in the rearview mirror. He was still frowning. "You don't remember me, do you?"

The bottom dropped out of my stomach. I wondered what Adrienne had said to this man the last time she met him; I couldn't begin to guess, except that it was probably awful. But Adrienne wouldn't have wondered. Adrienne wouldn't have cared at all. I shrugged and looked away.

"I guess not. Should I?"

I could feel Benny staring at me for several seconds longer. Then he shrugged and put the car in gear.

"Guess not," he said. "I guess remembering isn't your job."

The ride to Kurt Geller's downtown office took twenty minutes, with another awkward moment at the curb as Benny opened the door and extended a hand to help me out of the back seat. This time, I swallowed the urge to say thanks. I wondered if Geller could get someone else to drive me home, and then wondered if that might be worse; for all I knew, Adrienne might have been shitty to that person, too. Maybe even shittier. My feet were already beginning to hurt again as I clicked through the lobby doors. Someone called Adrienne's name, and I turned to see a slender woman in a skirt suit, holding a hand up in greeting.

"I'm Ilana, Mr. Geller's assistant," she said. "He sent me down to get you."

"Have we met before?" I asked cautiously, still paranoid from the encounter with Benny, but she only smiled politely.

"I don't think so. I wasn't with the firm yet back when your husband . . ." She caught herself and stopped midsentence, frowning sympathetically. "Excuse me, I'm so sorry. This must be very difficult for you."

"Thank you," I said.

"If you'll just follow me," said Ilana, and gestured at the elevator bank. We rode in silence, a long way up. When the doors opened, I followed her again. Past a receptionist who glanced up with recognition in her eyes—I nodded at her; she nodded back—and into the office where Kurt Geller stood behind a desk to shake my hand. I had seen pictures of him, too, but was still thrown by the look of him. In Copper Falls, people were young, middle-aged, or old, and it was never hard to tell who was what; every painful year etched itself onto your face like a claw mark. Geller was like something from another planet; he could have been anywhere from a prematurely gray thirty-five to a well-preserved sixty, agelessly handsome in a way that I had never seen in real life. He nodded at Ilana, who left, shutting the door behind her.

"Please sit," he said, and I did, collapsing into the nearest chair. I took off the hat and sunglasses, still paranoid, maybe even expecting

Geller to point and howl at me like the gangly guy at the end of *Invasion of the Body Snatchers*. He did point, but at the empty chair beside me.

"Feel free to set your things there," he said. His smile stayed in place, but softened. "It's a pleasure to see you, Adrienne, although of course I'm terribly sorry it's under these circumstances. I valued my relationship with your husband, and I intend to see to your case personally." He pressed his lips together. "I understand Ethan may have been . . . found?"

"They said they don't know for sure yet," I said. "But Dwayne—the man I shot, who broke into my house—he said—"

"I understand," Geller said. "I'm terribly sorry. We'll need to discuss all that, of course, but let's get the business end out of the way. My pre-trial fee has increased a bit since your husband's case—"

"The cost doesn't matter," I said, and heard Adrienne's voice coming out of my mouth. She'd said those same words to me any number of times, always with a carelessness that shocked me, it seemed so alien. But Geller just nodded. He scribbled a number on a slip of paper and slid it across the table to me. I counted the zeros, keeping my expression neutral. Pretending I wasn't shocked at all to learn that the man in front of me cost as much as a three-bedroom house.

"Would you like me to write the check now?" I said.

He waved a hand in the air. "That's all right. We have a lot of ground to cover. Tell me the whole story about what happened last night."

And I did. I mean, I told him *a* story. Not a true one, but a good one. A fairy tale in which the beautiful princess wakes up alone in her castle in the middle of the night, the tip of an intruder's knife hovering gently at her throat. Only with a crowd-pleasing modern update: in this story, the prince was gone, and the princess had to save herself with some quick thinking and a well-placed bullet.

He said Ethan was dead.

He said he wanted money.

He didn't know we kept a gun in the safe.

I told the story. I told it well. I told it so well that even I believed me, and why not? This was exactly the kind of game I'd always loved best, that used to occupy me for hours and hours on those dusty summer days in the junkyard. I had always been so good at convincing myself that I was someone and somewhere else—and I had always preferred to do it alone. Other people always ruined it, poking holes in the fantasy until it fell apart. Other people always wanted to tell you why your story was wrong and fake and stupid, and that you were fooling yourself, and that no amount of pretending would ever change who and what you are. A princess? A hero? A happily-ever-after? In your dreams. Maybe after a million dollars of plastic surgery.

Kurt Geller listened while I talked, making notes periodically, mostly nodding along. When I finished, he tapped his pen against the paper where he'd been scribbling.

"When did you buy the gun?" he asked.

I frowned, feeling a flare of resentment at this expensive man, poking a hole in my story. Asking a question I didn't know the answer to.

"I can't think," I said. "We owned it legally. That's what matters, isn't it?"

"And when you shot him, where was he standing? In relation to you, that is."

"A few feet away. Between me and the door."

Geller nodded. "Blocking you from leaving. Understood. And you shot him in the chest?"

I closed my eyes, saw Dwayne stagger forward. The hole in the front of his shirt, going red around the edges. "Yes."

Another nod. "That's good." He looked again at his notes. "Before this, you'd been alone in the house for, what, nearly two days? You didn't think to wonder where Ethan was, why he hadn't called?"

"It's not unusual. I mean, it wasn't. He was away pretty often. Sometimes, especially if it was a short trip, he didn't bother to keep in touch." I hesitated. "And sometimes I didn't want to hear from him anyway."

The tap-tap-tapping of Geller's pen against the paper stopped. He raised his eyebrows. I let the silence stretch between us for two beats too long. It made sense if I seemed reluctant to tell this next part, but I didn't have to pretend to hesitate. I didn't want to say it. Saying it meant I had to think about it, about the two of them together. I squirmed.

Geller leaned forward, and the smile disappeared. "Adrienne," he said, "I'm going to tell you what I tell all my clients. Don't lie to me. When you lie to your lawyer, you make me the stupidest one in the room. That's bad when it's just the two of us. It's worse if this goes to trial. Whatever it is—"

"You know I had an affair," I blurted, and the lawyer eased back into his seat.

"Go on."

"I had an affair with Dwayne Cleaves. He was the handyman at the lake where we stayed in the summer. I was bored and unhappy, it was impulsive, and I just . . . I don't even know." I thought Geller might scold me for waiting so long to tell that part, but he just nodded.

"Okay," he said. "And you had a visit from the Maine State Police yesterday, correct? Because Dwayne Cleaves was already wanted for questioning in the murder of his wife?"

"That's what the detective said. His name was Ian Bird."

Geller blew a breath out through pursed lips.

"Okay. Look, Adrienne, here's the thing." He sat back in the chair, a strange look on his face, and I felt my stomach knot up. Braced myself. The finger was going to come up now, he was going to point and scream: *Here's the thing. YOU'RE NOT ADRIENNE.*

Instead, he shrugged a little, and said, "I'm not worried."

I blinked. "You're . . . not."

"Dwayne Cleaves killed two people, including your husband. He drove Ethan's car down to the city, broke into your home with a stolen key, threatened you with a weapon, tried to rob you. It's clear-cut self-defense. So assuming that ballistics tell the same story, and based on what my sources in the department told me this morning? No, I'm not worried. The DA is up for reelection next month, and the brass is already lukewarm on her after that department probe she launched over the summer. The last thing she wants is to poke that beehive by dragging the police into another high-profile loser of a case."

"I don't understand," I said, because I didn't, and Geller shrugged.

"I don't mean to be insensitive. But you must realize, you're a highly sympathetic defendant. You're a beautiful young woman who just lost her husband, who had the courage to shoot a killer who broke into her home in the middle of the night."

"And the affair?"

"Again, not to be insensitive . . . but it's the #MeToo era, Adrienne. If someone tried to use that against you, we'd mop the floor with him."

I gripped the arms of my chair as hard as I could. Geller looked at me sympathetically.

"It's a lot to process," he said. "Can I get you a tissue?"

I just nodded.

But I wasn't fighting back tears. I was struggling not to laugh.

Geller crossed the room and pulled a box of Kleenex from a shelf, then extended it to me.

"I'm sorry for your loss," he said. "And for what you went through. I know this wasn't an easy conversation, and I appreciate your honesty. It's rare for a client to be so forthcoming so immediately."

"Thank you," I said, taking a tissue. I brought it to my face, then realized that Geller was still standing over me, still staring.

"It really makes me wonder," he said, his voice mild as ever, "why I'm so sure right now that there's something you're not telling me."

The world shrank to a point. My blood roared in my ears, which felt like they were on fire, as I stared up at Geller with my mouth open and my eyes wide. The tissue fluttered out of my hand and onto the floor. He stooped to pick it up, setting it gently back in my hand. My fingers curled automatically, but they were the only part of my body that seemed to be working. My jaw still dangled off its hinges, and my legs had gone entirely numb. Geller just meandered back behind his desk, settling again into his chair. His ageless face, so handsome a moment ago, seemed terrifying now, like a mask from behind which the real Kurt Geller was watching me. Seeing me. Seeing everything. Only the look in his eyes was familiar: it was the same one I'd seen on Benny's face, on the faces of the police, even in Anna's guarded expression as we made halting chitchat on the street. I'd been too distracted by my own lies, too worried about being found out, to understand what it meant. Now I couldn't understand how I'd taken so long to realize: it wasn't *me* that people didn't trust. It was Adrienne.

Every person Adrienne knew, from her SoulCycle buddy to her lawyer, absolutely fucking hated her.

"As I said," Geller was saying, "I'm not worried about your case, per se. And if the DA tries to pursue this, I can try to discourage her in half a dozen different ways. But I would like the truth, Adrienne."

Finally, I managed to close my mouth. I swallowed, hard.

"Well, you're not getting it," I said, and Geller's eyebrows shot up. I could hear the rage in my voice, rage that was all mine and didn't sound like Adrienne at all. But I couldn't dial it back. I wouldn't. I had to see, to know what would happen if I didn't play my role just right. People were always ready to let Adrienne know what was expected of her. What if she defied expectation?

"Even if I wanted to tell you everything, I couldn't," I said. "I know Ethan is dead in a burned-out junkyard in the middle of nowhere. I know Dwayne killed him. But I don't know the truth. I don't know why, and now nobody ever will, because I didn't wait around for Dwayne to explain his motivations or make excuses before I pulled that trigger. You want the whole story? The only person who could've told it to you is dead. I'm fine with that. If you can't stand the uncertainty, then maybe I should find another lawyer."

He blinked. I held my breath.

Then he smiled, the surprise wiping itself off his face, and said, "Oh, that won't be necessary. And yes, I'll take that check now."

After it was all over, with the money in Geller's hands and with nothing to do but wait and hide and hope, I would think again and again about that reckless moment in the lawyer's office. That span of a minute where I'd cracked open the door on my old life and allowed Lizzie to peer out, to speak, to be seen. A completely unnecessary and dangerous risk, but one I had to take—if only to prove the truth to myself. Because I think I knew, even before I tried, that nobody would see her hiding there. I think I knew way back, before I ever pulled the trigger, maybe even before Adrienne came into my life at all. I was good at pretending, at imagining. When I looked at myself, I could see possibilities. But I think I knew nobody else would.

People see what they expect to see, once they think they know who you are. Their ideas are a ghost that floats ahead of you into every room, waiting until you arrive and then clinging all over you, grimy, opaque. It builds up around you over the course of a lifetime, layer by layer, until the ghost-you made of other people's judgments is all anyone sees. The redneck cunt. The junkyard jezebel. The privileged bitch. And you're stuck at the center, invisible. Trapped. Screaming, *I'm in here,* but the sound of your own reputation is so loud that nobody will ever hear you. By the time Lizzie Ouellette had that gun in her hands, she was like a costume I couldn't take off, and nobody will ever miss the girl who lived inside it. Nobody even knew her.

Maybe my new costume will fit better.

Maybe I can be a better Adrienne Richards than Adrienne Richards ever was.

I held her phone in my hands and tapped the screen once, twice. Hesitated. Below my hovering finger, a dialog box asked, *Are you sure? This action cannot be undone.* It made me think again of that hairstylist, frowning as I explained what I wanted. Was I sure?

I wasn't. I wasn't sure at all. This was uncharted territory. Until this moment, I'd been guided by the question of what Adrienne would have done, because doing what Adrienne would have done, no matter what it was, was important. I knew this. I had known it from the moment I pulled the trigger, that getting away with this meant staying the course. Staying in character. If I was going to be Adrienne, I had to make Adrienne's choices, not mine. And this choice, this undoable action, was not what Adrienne would have done. Not at all. Not ever.

But then again, Adrienne wasn't exactly herself these days. Adrienne was in shock. Adrienne had been through a traumatic experience, and if she was acting strangely all of a sudden, didn't she have the right? Could you blame her? Would you even wonder why?

"Fuck it," I said aloud, and jabbed my finger at the screen. The dialog disappeared, replaced by a new message.

Your account has been deleted.

PART 3

SIX MONTHS LATER

CHAPTER 27

BIRD

The knife was in a plastic bag, stamped with a case number and capped by a red security strip that indicated it hadn't been opened since the previous year. Bagged, tagged, and forgotten. It looked like any hunter's knife, utterly unremarkable—unless you knew, as Bird did, that it had been used not too long ago to cut off a woman's nose.

The officer behind the desk was neatly dressed in uniform but looked more like a librarian than a cop, her hair pulled back into a small, nubby bun at the nape of her neck and her eyes large behind a pair of small, round glasses. She pushed a clipboard at Bird.

"Sign for it, and it's all yours," she said. "Took you long enough to come get it."

Bird shrugged. "I'm not exactly in the neighborhood," he said. "Hopefully it wasn't taking up too much space on your shelves."

The woman smiled. "Not a problem. You all set? Need a chain-of-custody form?"

"No need," Bird said. "We closed the case; I'm just tying up loose ends. This fella here"—he brandished the knife—"is going straight into a box."

It was a cool April day in the city, blustery and half-gray. The afternoon sun peeked in and out from behind the clouds, lukewarm and colorless as weak tea. Bird turned his face to it all the same. The state of Maine was still thawing out after a long, bleak winter, but a couple hundred miles south, you could feel spring coming down the pike. Longer days, milder temperatures, the smell of damp earth in the air. The Sox were at Fenway, playing their home opener. Bird could stop for an early dinner, catch the end of the game, and still be home before dark.

He drove back out of the city, putting a little distance between himself and Boston's rush-hour snarl. It was six months to the day from the last time he'd driven this route, leaving Adrienne Richards's house and heading north, and leaving her to shoot Dwayne Cleaves in what Boston law enforcement immediately decided was an open-and-shut case of self-defense. Bird had been surprised at the time by how little attention it got, particularly in the press, particularly with an obnoxious, publicity-hungry, highly telegenic survivor like Adrienne Richards at the center of it all. You couldn't deny, it was a juicy story. The residents of Copper Falls were inundated for days, slamming doors in the face of every reporter who made the trip north in hopes of getting a comment from Lizzie's friends and family. Nobody talked, of course. Eventually, the reporters left. But Adrienne—you'd think she would milk her fifteen minutes of fame for all it was worth. Instead, she'd declined all interview requests and virtually vanished from the public eye. The tabloids screamed for a while to know where and what she was hiding, but eventually, they got bored and found another story to chase. The screaming stopped. Life went on. Except for Ethan Richards, of course, but nobody even pretended to be too broken up about that.

Not that Bird had been keeping close tabs. He'd had more than enough to occupy him in the intervening months after closing Lizzie

Ouellette's case, months spent following up on the leads from his conversation with George Pullen. The centenarian Pullen couldn't tell you what he'd had for breakfast that morning, but he still remembered the early 1980s and Laurie Richter with razor-sharp clarity. Most of all, he remembered that a buddy of his had been acting odd that summer, and got odder after the girl went missing. Staring into space, staying up all night, disappearing for days at a time. Pullen didn't know what to make of it, he said; he wasn't even sure the friend knew Laurie, who was much younger than either of them and kept mostly to herself. But it was weird enough that he asked where the buddy was always running off to, and when he did, the man had gotten wild around the eyes—"Like a spooked racehorse" were Pullen's exact words—and said he'd been fishing at a quarry out near the Forks. He described the place in painstaking, almost reverent detail. The clarity of the water, the mottled colors of the rock, the way you could perch on an outcrop and look straight down into the depths. It was peaceful, he said. So peaceful. When Pullen asked about the fish, the buddy gave him a funny look and said he didn't know—he'd never caught one.

Thanks to that conversation, Bird had pinpointed four slate quarries in the area that he thought were worth a look.

They found Laurie Richter's car sunk in the third place on the list. Her body, what was left of it, was locked in the trunk.

There were still months of work ahead before Bird caught another break, complicated by the fact that George Pullen's buddy, unlike George himself, was no longer alive to spill his guts. But the discovery of the car ignited renewed interest in the case, and in the end, George Pullen lived long enough to find out that his buddy wasn't guilty of anything but not wanting to break his kid sister's heart.

The buddy's nephew, on the other hand—the kid sister's kid—was a goddamn murdering bastard.

Not much of a liar, though, Bird thought with a smirk. Once they'd gotten the guy in custody, he confessed within minutes. He was just tired, he told them. All those years, keeping that terrible secret, waiting and wondering if someone would figure it out. It was a relief, finally, to tell the truth.

Bird's mind was still meandering through a half year's worth of memories—Lizzie Ouellette, Dwayne Cleaves, Adrienne Richards, Laurie Richter—as he pulled off the highway and followed the signs for a chain restaurant, the most reliable bet for a decent burger and a seat with a view of the TV. If not for the fact that he'd just been thinking of her, he might have come and gone without ever recognizing the woman sitting at the bar. She was four seats down, beside the wall, her body angled slightly toward him, her face upturned. She was sipping a beer and gazing at the television, where the Sox were down by one run. Her hair was different now, cropped to her shoulders and colored a reddish brown, but there was no mistaking her face. Bird shook his head in amazement.

When Adrienne Richards had disappeared from the public eye, everyone assumed she was living a life of private luxury at some seaside retreat. But now here she was: in a suburban Chili's, drinking Coors and watching baseball.

He almost turned around and left. It wasn't just that he wanted to avoid the inevitable awkwardness once she spotted him, if she spotted him. It was the look on her face: not happy, exactly, but comfortable. At ease. At home. Crazy as it was, Bird felt like he'd be intruding.

Then she looked up, and her eyes went wide, and the sip of beer she'd been about to take tipped down the front of her shirt instead.

"Shit," she hissed, slamming the bottle onto the bar and fumbling for a napkin. Bird crossed the distance between them, his hands raised apologetically.

"Hey," he said. "Sorry."

She was blotting the spilled beer from her shirt, and lifted her eyes only briefly to meet his.

"Hi, Detective Bird," she said. The corners of her mouth tugged down; she wasn't happy to see him.

"Hi, Mrs. Richards," he said, and she hurriedly shook her head, eyes darting around the bar. Fearful of attracting attention.

"Don't," she said. "It's Swan, now, anyway. My name."

Bird looked around, too; her nervousness was palpable enough to be contagious, but all the other patrons had their eyes on either the television or their drinks. He lowered his voice anyway.

"You changed your name?"

"Changed it back. Adrienne Richards just had a lot of . . . baggage," she said, and he laughed in spite of himself.

"Adrienne Swan," he said, trying it out. "Sure, makes sense. It sounds nice. Swan. Pretty birds, too."

"They murder a dozen people per year," she said.

"You're making that up," Bird replied, but in fact, he couldn't tell, and that bothered him. When he'd questioned this woman six months ago, he'd been able to read her easily; he still remembered the confident moment when she'd lost control, said a little too much, and he was sure he'd gotten the truth. Now, he stared at her face and had no idea if she was joking or not. She gazed back at him, expressionless—and then the corners of her mouth twitched, and she shrugged.

"Look it up if you don't believe me." She took a long sip of beer, then turned to face him, frowning. "God, I'm sorry. Is this even . . . allowed? Me talking to you, you talking to me? It's weird."

Bird winced. "Look, *I'm* sorry. Really. I shouldn't have come over. I was about to leave, actually, but I wasn't even sure it was you at first. You look . . . different."

"Yeah, well, it's been that kind of year," she said. "This shit puts lines on your face that no amount of Botox can fix."

"I didn't mean it like that," he said, but she just shrugged again. "Anyway, sorry I startled you. Really. I'll leave you to it." He turned to go, and her voice floated over his shoulder.

"Weren't you sitting down?"

"I can always go somewhere else."

"No," she said, and hesitated as he turned back to look at her. She chewed her lip, considering her next move, then abruptly nodded at the chair next to her. "Look, I came here because nobody knows me. The odds of us running into each other—it's just too weird. It feels like, I don't know, some kind of test. The universe, or something. So sit down if you want to, and I'll buy you a drink. If you want to. Unless you're on duty."

Bird hesitated. Even if he'd expected to see Adrienne Richards, no, *Swan,* here, he would not have expected an invitation to sit and drink with her. He hadn't exactly been nice to her when they'd last seen each other, and he hadn't exactly been sorry about it, either. The case was closed, but if he thought about it—and he did think about it, every so often—he thought that she might have always known a little more than she was telling. He thought she might have gotten away with something.

But he also thought, back then, that she was a real pill. An entitled bitch, even. Eminently dislikable.

Now he didn't know what to think.

"All right, thanks. Sounds fun," he said, and realized, incredibly, that it kind of did.

Adrienne signaled the bartender and kept her eyes on the game while Bird ordered.

"I'll have what she's having," he said, and watched with amusement as the bartender said, "Sure," and plopped a longneck down in front of him without so much as glancing at the minor celebrity sitting in the next seat over. Not a glimmer of recognition. He took a pull from the bottle and looked over to find Adrienne watching him.

"You think it's weird that he doesn't recognize me," she said.

"A little," Bird replied, and she smiled.

"People see what they expect to see," she said. "And if they don't know what to expect, they see whatever you show them. It took me a little while to figure it out. Back when everything happened, reporters were always trying to follow me around, and I used to put on this outfit to avoid the cameras. Big sunglasses, big hat, this big woolly wrap thing, you know, like a sweater made out of a blanket. The 'in-cognito' look." She mimed the quotes with her fingers. "And for some reason, I thought this would work."

Bird chuckled, and so did she.

"It was ridiculous," she said, laying the back of her hand against her face and lifting her chin like a model. "'Oh no! Please, no photographs! I'm famous! Don't look at me!'"

"Funny how that works," Bird said.

"It's like a secret code. What to wear when you want to be photographed looking like you didn't want to be photographed."

"Seems like you worked it out."

"Seems like it," she said. "For the time being, anyway. I have this feeling that in six months, there won't be any attention left for me to dodge."

"You say that like it's a bad thing," Bird joked, and she shook her head.

"No, no. It's what I want. It's all that I want." She turned to look at him, studying him. "Detective Bird, what's your first name?"

"Ian."

"Ian. Ian, why are you here?"

"Tying up a loose end," he said. He would not tell her about the knife, still in its bag, sitting in a lockbox in the cruiser's trunk. She might even recognize it, he thought. According to the police report, she'd woken up around two o'clock in the morning to find Dwayne Cleaves in her bedroom, standing over her, the blade glinting silver in his hand.

"Something to do with—"

"Yeah," he said.

"I guess you're not allowed to talk about it."

"Did you want to talk about it?"

"No." She took a long drink. "I'd be happy never to talk about it again. Congratulations, by the way."

Bird drained his beer. "Thanks. What for?"

"Laurie Richter? I read somewhere that you caught the guy. That case was . . ." She shook her head, trailing off. He wondered what she'd been about to say, how she'd even known about it. Adrienne Richards didn't seem like the true-crime type, but maybe that was a failure of his own imagination. *People see what they expect to see,* he thought.

"Oh yeah. Well, thanks. I got lucky."

She gave him a funny look. "I'd guess it was more than that. Do you want another beer?"

He looked at his watch, at her face.

"I will if you will," he said.

The conversation grew easier as he talked about Laurie Richter, the series of lucky breaks—and yes, okay, the hours and hours of legwork—that had led him first to her body and then to the son of a bitch who'd killed her. He told her about the confession, about how the old man sat up just a little straighter as he unburdened himself, finally free of that weight, a young man's terrible secret that he'd been keeping for much too long.

"Forty years," Adrienne said. "Jesus."

"Long time to carry something like that," Bird said, nodding. "But what about you? I mean, how have you been doing with everything?"

"The lawyers handled most of it," she said. "Ethan was pretty organized; he had everything all planned out for, you know, if something happened. Once they identified the body, all I had to do was sign things."

"Was there a funeral?"

She shook her head. "Private service. Just me and the lawyers. It just seemed like, after what happened . . ."

"You don't have to explain," Bird said quickly, but she seemed not to hear him.

"It was so strange," she said quietly. "There were all these condolence cards, so many flowers, but all from, like . . . corporations.

People were sorry to lose Ethan's money. I don't think anyone cared at all that he was gone."

Bird didn't say anything, and she took a drink, setting the bottle down with a light clunk.

"Anyway, that's all over. Or will be. The lawyers said it should be settled soon."

"You do anything for the holidays?" Bird asked, hoping for a subject change, and Adrienne's mouth twitched.

"I went south for a little while, actually," she said. "I saw my mother. Not that she knows it. She's in a home. Alzheimer's."

"Sorry to hear that. How's she doing?"

"She's okay," she said. "But I think . . . I think I want to move her. She should be somewhere better. Somewhere nicer."

Sometime later, Bird glanced outside and realized that the sun had fully set. The bar was buzzing now with the after-work crowd, the afternoon sports fans long gone after a disappointing loss for the Sox that neither he nor Adrienne had seen. There had been another round of beers, and another—at some point Adrienne had switched to water, while Bird threw caution to the wind and ordered a whiskey—and their chairs had somehow pivoted so that they were sitting very close now, so close that their knees kept brushing together, close enough that he could smell her perfume. *What is this? What's happening?* Bird thought, and then wondered if he was only imagining things. Maybe nothing was happening at all. Maybe he was just buzzed, more than buzzed—"buzzed" was receding in the rearview mirror as he rounded the corner and entered the long home stretch toward *drunk*—but she was staring at him with her eyes wide and her lips slightly parted, and that was happening, and so was the tugging sensation low in his abdomen, that gut sense of something electric in the air. He lifted his hand, which was moving so slowly that seemed like it might belong to someone else, and watched it close the distance between them to gently touch her knee. She lowered her eyes, looked at the hand on her leg, looked back up at him. Her parted lips began to move.

She said, "Do you want to get out of here?"

What is happening? What is happening? What the actual fuck is happening? his brain said.

"Yes," he said. "Yes, I do."

Her knee disappeared from beneath his hand as she stood up and pulled her jacket on. He followed her outside, the two of them pausing awkwardly in the parking lot as he realized that he had no idea where to go. There was a silence punctuated by the whooshing of traffic on the nearby road, the ticking of a streetlight from green to red.

"Your place?" he asked.

"No," she said. "Not there. I can't. And anyway, it's far."

"My . . . car?" he said, and started to laugh, and so did she, the tension between them dissolving. She leaned into him and he wrapped an arm around her.

"My back seat glory days are over," she said. "But look, look at that." She pointed, and Bird looked, and saw the familiar logo of a discount motel chain looming on a lighted sign above their heads. Right next door, less than fifty yards away.

"It's fate," he said, and she guffawed.

"It's a cosmic joke."

"Not fancy enough for you?"

"Fuck you," she said. "Let's go. It's cold out here."

Ten minutes later, Bird was sliding a key card into the electronic lock, Adrienne hovering close behind. He was about to make another joke—something about the probable lack of champagne and caviar on the room-service menu—but when he turned to let her through the door, she was right there, right beside him, and then the door was closed and locked and her body was pressed against his, their lips brushing hungrily past each other as he fumbled in the dark for a light switch.

"Leave it off."

The sign for the hotel loomed like an oblong moon outside the window. She stepped away from him and stood in front of it, sil-houetted, her arms raised as she pulled her shirt over her head. He shrugged out of his jacket.

"I want to see you," he said, and she laughed.

"Maybe I don't want to be seen."

He went to her, his hands finding her shoulders, dropping to encir-cle her waist. He could smell the warm, sweet scent of her body un-derneath the lighter note of her perfume or shampoo, and the tugging sensation in his low belly became a throb. He pulled her to the bed, pulled her down, the softness of her skin against his lips, the scratch of the cheap motel comforter against his back. Her hands were at his waist, undoing his belt, sliding his pants down over his hips. He felt the brush of her fingertips and said, "Oh," and then there was no more talking.

When they'd finished, he reached out to flip on the bedside lamp. This time, she didn't object, only nestled deeper into the crook of his arm. He looked down at the top of her head. The auburn color was nice, but it had always struck him funny, how the rules were so different for women that way; if you were a girl and you didn't like the hair God gave you, you could pick any color you liked out of a box. But men, never. There was something vaguely suspicious about a guy who dyed his hair, even if it was just to cover the grays. Un-dignified. He yawned, feeling warm and sleepy, the first hints of a headache starting to creep around the corners of his eyes. The whiskey had been a mistake, but then again, if he hadn't had the whiskey, he might not be here, in a postcoital moment as wild and unexpected as it was nice. It *was* nice. The past few months had been professionally productive but personally lonely. He'd been on a handful of first dates that had netted one night of mediocre sex, zero second meetings, and the uncomfortable feeling that this was probably his fault. He yawned again. Maybe he'd sleep here awhile before heading back. Beside him, Adrienne yawned, too.

"That's your fault," she said. "It's contagious. I should go. I can't sleep here."

"I mean, you *could*."

She smiled. "No. It's a bad idea."

"At least don't move just yet," he said, and squeezed her closer. "I like having you here. You're very . . . warm."

"Five minutes."

He nodded. "Okay. Five minutes." For a while, neither one of them spoke. Bird turned to rest his chin on the top of her head.

"So, what are you going to do now?" he said finally.

"Well, for the next five minutes, nothing," she joked.

"No, I mean—"

"I know what you mean." She sighed. "And I don't know. People keep suggesting things. All these options. But I don't like any of them."

"Some folks I know thought you might get a book deal," Bird said, and she laughed.

"One of the many options. They offered. Hard pass."

"You don't want to be famous?"

She scowled. "God, no."

"Come on. Be honest."

"I am. I guess it probably sounds weird to you. But Adrienne Richards, she's the one who wanted to be famous. And I'm not her. I left that person behind."

Bird closed his eyes. His breathing began to slow, and he thought it wouldn't be so bad to just drift off. Drift off and wake up alone. The five minutes he'd asked for were ticking away, and while neither one of them had said so, there was a cycling-down feeling in the air. The end, not the start, of something. He should stay awake to see it through, but his eyelids were so heavy.

"You want honesty?" Adrienne said. "You want to hear something really fucked up?"

"Mmm," Bird said.

She said, "I once told my husband I hoped he died."

Bird's eyes cracked open, and he rolled to one side to look at her. She was lying on her back, her gaze fixed on the ceiling.

"Jesus, seriously?"

"The thing is, I still don't know if I really meant it. I don't think I did. But then everything went to hell. And now he's gone."

"You feel like it's your fault."

"It's definitely my fault," she said, so matter-of-factly that all Bird could do was silently agree. Not that Ethan Richards's death was all her fault—a thing like that never was. But you could also see how things might have been different, if she'd made different choices. If anyone had. There was blame enough to go around.

"Do you miss him?" Bird said, and now she did look at him.

"That's a weird fucking question," she said.

"It is," he said. "I don't know why I—"

"No," she said. "I'm glad you asked, because I want to say this. I want to tell someone that, yeah, I miss my husband. I do. I miss him, and at the same time, I know we couldn't have gone on together. Something was always going to happen—maybe not this, but something. We were like a homemade bomb. You know? Where you've got these two things, they're nothing on their own, but then you put them together and you get a toxic sludge that kills everything it touches."

"Uh," said Bird, and she laughed, shaking her head.

"Yeah. I know. And that was our marriage. But we'd already been put together. That's the thing. Even if we broke up, we couldn't . . . un-combine."

"Until death did you part," Bird said.

"Yeah," she said. "Until then. I should go."

The comforter fell away as she sat up, turning away from him. He laid a hand on her back.

"I'm sorry," he said.

"For what?"

"For your loss. Whatever that means to you."

She turned fully toward him, leaned in, touched her lips to his. "Thank you."

He watched as she stood, slipping her bra straps back over her shoulders, reaching behind her back to clasp it. There was a tiny scar on the inside of her right breast, paler than the surrounding skin and slightly wrinkled.

"Chicken pox?" He pointed.

"War wound," she deadpanned.

"From another life," he joked back, and maybe it was just how fuzzy-headed and sleepy he was, but he would never quite understand what happened next: she blinked at him, then threw her head back and laughed like he'd made the funniest joke there was. But if there was anything he'd learned tonight, it was that there was a lot he didn't understand about Adrienne Richards. He watched her put her shoes on and shrug her jacket over her shoulders. She pulled an elastic from the jacket pocket and twisted her hair into a knot, taking a last look around the room.

"So. Same time next month?" he said, because he felt like he had to say something, and this time she didn't laugh.

"Wouldn't that be a thing," she said, smiling in a way that said, *We both know this will never be a thing.* For a moment, she paused, shifting her weight, and he thought she might ask for his number after all, or at least come to kiss him goodbye. Then she shrugged, turned away, and opened the door.

"Adrienne," he said, and she stopped, her hand still on the doorknob. Not turning back, but looking, glancing back over her shoulder. Lips lightly parted, her cheeks still pink from the heat of sex, her hair coiled messily on top of her head. Pale blue eyes fringed with heavy lashes, open wide. As if caught by surprise.

"Good luck. I mean it."

She nodded.

Then the door closed, and she was gone.

CHAPTER 28

LIZZIE

My name is Lizzie Ouellette, or it was, before I gave it away. Another woman has it now; it's written six feet above her head on a stone in the Copper Falls cemetery, where she's buried wearing whatever the mortician's wife decided was most appropriate. Old Mrs. Dorsey would have done the job, riffling my closet for a burial dress just like she riffled through my mother's all those years ago, testing the weight and weft of the options with her arthritic fingers while my father nodded mutely along, going with whatever she suggested. She would've been careful, even though it hardly mattered. After the wreck I made of the new Lizzie's face, a closed casket was the only option. I wonder sometimes what she chose, though. If she ran her fingers over the silky green gown, squinted at the label, wondered at how I'd come to own such a thing. If people whispered after the funeral about all those beautiful, expensive dresses, things that had no earthly business in my closet. All my nicest clothes were things Adrienne had given me. I wonder if that's how it ended for her: moldering in a grave with some-one else's name on it, wearing a dress she'd tried to give away, while I continued on in the life I'd stolen. All wrapped up in her identity like a little girl playing dress-up.

It was late spring, the grass in the cemetery fresh and green, when I arrived back in Copper Falls. Wearing my Adrienne-Richards-in-disguise disguise, driving her ridiculous car. It was risky, returning to the scene of the crime like some kind of murder mystery cliché, but I think I always knew I would. I had to. There were things I needed to do, and things I needed to prove. I needed to show myself that Lizzie was so dead, so gone, that she could cut a perfumed path right in front of their stupid noses and they'd never even notice. I needed to go back, if only to know for sure that I could never really go home. To lay my hand on the headstone and trace the shape of a name I'll never write out again. To look at the two stones just beside it, one large, one small, both bearing the same name, and feel a sad sense of satisfaction at the idea of them keeping each other company. To drive past all the places I used to live, and see that I wasn't there anymore. To watch through someone else's eyes as life went on without me.

It turned out that I was half-right: nobody saw Lizzie that day. Not in the aisles of the grocery, where I once made a spectacle of myself shouting at Eliza Higgins. Not at the local ice cream shop, where Maggie was still scooping, still scowling, and still giving dirty looks to anyone who asked for flavor samples. Not at the cemetery, where I knew I shouldn't linger, but couldn't help pausing to lay a small bouquet of jewelweed and clover on the baby's grave. Not at the post office, where I slid a postcard and an envelope filled with cash into another, larger envelope, no signature, no return address. I dropped it into the mail and then wondered if maybe I shouldn't have. I wondered what I was more afraid of: that he wouldn't understand, or that he would.

Nobody saw Lizzie. But I had forgotten how Adrienne, in that stupid hat and those giant sunglasses, always drew attention in a way that I never could, never did.

I didn't realize she was following me until I was on my way out of town, stopped at the gas station to top off the Mercedes's tank. I didn't hear her footsteps behind me; I didn't realize the voice that called out, "Hey, you," was meant for me. But then a finger jabbed into my shoulder blade, hard, and I turned to see Jennifer Wellstood, legs braced, hands on hips, glaring at me with utter loathing on her face.

"Remember me?" she said, and I had to fight the urge to laugh, because of course I did. I did, and what I wanted to say was, *Bitch, I remember everything.*

I remember the way you chewed the inside of your cheek while you curled my hair on my wedding day, and told me you thought my dress was nice, even though it wasn't white.

I remember the ridiculous look on your face when I caught you with my husband, and how after I stopped being pissed, I couldn't stop laughing, wondering where the hell you got the idea that it took two hands to jerk someone off.

I remember the time you got drunk at a party and dared Jordan Gibson to let you wax off his back hair, and he was so wasted that he actually let you try.

I remember that I liked you, in spite of everything.

I remember that you were more decent than most.

But Adrienne Richards wouldn't remember Jennifer, and if she did, she would never admit it. So I gave her Adrienne's tight-lipped smile, and I kept Adrienne's sunglasses on, and I used Adrienne's snottiest voice to say, "Oh, I'm sorry, no. I don't."

Jennifer let out a short bark of laughter and shot back through gritted teeth, "Yeah, well, I remember you. Fucking hoity-toity bitch. You've got some fucking nerve, coming back to this town. Haven't you done enough?"

"Excuse me?" I said.

She was yelling now. "Lizzie and Dwayne are dead because of you.

Nobody wants you here. So why don't you get in your car and leave, and never come back!"

"Oh, I intend to," I simpered, even though my heart was pounding. "Don't you worry, honey. You'll never see me again."

I turned away, got back in the car. As I twisted the key in the ignition, a hand smacked against the driver's-side window so hard that it made me yelp. I looked up: Jennifer was standing beside the car, glaring at me through the glass. Her face twisted in a funny way, and for one wild moment, I wondered if she'd recognized me after all. Instead, she opened her mouth and yelled, "And your hair still looks like shit!"

I laughed most of the way out of town.

Cried too, just a little.

As much as Copper Falls hated me, they still hate outsiders more.

But I can live with that. I'm sure I can. That's the nice thing about being dead. I don't have to care anymore, about any of them, save one—and he'll be okay. I will be sure that he is. I think he knows I'm in a better place.

I just wish it weren't so lonely.

I didn't lie to Ian Bird when I said I'd been to see Adrienne's mother. I did. I wanted to. The press had stopped harassing me sometime before Thanksgiving. By mid-December, there was snow on the ground and only the occasional footprint in it from a photographer hoping to snap a picture of me as I came or went, a preview of the moment I knew would come, someday, when nobody cared anymore about Adrienne Richards. Kurt Geller looked at me strangely when I told him my plans, but I was getting used to that, the way the people in Adrienne's life flinched when she did something unexpected. I was learning that I could push back.

"Is there a reason I shouldn't visit my mother?" I asked, and he pursed his lips.

"I suppose not," he said finally. "I wouldn't leave the country just now, if I were you, but South Carolina—"

"North," I said immediately.

"Of course," Geller replied smoothly. "My mistake."

I smiled and told him there was no need to apologize, but I wondered, the way I always do. If he suspects something, if he's testing me. Toying with me. I don't think Kurt Geller has ever really trusted me, but perhaps he never trusted Adrienne, either. I also don't think he cares much, as long as the checks keep clearing and he gets his commission from the breakup of Ethan's estate. And then I think about what he said to me that day, before I left—a gift, although he'll never know it.

"You look so tired, my dear," he said. "Of course, nobody would blame you for letting certain things fall by the wayside, and tragedy can be so aging. But have you considered a little Botox, perhaps? Just to make you look more like yourself again. I can recommend an excellent dermatologist."

"That won't be necessary," I said, in a tone I hoped sounded offended. It was a page straight out of Adrienne's playbook, to insult a woman's looks in the guise of concern; even I knew that "tired" was not-so-secret code for "pale, saggy, and old." But what I really felt wasn't offense. It was relief. I had wondered when it might happen, when someone would look past Adrienne's hair and clothes and sunglasses and notice that a changeling had taken her place. Every time someone squinted at my face, every time someone stared a little too long, I would feel the tickle of fear: *They see me.*

But of course they didn't. They just saw a woman whose features had always been a continuous work in progress, and wondered what kind of work she'd had done. Adrienne was the type who would go out of town for a weekend and come back *tweaked,* her face subtly manipulated in a way you couldn't quite put your finger on. A slimmer jawline? A smoother forehead? It was what made Geller's suggestion such a brilliant joke: Adrienne hadn't looked like herself in years.

I was safe.

I also understood, finally, why the man's perfectly ageless face never seemed to move.

The flight south was my first time on an airplane, and as the wheels lifted off the tarmac, I felt terrified and elated. Weightless. I flew first class because Adrienne would have, but also because I wanted to. A flight attendant poured me a glass of champagne and asked whether I was going home for the holidays. I told her I was going to see my mother, and it was funny, how it didn't feel like a lie. How it still doesn't. The director of the nursing home met me at the door and warned me that the visit might be challenging, and it was, but not the way they were afraid of: Margaret Swan threw her arms around me with a broad smile and exclaimed, "Oh, it's you!" and I hugged her back, hard, feeling like something was cracking open inside me. I put my face in her shoulder. I heard my voice break as I said, "Mom," even though I knew that Adrienne always called her "Mother."

Of all the things that Adrienne never appreciated, all her castoffs and hand-me-downs, this is the one that makes me angry. And grateful. And afraid.

After visiting hours were over, I stopped in a washroom. One of the orderlies who'd escorted me in was standing at the sinks in her white clogs and scrubs, scraping a fingernail over her front teeth. She flashed me a smile, the nasty kind that curls the lips but doesn't reach the eyes, and said, "You know she's just faking it, right? They all are. We tell them a few minutes ahead of time that they're going to see whoever, and then they pretend to recognize their daughter or son or wife or whatever. You do know that, don't you?"

The thing is, I did know. Of course I fucking knew. I could see it behind Margaret's eyes in the moments before she hugged me, that fear of making a misstep. Of not knowing what's expected. Like trying to sing along to a song whose lyrics you've forgotten, hoping the noises you're making sound enough like the words that nobody notices, wondering if the shape of your mouth is betraying you, going "ooooh" when it should be "aaaah." Yes, I know what someone looks like when they're pretending.

But for God's sake, even I know you don't say that to a person. Not out loud, not in a place like this, not about someone's mother. Adrienne would have been furious. Not for her mom, but for herself. Jesus Christ, the rudeness. The lack of respect. She would have drawn herself up, standing tall like a regal ice queen, looking down her nose at the woman and sniffing, "Karen, I'd like to speak to your manager."

That's what Adrienne would have said.

What I said was, "Go fuck yourself, you rancid fucking cunt."

I still hear Adrienne's voice in my head, but that doesn't mean I always use it.

I really do want to move her somewhere nicer. Margaret. Mother. Mom, maybe.

Before I left, on the last day of my visit, Margaret Swan leaned forward and took hold of both my hands.

"You're a sweet girl," she said. "You remind me of my daughter."

I tell myself that I can live this way. Rick Politano says the estate will be settled soon, and once Ethan Richard's assets are distributed, I can go anywhere I want to. I should be relieved, I know. Excited, even. But that word, "anywhere," contains so many possibilities, too many, and it paralyzes me, especially when it's followed by those next two. *Anywhere I want.* As if I know what I want. As if I know who I am. Could I still follow Lizzie Ouellette's dreams, and be happy? I'm afraid to find out. I'm afraid to scratch the surface. I'm afraid that whoever I really was, she smothered and died somewhere inside, small and forgotten, while I was playing dress-up in Adrienne's skin. That if I try to peel the layers away, she'll rot and fall to pieces the moment the light touches her.

I still sleep in the house where Adrienne lived, where Dwayne died, and yes, I'm afraid of that, too. Afraid to stay here, afraid to leave. It's morbid that I haven't moved, I know, but it's the only place I have now that feels even a little like home. Like mine. I wasn't here with Dwayne long enough for his memory to chase me around every corner. I keep the door to the office closed. I pretend there's nothing behind it. I never did clean up the blood, and now it's been too long; the carpet will have to be replaced, the floor refinished where it soaked in beneath.

I shouldn't stay. I know that. Maybe not in the city, but definitely not in this house. I know people think it's strange that Adrienne Richards is still living in the house where she shot her lover to death. I know I should downsize. I should listen to the people who are so eager to tell me what to do, and do what they tell me. Advisors and consultants. Realtors, like the one who sold this place to Ethan years ago, who called me the day after the death notice ran. He wanted to offer his condolences . . . and his honest opinion that the house was much too big for one. I told him it was too soon, muttered something about walls full of memories, the kind of schmaltzy shit that Adrienne sometimes posted on social media when she had nothing else to say. But the truth is, it's the emptiness of the place I like. There's something comforting about all that space, like a cushion between myself and the world. At night, I pour a glass of wine and look out at the sparkling city. I could lose myself here, or maybe find myself.

Or maybe someone will find me first, and put an end to all of this. I think about Jennifer Wellstood, staring into my face, shouting at me without seeing me. I think about Ian Bird, his fingers grazing my body, his breath hot and urgent as he whispered Adrienne's name in my ear. I think about the man he caught, the one who killed Laurie Richter, so desperate under the decades-long weight of his crimes that confession was a relief.

If I believed in fate, I'd say that story was a message from the universe. A warning of things to come. But then again, if I believed in fate, I'd probably think that all of this was meant to be. That I was always going to pull that trigger, and then pull it again. That Adrienne came into my life just so I could step into hers, and was it really my fault if I was only following the path that destiny set out for me?

But I don't believe in that stuff. It was my hands holding the gun, my choice to take this life. I'm no victim of circumstance. And I've carried worse burdens than this.

I stopped going to that Chili's, though. Just in case.

I don't know how long this will last. I've been lucky; maybe I'll stay that way. Sitting in this enormous house, drinking a dead woman's Sancerre, petting the cat, who doesn't seem to mind at all that I'm his family now. He didn't have a tag or anything, so I went ahead and named him; whatever they used to call him, he's Baxter now. I know what you were probably expecting, and no, I didn't name him Rags. Are you fucking kidding me? Jesus, like I want to relive that memory every time I open a can of Fancy Feast. Like I ever want to think about Rags again, or the junkyard, or Dwayne.

I do still think about Dwayne.

Adrienne's gym bag is still in the closet, still stuffed with cash and diamonds and a toothbrush if I ever need to run. I'd head north, I think. After all of this, I still prefer the cold. I like a hard winter, the slap of the air on a dark, frigid morning, the eastern sky just beginning to blush with light. The groaning of the lake as the ice settles. A fresh blanket of new snow, the trees heavy with it, the whole world sparkling white and clean. I'd take the cat with me. I'd leave everything else. This is what I would do, *will* do, if someone gets curious. Or if I slip up. Or if I can't bear it anymore.

But I'm going to try. This life I've taken should be lived by someone; it might as well be me. And as for Lizzie Ouellette, let me tell you: she was nothing but trouble. She was the trash someone should've taken out years ago. That redneck bitch, that junkyard girl. She's gone, and good riddance.

No one will miss her, not even me, and that's the truth.

I almost believe it.

EPILOGUE

BIRD

The junkyard that had been Lizzie Ouellette's childhood home was nothing but a vacant lot now, black and bare as a socket where a rotting tooth had fallen out. Bird pulled to the side of the road and got out, leaning against his cruiser, staring across the narrow street at the empty space. He didn't need to go any closer to be sure that the place had been abandoned, left to be reclaimed in due time by the creeping perimeter of forest surrounding the lot. The woods were lush and green, and a few tentative tendrils of weedy growth were already beginning to find purchase in the cracks and crevices that had once been buried under piles of scrap. Soon, the place would look like nothing at all, just part of the landscape—except to the people who'd always lived here, who would always remember what it used to be. Bird took a deep breath and smiled as he exhaled. The last time he had stood on this spot, the air had been full of floating ash, unbreathable even with a mask on. It smelled different now. Sweet, even a little bit heady, like grass that had been freshly mowed after a long day warming in the July sun.

Earl Ouellette was staying in town, in a small apartment above Myles Johnson's garage. Bird thought he saw Johnson as he got out of his car, a shape standing in the shadows just inside the house, behind a dirty screen door. He waved. The shape disappeared. Bird wondered how the man was doing, understanding as he did that it would be pointless to try to find out. The cops he'd seen on this visit had been polite enough, but there was a palpable sense running underneath the pleasantries that they wanted him gone, that Bird's presence in town was just a reminder of things they were all trying very hard to forget. *Fair enough*, he thought. With any luck, this would be his last trip to Copper Falls.

Earl stepped out as Bird climbed the stairs to the apartment door, lifting a hand in greeting. Bird looked up, squinting in the sun.

"Earl. How are things?"

Earl shrugged, stepping aside to let him pass. "I've been doing all right. Yourself?"

"All good. Thanks for taking the time."

Earl followed Bird inside. The apartment was dingy but neat. A sagging sofa along one wall was the only piece of furniture in the place, and Earl settled at one end while Bird looked around the room: there was a stack of clothing folded up in one corner, and a countertop along the front wall with a few papers stacked on top, a hot plate, a sink, and a smallish fridge. His eyes slid over the papers—insurance, it looked like, and a large white envelope with the name POLITANO ASSOCIATES stamped in one corner—and bent to examine the fridge. Two pictures were pinned there with a magnet, in between a business card for an insurance adjuster and an old-timey postcard that read GREETINGS! FROM ASHEVILLE, N.C. One of the photos Bird had seen before, the one of Lizzie in her yellow dress, gazing back over her shoulder. In the other, she was younger, a little girl with scabby knees, sitting unsmiling on the steps of a trailer with a raggedy-looking cat in her arms.

Behind him, Earl cleared his throat, and Bird peered back.

"Nice photos," he said.

"Ayuh. I only have the two," Earl said.

Bird indicated the postcard. "What's in Asheville?"

Earl's mouth gave a funny little twitch, like he'd started to smile, then thought better of it and hauled it back in.

"Friend of mine."

Bird waited for more explanation, but Earl just sat, letting the silence play out. *Not one for small talk*, Bird thought. Well, that was fine. His own father had been the same way. And there was no need to linger here. He shifted his weight to fish an envelope from his pocket.

"Well, I'll just get to it. Like I said on the phone, victims' compensation finally approved this. I'm sorry for the delay. It doesn't usually take this long."

Earl took the envelope with a nod, and set it aside without opening it.

"Appreciate it. You didn't have to come all this way."

Bird shrugged. "It's better this way. Gives me a chance to check back in with the family, see how they're getting on. Anyway, hopefully the money will be a help to you."

Earl's mouth twitched again and he nodded, saying, "Every little bit helps," but Bird couldn't help noticing that he still hadn't bothered to look at the check. Like it didn't really matter. It was a weird show of confidence for a guy who was living above a garage and spending his nights on a sofa. He glanced at the fridge again.

"How about your insurance, on your business? They come through for you?"

"We been back and forth on it. They tell me it takes longer when it's arson, even if t'wasn't you who done it."

"You think you'll get back what the place was worth?"

Earl did smile then, but only a little. "Hard to say. Lot of memories there. Hard to put a number on a thing like that."

"Well, if there's anything else I can do . . ."

"No need, Detective. I got folks looking out for me." He pressed his lips together, nodding a little.

"That's good," Bird said, but Earl didn't seem to hear him. He was still nodding.

"My Lizzie always looked out for me," he said.

Bird nodded, too.

"I'm so sorry," he said.

Earl said, "Ayuh," and stood up.

So that was it, Bird thought. A brief conversation, all things considered, but sometimes they were like that. It wasn't just the local law enforcement; the families of the deceased weren't always happy to see him, either, especially not after so much time had passed. Some labored through a few minutes of pleasantries before something hardened behind their eyes and Bird found himself shooed out the door. Some never opened the door at all. He understood. Not everyone appreciated the reminder of what was lost. For some people, the only thing to do was leave the past behind, let the dead rest, and carry on without them. Earl Ouellette was doing that. Bird would do the same, although he'd make one more stop before he left. Just a quick one, at the place where they'd buried her, to say hi and goodbye and I'm sorry.

I'm sorry, Lizzie.

He crossed the room, past the minifridge, his eyes drifting one last time over the postcard, the pictures. "Take care, Earl," he said, but his gaze lingered on Lizzie's wedding photo. Looking back over her shoulder, lips slightly parted, as if caught by surprise. The expression on her face was cautious, but her blue eyes were pale and fierce. She looked aware, awake, *alive*, and in the periphery of his memory, something flickered. Something familiar. A shadow shaped like a woman. Hair twisted up on her head, the flush of exertion on her cheeks. But she was walking away from him, already fading. A phantom. A ghost of a ghost.

"Take care, yourself," Earl said. The door creaked as it swung open.

Bird stepped through, back into the warmth of the afternoon, and for one moment, he felt an unanswered question on the tip of his tongue. Something left unsaid, maybe even something important. But it was too late: the door was already closed behind him, and the sun, so hot and bright and glaring, made him feel like he needed to sneeze. He squinted, sniffed, then descended the steps to his car, opened the door, turned the ignition. A left out of the driveway, another left onto the town's main street, and then he was flying. Past the Copper Falls ice cream shop, where a lemon-faced old woman was taking orders through a window. Past the municipal building, where Sheriff Ryan stood outside and raised a hand as the cruiser passed by. Past the hill-top church, with its shaded graveyard beside, and though Bird had planned to pause here, he didn't. To stop by Lizzie Ouellette's grave seemed suddenly unnecessary. An empty gesture, a knock at the door of a house where you already knew nobody was home. It was enough to have thought of it, he decided, and the cruiser picked up speed. Going, going.

I'm sorry, Lizzie.

It happened just one more time as he passed out of Copper Falls: the briefest sense, only a heartbeat long, that there was something he might have forgotten. But when he searched his mind in the place where the flicker had been, whatever it had been, there was nothing there at all.

ACKNOWLEDGMENTS

Thank you to the friends and fellow writers who offered early reads, valuable advice, sanity checks, and general cheerleading while I worked on this book: Leigh Stein, Julia Strayer, Sandra Rodriguez Barron, Phoebe Maltz Bovy, Amy Wilkinson, Katie Herzog, Jesse Singal, and Nick Schoenfeld.

Thanks to my mom, Helen Kelly, the most enthusiastic beta reader in the world.

I owe a tremendous debt to these subject matter experts: Lennie Daniels, retired New York state trooper, answered my questions about criminal investigations and law enforcement procedure in rural enclaves. Andrew Fleischman, defense attorney and A+ Twitter follow, provided legal expertise (including Kurt Geller's best line). Joshua Rosenfield (a.k.a. my dad) rounded it out with medical knowledge. Any inaccuracies or creative liberties are my fault, not theirs.

Thanks to Margaret Garland for connecting me with Lennie.

I am exceptionally grateful to Yfat Reiss Gendell for being my agent throughout seven years, multiple genres, two Comic Cons, and a global pandemic.

It was an incredible privilege to work with Rachel Kahan, whose insight and enthusiasm made this story better. Thanks also to the incredible team at William Morrow who turned this messy manuscript into a book.

Thanks to my brother, Noah Rosenfield (to whom this book is dedicated), for always being game to bat an idea around. A TV show where some dogs are police officers, and some are just dogs: is this something?

And finally, thank you to Brad Anderson, who in no way resembles any of the various terrible husbands in this book. Except for the beard. I love you.

PROLOGUE

CHRISTMAS EVE, 2014

She knows he's there even before he speaks. She feels the weight and warmth of him as he sits down beside her, the firm press of his hip against the small of her back. His fingers curl gently over her shoulder as he leans in, and she smells his breath, warm and sweet, tickling her ear and sending a delicious chill down her spine.

"Miriam," he says. "Are you awake, my love?"

"Yes," she whispers. For him, she is always awake. She always has been. Ready to rise at the touch of his hand, ready to offer her mouth to be kissed. She rolls toward him, reaching out, and feels him catch her by the wrist. He has strong hands. A workingman's hands. It has been a long time since he was up at dawn to labor at the docks, a long, long time, but the calluses, those relics of labor long since abandoned, never went away. Her own mother once shuddered over those hands—"Your beautiful skin, Miriam! How can you bear it?"—but Miriam would only smile and shrug, because the truth was, she loved the feel of his fingertips, the light scrape against her skin. When he touched her, it felt the way she imagined it would to be embraced by an animal, something big and powerful like a bear, holding her gently between its huge rough paws. He could have torn her to pieces.

But he didn't. He wouldn't.

"Will you come to bed? Isn't it very late?" she asks, squinting at the place where she thought her bedside clock should be, but isn't, which is strange. The room is dark, all shadow, with only the barest glimmers of moonlight shimmering outside a window that is beginning to feather with frost. Her husband is somewhere among the shadows, but she cannot see his face, only the back-and-forth movement of his head as he shakes it, No. He is wearing his hat, she can see the curve of it, and she hears the light crunch of canvas as he shifts beside her. His coat, she thinks. He's wearing his coat. But why? She shivers again, this time with confusion, her skin suddenly crawling. Why is he awake in the middle of the night? Why can't she see his face?

But then he laughs, and after a moment, she laughs, too, and the creeping sensation of dread disappears.

"Did you forget?" he asks gently. The hand holding her wrist unclasps, winding its fingers through hers.

"Forget?" she repeats, feeling stupid. "I don't—but I've only just woken up. What is it?"

"It's our night. Our special night. The reach has frozen over."

"It has?"

"Darling," he chides, "you did forget."

Her whisper is indignant. "I did not."

"No?"

"Of course I remember."

"Then let's go." The shadow shifts off the bed with a creak, and she hears him moving across the floor. She slips her legs out from beneath the covers, setting her feet carefully side by side, curling her toes into the braided rug. The air is cold against her bare legs, startlingly so, but her mind still feels clouded and half-asleep. She blinks, trying to clear the cobwebs, trying to make the hulking shadows resolve into familiar shapes. An armoire there, the bed-post here. Her things. Her room. Why does it feel so unfamiliar? A person shouldn't feel so lost, so confused, sitting on the edge of her own bed.

One of the shadows moves.

"Theo?" she says, and sees the bob of his head, the peaked brim of his cap as he passes in front of the window to kneel beside her.

"Here, let me help you," he whispers, and she lifts her feet obediently at his touch, one at a time, feeling them disappear into the warm depths of a pair of fur-lined boots. She feels his breath again as he tightens and ties the laces, this time against her bare legs below the hem of her nightgown, and feels herself flush. Not with embarrassment, but anticipation. Their special night.

Of course she hadn't forgotten. Not now, not after so many midnight trysts that she knew the way by heart, stealing out in the black and bracing cold, down to the water's edge. She would hug the wall along the staircase, treading carefully to avoid the creaky spots, waiting at the bottom to be sure that the coast was clear—only no, she thinks, shaking her head, that was before. She'd been only a girl then, breaking her father's rules, giddy and defiant. But it's her house now. Her own, and her husband's. She could make as much noise as she likes. Except—

"The children," she exclaims suddenly, her voice loud in the dark, and he puts a hand to her cheek.

"Shh. They're asleep. They'll be fine."

She blinks again and loses time. One moment, she was rising to her

feet, shuffling in the heavy boots toward the bedroom door. The next, she is outside, the wind whipping at the hem of her nightgown, the flagstone path through the garden at her feet.

A fog has crept in, blanketing everything, blotting out the dark sky and the glittering stars. Only the moon is still visible, casting its bleak light as if through a veil. There is a blanket over her shoulders, and she pulls it around her, gazing uncertainly into the night—but there, there he is. A lamplight bobs in the distance, a soft whistle summons her from where she stands. She begins to walk. She knows the way, whether he's beside her or not.

The house looms behind her, huge and dark, as she descends the first set of steps. Down the hill, through the formal gardens where she had once played hide-and-seek as a girl. Past the massive topiaries, now bare and overgrown, that would be trimmed come springtime into perfect spheres. Past the long, high wall where you could pick up a path that led into the woods, or descend another, longer set of steps to reach the long pier that stretches into the bay.

This is where she used to walk out to meet him, in the shadow of the hedges, where a hulking juniper and the sheer stone wall kept her hidden from prying eyes. Not that anyone is awake in the house now, nor could anyone have seen them through the thick and drifting fog. When she looks back, the house is hardly there at all. It would be nothing but a looming shadow, if not for the single light shining from a window on the top floor.

She frowns. Something darts through her mind, a flicker of memory that is gone as quickly as it came, leaving behind a sense of unease. Something about the light. Something not quite right. She hesitates . . . but he appears again beside her, and the flicker chases itself away.

"Scared of the dark?" he says, and she giggles. A silly question. He knows better.

"I was just . . ." she says, and leaves the sentence unfinished, realizing she doesn't know how it ends.

He looks at her curiously and reaches out with the hand not holding the lantern. "Should we walk hand in hand?"

"Like we used to," she says, almost like a question, and he nods. "That's right, my love."

The darkness closes in as they walk between the trees. The flickering lamp, where is it? Has the light gone out? When she looks down, she sees that his other hand, the one not holding hers, is empty. No matter. There's moonlight, just enough. She can see the broad white expanse of the reach up ahead, where the path ends and the cove begins, where they will step together onto the ice. There's another flicker, this one stronger: *I dared him,* she thinks suddenly, and the memory fills her with delight as she moves forward, more quickly now, tingling with the thrill of what has been and the anticipation of what comes next. That had been the first time, on a night even colder than this one. She had walked onto the ice herself and dared him to follow, turning away without even waiting to see if he would. She knew he would. She had been sure where he was afraid, sure enough for both of them. Not just of the way across the reach, but of what waited on the other side. The cabin, with its little stove and a cord of firewood at the ready. No bed, but a bearskin rug that would serve the necessary purpose. A hideaway for two. His hands slipping under her nightdress and around her waist, acquainting themselves with the curves of her body, the beautiful friction of his calloused fingertips against her skin. She had been so young, they both had, full of blazing passion, with a beautiful life ahead. A boy and a girl.

But Miriam is not a girl anymore.

And when she turns, her husband is no longer beside her. "Theo?"

The wind rises as the moon is swallowed by the fog, and she goes to pull the blanket tighter around her shoulders, but there is no blanket. It's gone, along with the moonlight, along with him. The flimsy fabric of her nightdress whips around her legs, and she shivers, looking down. There are her feet, warm in their boots, the laces knotted tightly. Below them, gritty snow over an endless expanse of white.

She is standing on the ice.

The wind blows harder. She peers into the murk, her heart beginning to race, her eyes searching in vain for the invisible shore. It could be ahead of her or behind, the fog so thick that she can no longer see or remember which way she came. She reaches out, frantic, looking once more for his hand, but clutches only the air. There's nothing and no one. Nothing but the wind, raw and tinged with salt. She calls his name as the fog parts, and then she sees him. Just a silhouette, hardly there at all.

He is not there at all.

Instead of his voice calling back to her, there is only the soft sound, somewhere very close by, of rushing water.

If she had been given another moment more, she might have come back. She might have remembered that it had been more than fifty years since she had walked this way, fifty years since she had last crossed the reach on a cold winter's night. She might have remembered that her husband wasn't here, couldn't be, because he was dead, and had been for many years. She might have seen that her own hands, clutched across her sunken chest, were gnarled and marked with liver spots; she might have felt the arthritic flare in her hips.

She might have realized who and what she was: an old woman shivering in her nightdress, lost and alone in the dark.

And she might have remembered that just yesterday, a man on the news had warned that climate change was still bringing warmer winters—and that in the past ten years, the reach had never fully frozen until at least February, if it froze at all.

But there isn't time. Not enough for a memory. Not even enough for a scream. Her shuffling feet have taken her the wrong direction, and the white ice beneath her isn't white anymore, but black and thin and groaning. The groan becomes a crack. A dark mouth opens up beneath her. Miriam gasps once at the cold as it rushes up to meet her. The dark mouth closes over her head.

In the great stone house standing high on the hill, the light behind the upstairs window goes out.